INTRODUCTION BY SAM HENDERSON

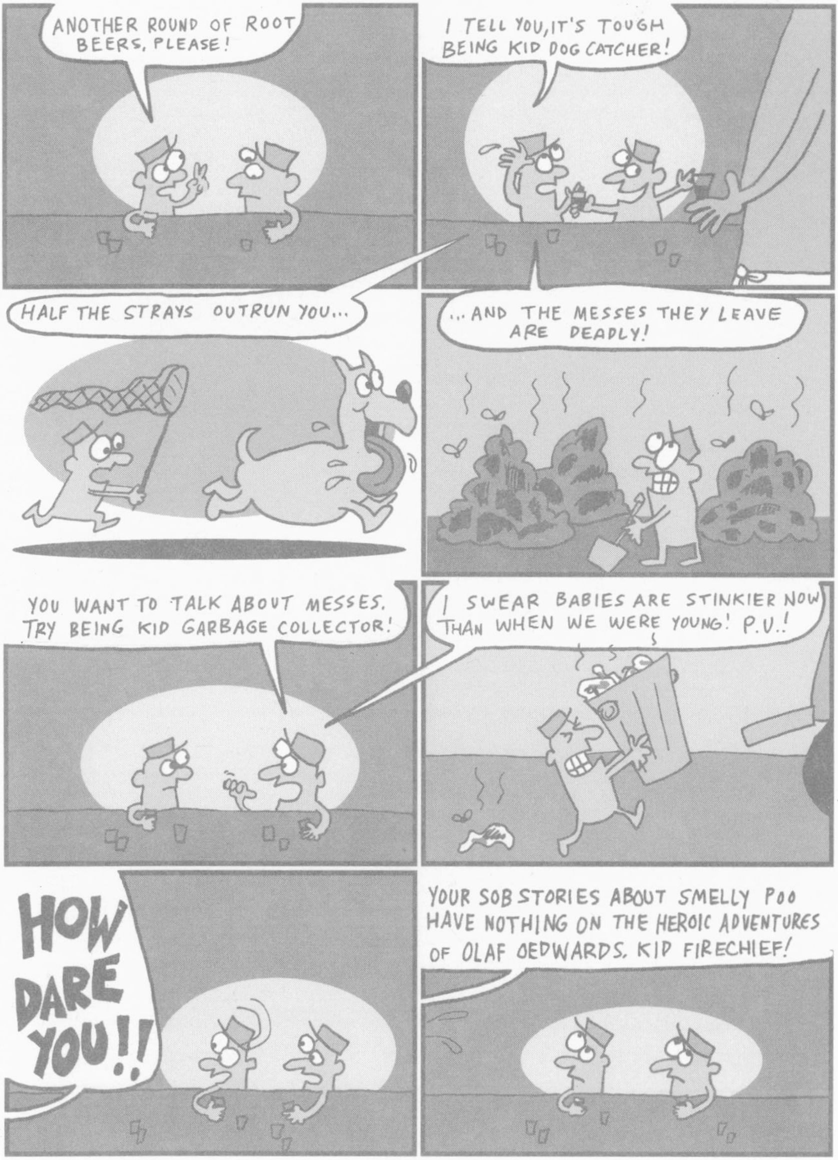
ANOTHER ROUND OF ROOT BEERS, PLEASE!
I TELL YOU, IT'S TOUGH BEING KID DOG CATCHER!
HALF THE STRAYS OUTRUN YOU...
...AND THE MESSES THEY LEAVE ARE DEADLY!
YOU WANT TO TALK ABOUT MESSES. TRY BEING KID GARBAGE COLLECTOR!
I SWEAR BABIES ARE STINKIER NOW THAN WHEN WE WERE YOUNG! P.U.!
HOW DARE YOU!!
YOUR SOB STORIES ABOUT SMELLY POO HAVE NOTHING ON THE HEROIC ADVENTURES OF OLAF OEDWARDS, KID FIRECHIEF!

HE'D GIVE YOU A TALKING TO IF HE WERE WITH US NOW!
IS H-HE...?
THAT'S RIGHT! HE'S WORKING! WHILE YOU'RE SITTING AROUND BLOWING YOUR ALLOWANCE ON SODAS, HE'S OUT SAVING LIVES!
I SHOULD ALSO POINT OUT THAT ON TOP OF THIS, HE KEEPS HIS ROOM CLEAN, UNLIKE TWO LAZY BUMS I KNOW! NOW GET HOME TO DINNER!
MOM ALWAYS HAS TO RUIN EVERYTHING!
©henderson 04

Other books by Steven Weissman:

"DON'T CALL ME STUPID!" ISBN: 1-56097-431-1
CHAMPS ISBN: 1-56097-372-2
WHITE FLOWER DAY ISBN: 1-56097-514-8

Editorial Co-ordinator: Gary Groth • Production: Paul Baresh
Production Manager: Kim Thompson • Promotion: Eric Reynolds
Published by Gary Groth and Kim Thompson

 This is a work of fiction and any similarity to persons living or dead is coincidental. Be fire safe! Map out an escape route at home and everywhere else you spend a lot of time. Never play with matches and, in case of emergency, always dial 911 (USA only).

Fantagraphics Books, 7563 Lake City Way NE, Seattle, WA 98115. Call our toll-free number for a free full-color catalogue of comics and related pop culture: 1-800-657-1100. Or visit our website at www.fantagraphics.com

Portions of this book have appeared in *Measles, Mammoth*, and *The Comics Journal*.

DEDICATED TO CHARLES WEISSMAN.

THANKS ANYWAY; SAM, CHRIS, GILBERT, JORDAN, REBECCA, LUCY, LUCIE, NOAH, HANNAH, EMILY, OLIVE, ETHAN, POWELL, LOY, MAITLIN, MICHAEL, MICHAEL, JACK, LUKE, KINLAY, MATS, DREW, JON, JENNY, JOHNNY, JESUS, LUPITA, JANET, YARITZA, CHARISSA AND FIREFIGHTERS EVERYWHERE.

ISBN: 1-56097-962-2 Printed in Canada

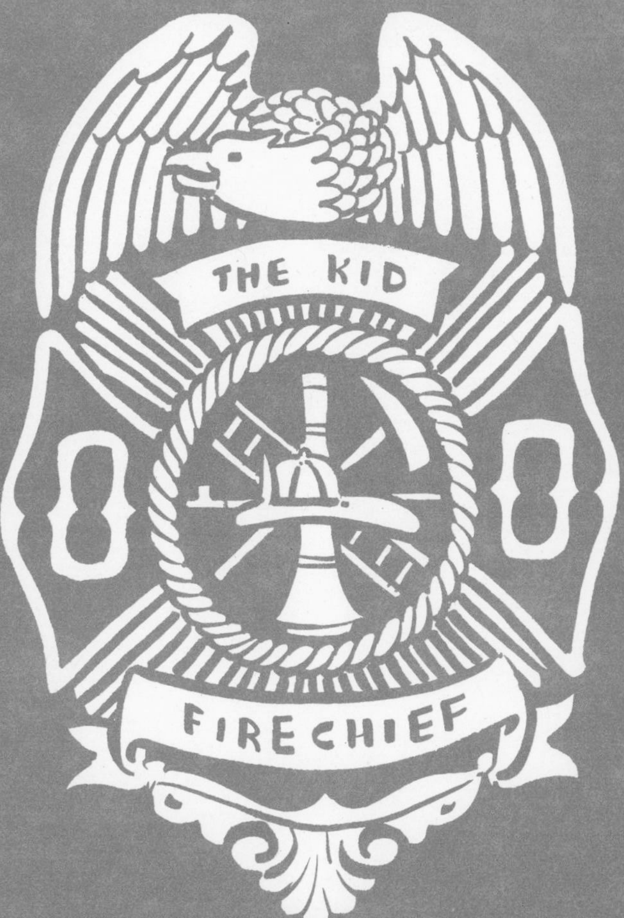
THE KID
FIRECHIEF

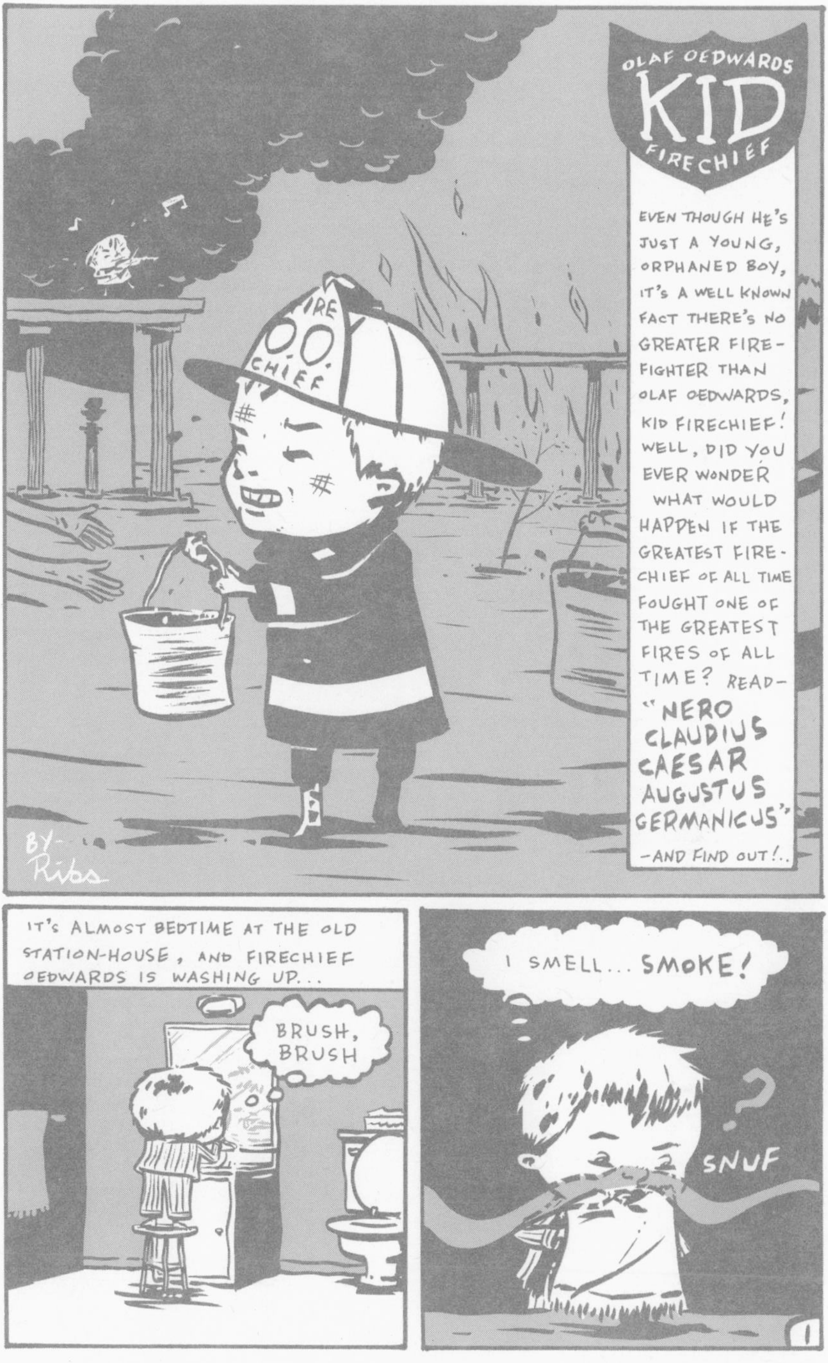
OLAF OEDWARDS
KID
FIRECHIEF
EVEN THOUGH HE'S JUST A YOUNG, ORPHANED BOY, IT'S A WELL KNOWN FACT THERE'S NO GREATER FIRE-FIGHTER THAN OLAF OEDWARDS, KID FIRECHIEF! WELL, DID YOU EVER WONDER WHAT WOULD HAPPEN IF THE GREATEST FIRE-CHIEF OF ALL TIME FOUGHT ONE OF THE GREATEST FIRES OF ALL TIME? READ–
"NERO CLAUDIUS CAESAR AUGUSTUS GERMANICUS"
–AND FIND OUT!..
BY- Ribs
IT'S ALMOST BEDTIME AT THE OLD STATION-HOUSE, AND FIRECHIEF OEDWARDS IS WASHING UP...
BRUSH, BRUSH
I SMELL... SMOKE!
SNUF
1

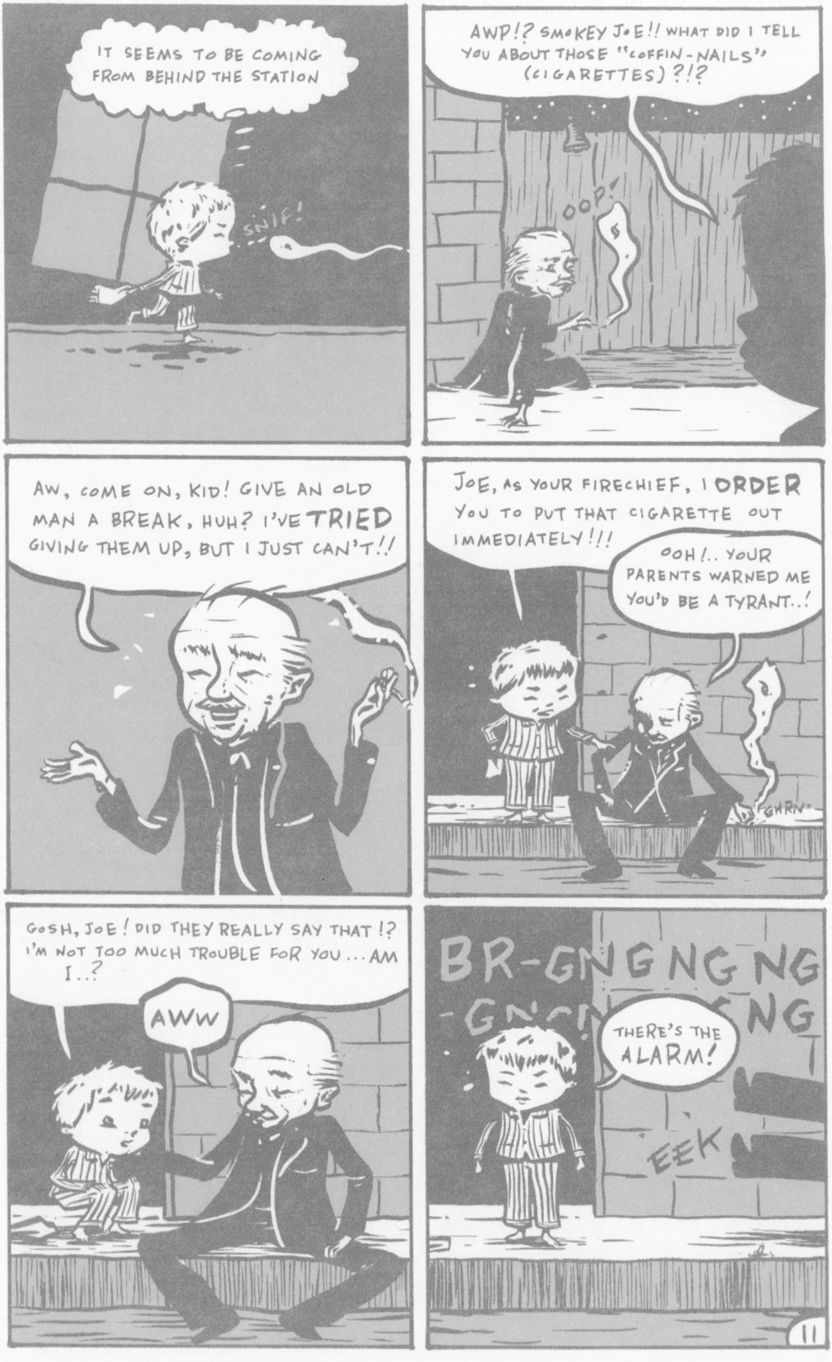
IT SEEMS TO BE COMING FROM BEHIND THE STATION
SNIF!
AWP!? SMOKEY JOE!! WHAT DID I TELL YOU ABOUT THOSE "COFFIN-NAILS" (CIGARETTES)?!?
OOP!
AW, COME ON, KID! GIVE AN OLD MAN A BREAK, HUH? I'VE TRIED GIVING THEM UP, BUT I JUST CAN'T!!
JOE, AS YOUR FIRECHIEF, I ORDER YOU TO PUT THAT CIGARETTE OUT IMMEDIATELY!!!
OOH!.. YOUR PARENTS WARNED ME YOU'D BE A TYRANT..!
GHRN
GOSH, JOE! DID THEY REALLY SAY THAT!? I'M NOT TOO MUCH TROUBLE FOR YOU... AM I..?
AWW
BR-GNGNGNG
NG
THERE'S THE ALARM!
EEK
11

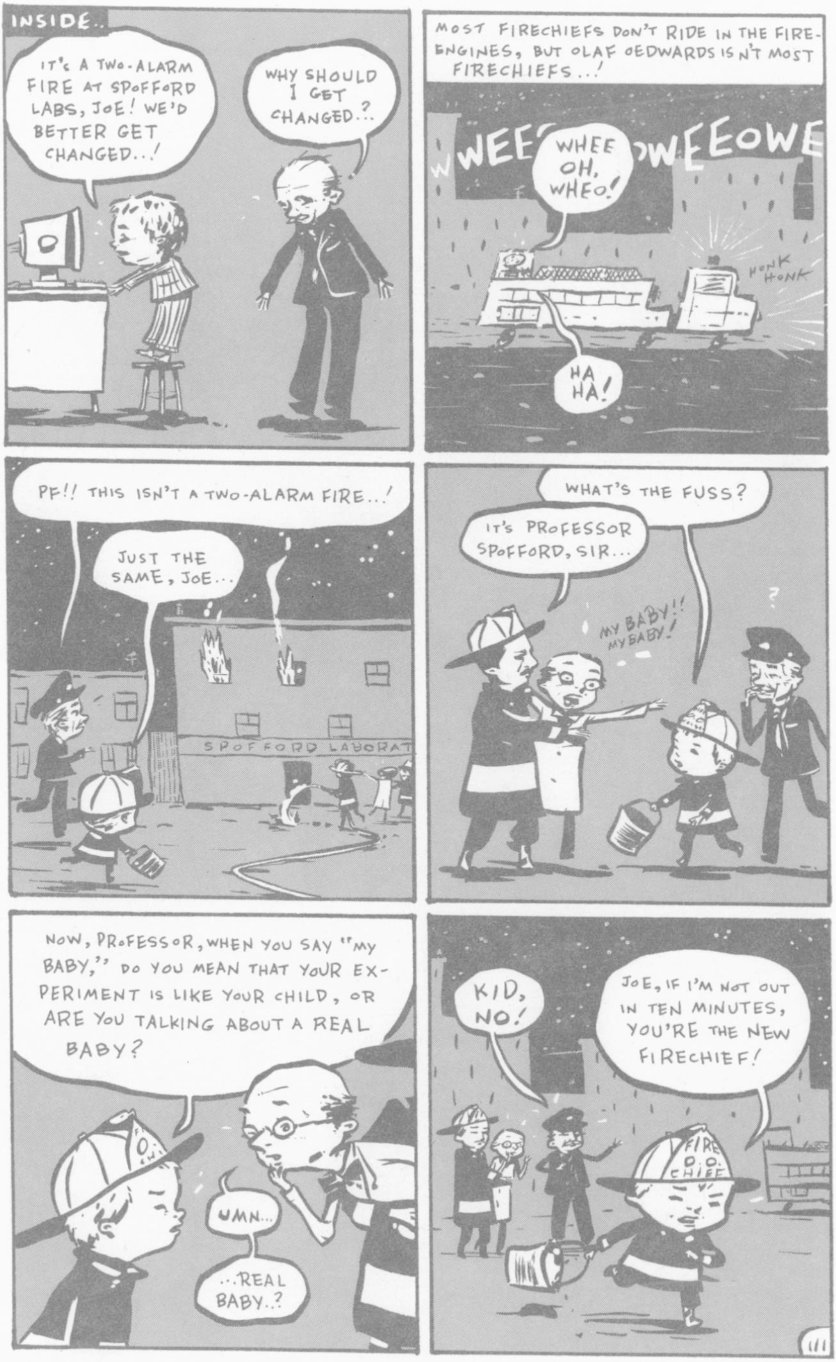

INSIDE..
IT'S A TWO-ALARM FIRE AT SPOFFORD LABS, JOE! WE'D BETTER GET CHANGED..!
WHY SHOULD I GET CHANGED..?
MOST FIRECHIEFS DON'T RIDE IN THE FIRE-ENGINES, BUT OLAF OEDWARDS ISN'T MOST FIRECHIEFS...!
WEEOWEEOWE
WHEE OH, WHEO!
HONK HONK
HA HA!
PF!! THIS ISN'T A TWO-ALARM FIRE..!
JUST THE SAME, JOE...
SPOFFORD LABORAT
WHAT'S THE FUSS?
IT'S PROFESSOR SPOFFORD, SIR...
MY BABY!! MY BABY!
?
NOW, PROFESSOR, WHEN YOU SAY "MY BABY," DO YOU MEAN THAT YOUR EXPERIMENT IS LIKE YOUR CHILD, OR ARE YOU TALKING ABOUT A REAL BABY?
UMN...
...REAL BABY..?
KID, NO!
JOE, IF I'M NOT OUT IN TEN MINUTES, YOU'RE THE NEW FIRECHIEF!
FIRE O.O. CHIEF

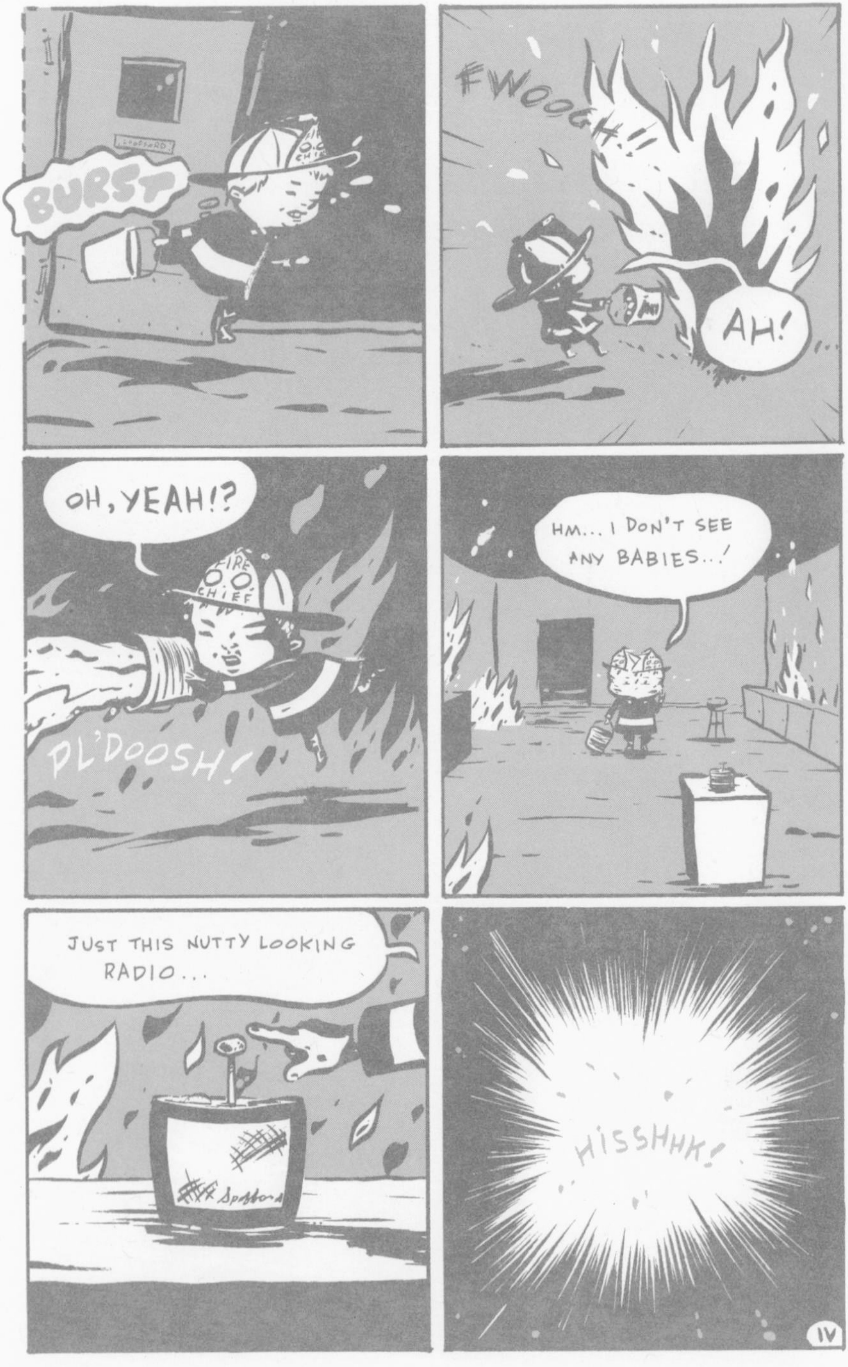
BURST
FWOOGH!!
AH!
OH, YEAH!?
PL'DOOSH!
HM... I DON'T SEE ANY BABIES...!
JUST THIS NUTTY LOOKING RADIO...
HISSHHK!
IV

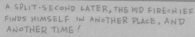

A SPLIT-SECOND LATER, THE KID FIRECHIEF FINDS HIMSELF IN ANOTHER PLACE, AND ANOTHER TIME!

WHA!?

WOW!! IF MY EYES AREN'T DECEIVING ME, I'VE BEEN TRANSPORTED TO ANCIENT ROME!!!

WHICH MAKES THIS A SPACE-TIME TRANSPORTER!

I'D BETTER HANG ON TO THIS GADGET SO I CAN GET HOME! GOOD THING I'VE BEEN STUDYING *LATIN*... I'LL TRY IT OUT NOW!

<HAIL, FELLOWS! IT LOOKS LIKE YOU COULD USE SOME HELP..!>

<BRACKETS INDICATE SECOND LANGUAGE>

<WE SURELY COULD, YOUNG MAN, BUT WHAT *YOU* POSSIBLY DO FOR US?>

<I CAN ONLY DO MY BEST, SIR! WHERE'S THE NEAREST SOURCE OF WATER?>

SHAKE SHAKE

SOON ENOUGH, OLAF OEDWARDS HAS ORGAN-IZED A WATER-BUCKET "RELAY" TO COMBAT THE WORST OF THIS CITY-WIDE BLAZE. BUT HE CAN'T HELP NOTICING...

<EXCUSE ME, WHO'S THAT FIDDLE-SCRATCHER UP THERE, AND WHY ISN'T HE HELPING US OUT?>

<YOU MEAN YOU DON'T KNOW!?>

<NO>

<THAT'S NERO CLAUDIUS CAESAR AUGUSTUS GERMANICUS!!>

HUH!?

<HE'S THE EMPEROR NERO!>*

*EMPEROR OF ROME: AD 54-68

V

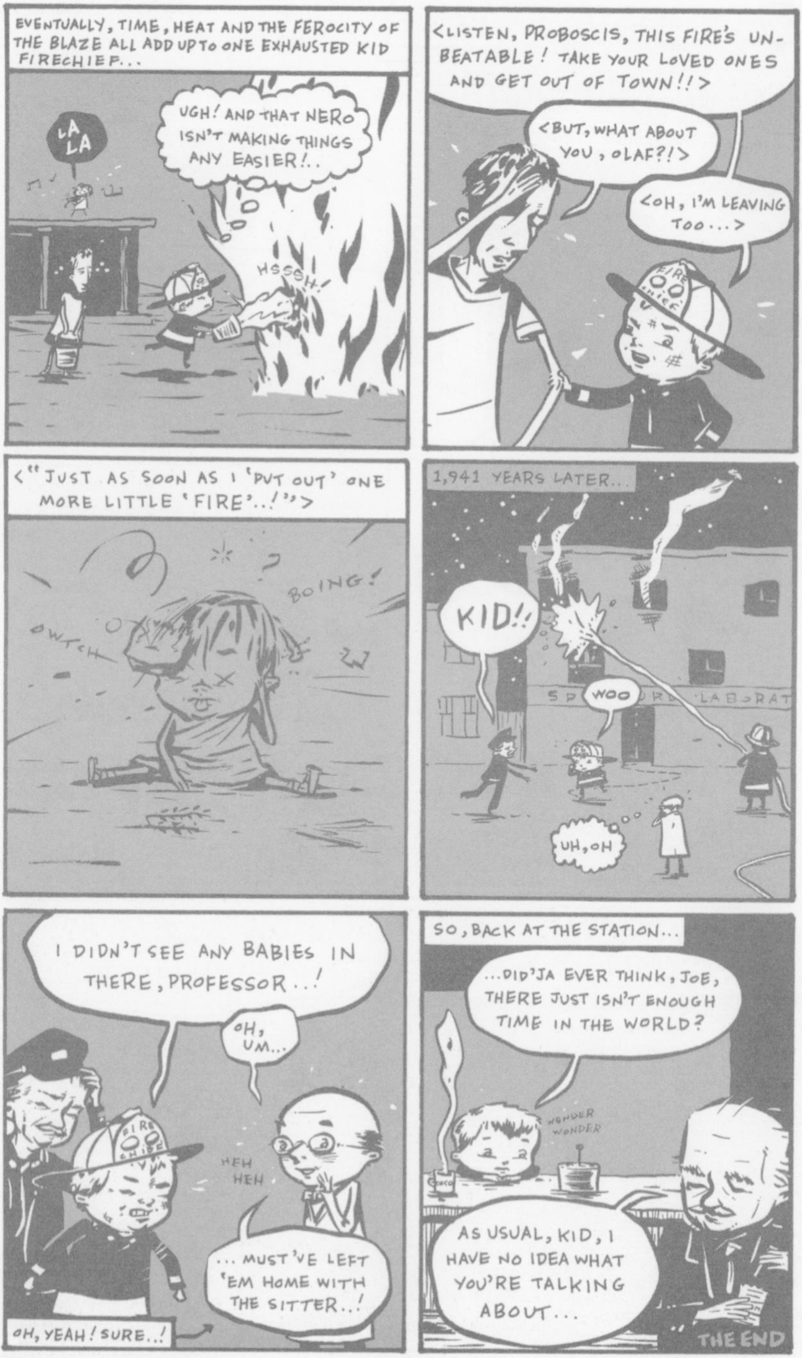
EVENTUALLY, TIME, HEAT AND THE FEROCITY OF THE BLAZE ALL ADD UP TO ONE EXHAUSTED KID FIRECHIEF...
LA LA
UGH! AND THAT NERO ISN'T MAKING THINGS ANY EASIER!..
HSSSH!
<LISTEN, PROBOSCIS, THIS FIRE'S UNBEATABLE! TAKE YOUR LOVED ONES AND GET OUT OF TOWN!!>
<BUT, WHAT ABOUT YOU, OLAF?!>
<OH, I'M LEAVING TOO...>
<"JUST AS SOON AS I 'PUT OUT' ONE MORE LITTLE 'FIRE'...!">
BOING!
OWTCH
1,941 YEARS LATER...
KID!!
WOO
UH, OH
I DIDN'T SEE ANY BABIES IN THERE, PROFESSOR...!
OH, UM...
HEH HEH
... MUST'VE LEFT 'EM HOME WITH THE SITTER...!
OH, YEAH! SURE...!
SO, BACK AT THE STATION...
...DID'JA EVER THINK, JOE, THERE JUST ISN'T ENOUGH TIME IN THE WORLD?
WONDER WONDER
AS USUAL, KID, I HAVE NO IDEA WHAT YOU'RE TALKING ABOUT...
THE END

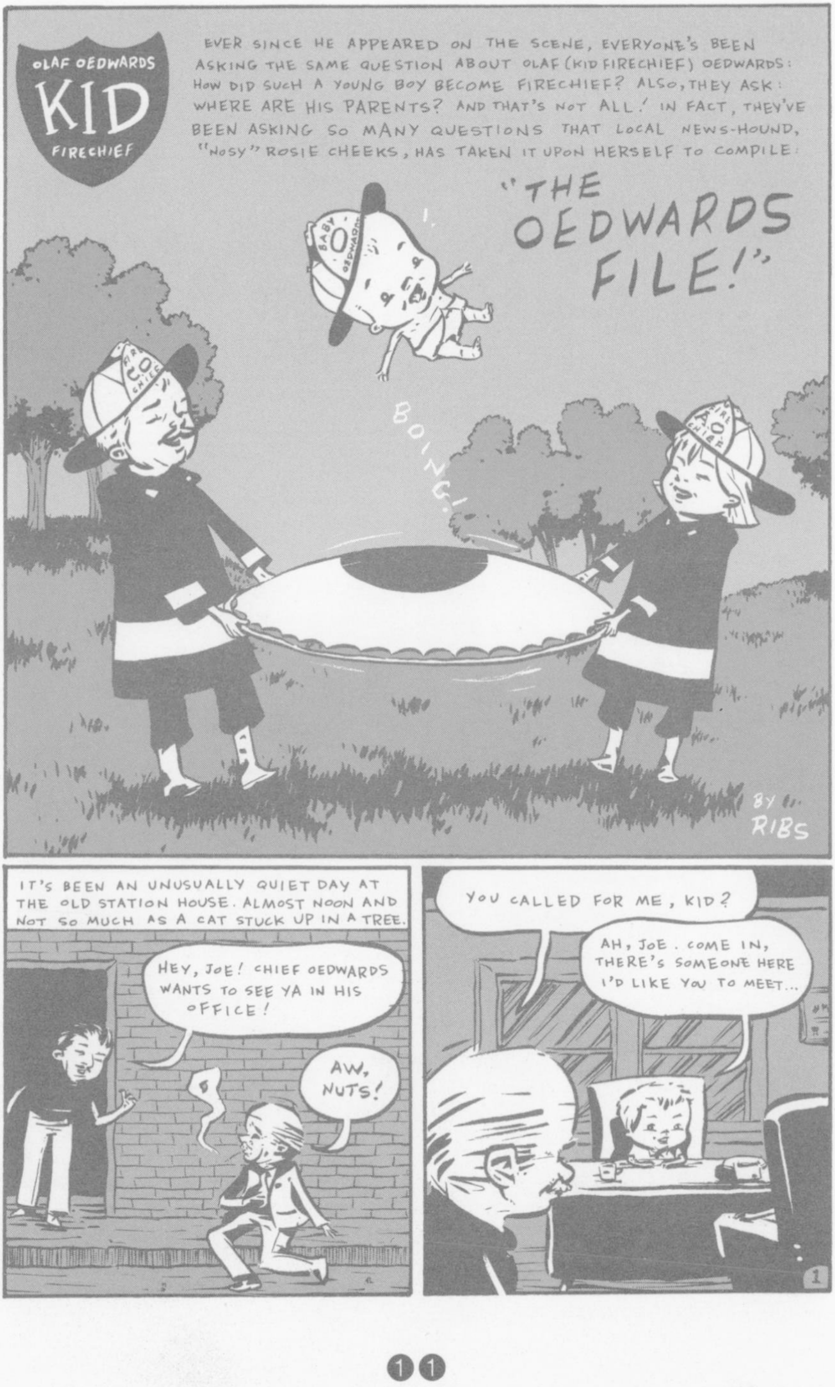
OLAF OEDWARDS
KID
FIRECHIEF
EVER SINCE HE APPEARED ON THE SCENE, EVERYONE'S BEEN ASKING THE SAME QUESTION ABOUT OLAF (KID FIRECHIEF) OEDWARDS: HOW DID SUCH A YOUNG BOY BECOME FIRECHIEF? ALSO, THEY ASK: WHERE ARE HIS PARENTS? AND THAT'S NOT ALL! IN FACT, THEY'VE BEEN ASKING SO MANY QUESTIONS THAT LOCAL NEWS-HOUND, "NOSY" ROSIE CHEEKS, HAS TAKEN IT UPON HERSELF TO COMPILE:
"THE OEDWARDS FILE!"
BABY OEDWARDS
BOING!
BY RIBS
IT'S BEEN AN UNUSUALLY QUIET DAY AT THE OLD STATION HOUSE. ALMOST NOON AND NOT SO MUCH AS A CAT STUCK UP IN A TREE.
HEY, JOE! CHIEF OEDWARDS WANTS TO SEE YA IN HIS OFFICE!
AW, NUTS!
YOU CALLED FOR ME, KID?
AH, JOE. COME IN, THERE'S SOMEONE HERE I'D LIKE YOU TO MEET...
1

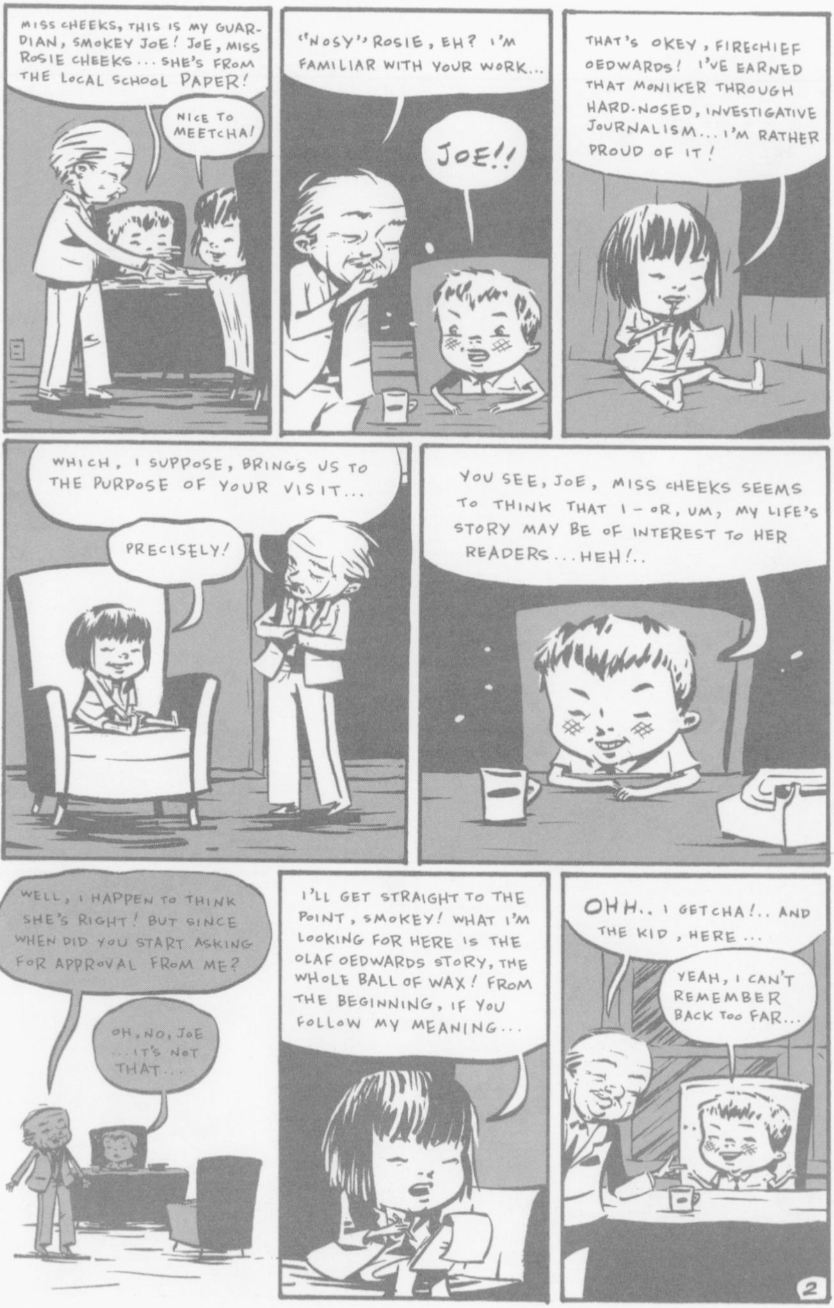
MISS CHEEKS, THIS IS MY GUARDIAN, SMOKEY JOE! JOE, MISS ROSIE CHEEKS... SHE'S FROM THE LOCAL SCHOOL PAPER!
NICE TO MEETCHA!
"NOSY" ROSIE, EH? I'M FAMILIAR WITH YOUR WORK...
JOE!!
THAT'S OKEY, FIRECHIEF OEDWARDS! I'VE EARNED THAT MONIKER THROUGH HARD-NOSED, INVESTIGATIVE JOURNALISM... I'M RATHER PROUD OF IT!
WHICH, I SUPPOSE, BRINGS US TO THE PURPOSE OF YOUR VISIT...
PRECISELY!
YOU SEE, JOE, MISS CHEEKS SEEMS TO THINK THAT I - OR, UM, MY LIFE'S STORY MAY BE OF INTEREST TO HER READERS... HEH!..
WELL, I HAPPEN TO THINK SHE'S RIGHT! BUT SINCE WHEN DID YOU START ASKING FOR APPROVAL FROM ME?
OH, NO, JOE ...IT'S NOT THAT...
I'LL GET STRAIGHT TO THE POINT, SMOKEY! WHAT I'M LOOKING FOR HERE IS THE OLAF OEDWARDS STORY, THE WHOLE BALL OF WAX! FROM THE BEGINNING, IF YOU FOLLOW MY MEANING...
OHH.. I GETCHA!.. AND THE KID, HERE...
YEAH, I CAN'T REMEMBER BACK TOO FAR...
2

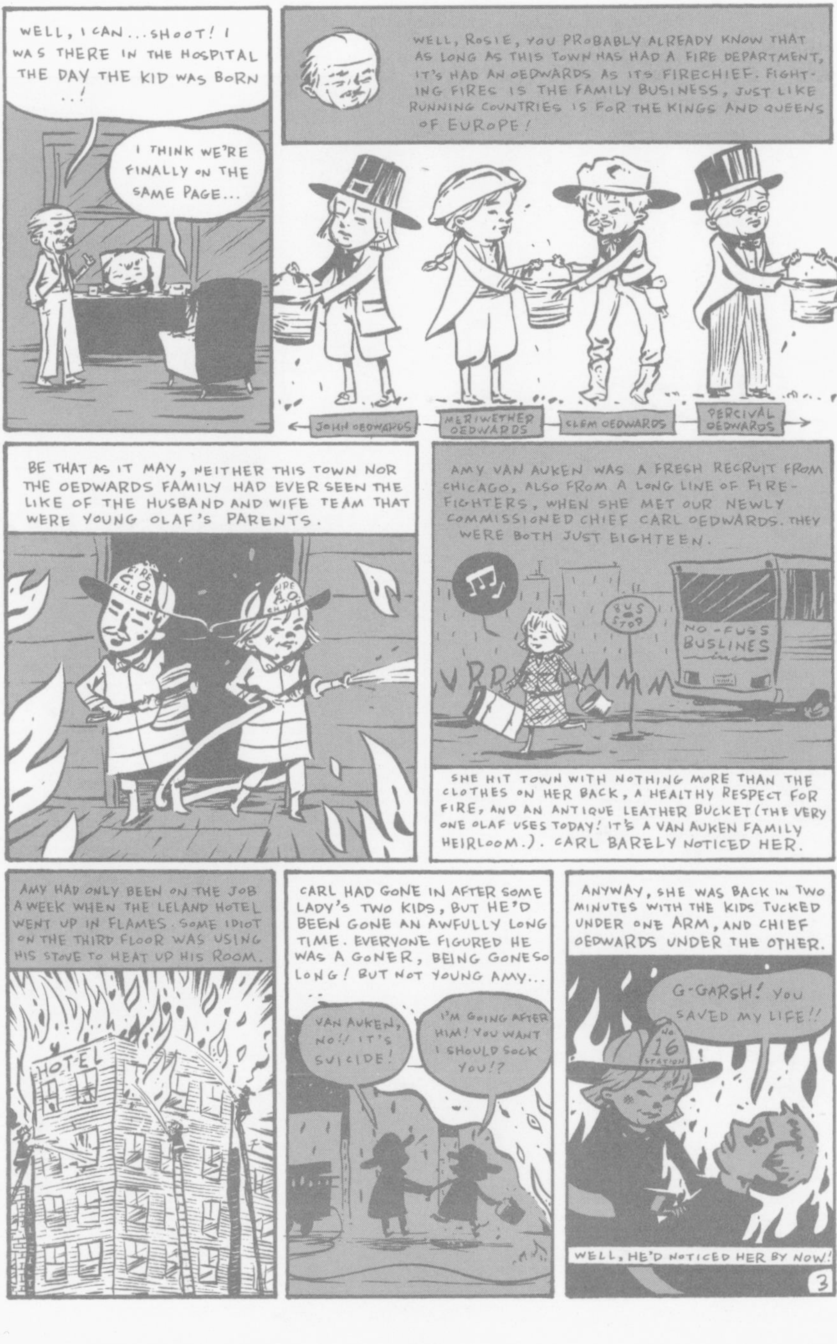
WELL, I CAN...SHOOT! I WAS THERE IN THE HOSPITAL THE DAY THE KID WAS BORN..!
I THINK WE'RE FINALLY ON THE SAME PAGE...
WELL, ROSIE, YOU PROBABLY ALREADY KNOW THAT AS LONG AS THIS TOWN HAS HAD A FIRE DEPARTMENT, IT'S HAD AN OEDWARDS AS ITS FIRECHIEF. FIGHTING FIRES IS THE FAMILY BUSINESS, JUST LIKE RUNNING COUNTRIES IS FOR THE KINGS AND QUEENS OF EUROPE!
JOHN OEDWARDS
MERIWETHER OEDWARDS
CLEM OEDWARDS
PERCIVAL OEDWARDS
BE THAT AS IT MAY, NEITHER THIS TOWN NOR THE OEDWARDS FAMILY HAD EVER SEEN THE LIKE OF THE HUSBAND AND WIFE TEAM THAT WERE YOUNG OLAF'S PARENTS.
FIRE C.O. CHIEF
FIRE A.O. CHIEF
AMY VAN AUKEN WAS A FRESH RECRUIT FROM CHICAGO, ALSO FROM A LONG LINE OF FIRE-FIGHTERS, WHEN SHE MET OUR NEWLY COMMISSIONED CHIEF CARL OEDWARDS. THEY WERE BOTH JUST EIGHTEEN.
BUS STOP
NO-FUSS BUSLINES inc
VRRRMMMM
SHE HIT TOWN WITH NOTHING MORE THAN THE CLOTHES ON HER BACK, A HEALTHY RESPECT FOR FIRE, AND AN ANTIQUE LEATHER BUCKET (THE VERY ONE OLAF USES TODAY! IT'S A VAN AUKEN FAMILY HEIRLOOM.). CARL BARELY NOTICED HER.
AMY HAD ONLY BEEN ON THE JOB A WEEK WHEN THE LELAND HOTEL WENT UP IN FLAMES. SOME IDIOT ON THE THIRD FLOOR WAS USING HIS STOVE TO HEAT UP HIS ROOM.
HOTEL
CARL HAD GONE IN AFTER SOME LADY'S TWO KIDS, BUT HE'D BEEN GONE AN AWFULLY LONG TIME. EVERYONE FIGURED HE WAS A GONER, BEING GONE SO LONG! BUT NOT YOUNG AMY...
VAN AUKEN, NO!! IT'S SUICIDE!
I'M GOING AFTER HIM! YOU WANT I SHOULD SOCK YOU!?
ANYWAY, SHE WAS BACK IN TWO MINUTES WITH THE KIDS TUCKED UNDER ONE ARM, AND CHIEF OEDWARDS UNDER THE OTHER.
G-GARSH! YOU SAVED MY LIFE!!
No 16 STATION
WELL, HE'D NOTICED HER BY NOW!
3

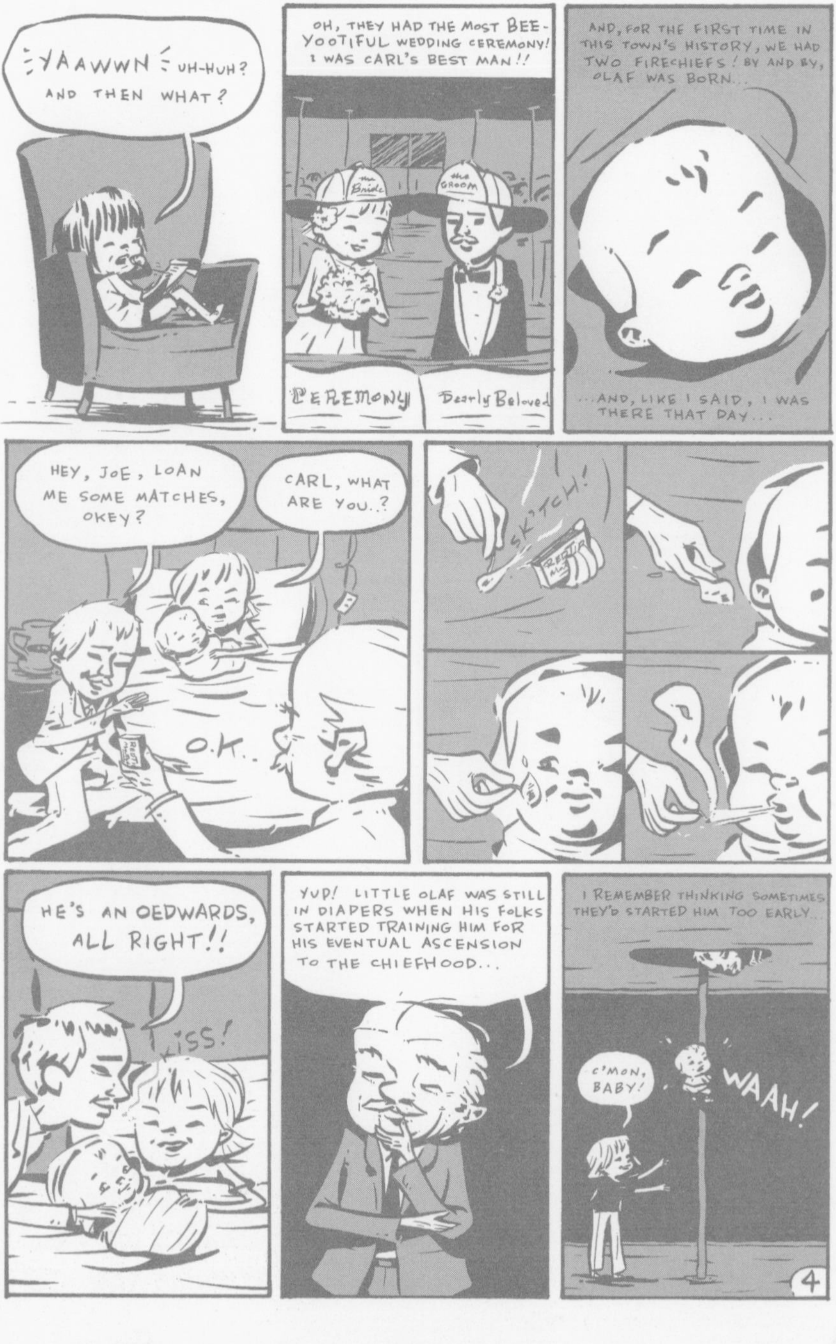
YAAWWN UH-HUH? AND THEN WHAT?
OH, THEY HAD THE MOST BEE-YOOTIFUL WEDDING CEREMONY! I WAS CARL'S BEST MAN!!
the Bride
the GROOM
CEREMONY
Dearly Beloved
AND, FOR THE FIRST TIME IN THIS TOWN'S HISTORY, WE HAD TWO FIRECHIEFS! BY AND BY, OLAF WAS BORN...
...AND, LIKE I SAID, I WAS THERE THAT DAY...
HEY, JOE, LOAN ME SOME MATCHES, OKEY?
CARL, WHAT ARE YOU..?
O.K...
SK'TCH!
HE'S AN OEDWARDS, ALL RIGHT!!
KISS!
YUP! LITTLE OLAF WAS STILL IN DIAPERS WHEN HIS FOLKS STARTED TRAINING HIM FOR HIS EVENTUAL ASCENSION TO THE CHIEFHOOD...
I REMEMBER THINKING SOMETIMES THEY'D STARTED HIM TOO EARLY...
C'MON, BABY!
WAAH!
4

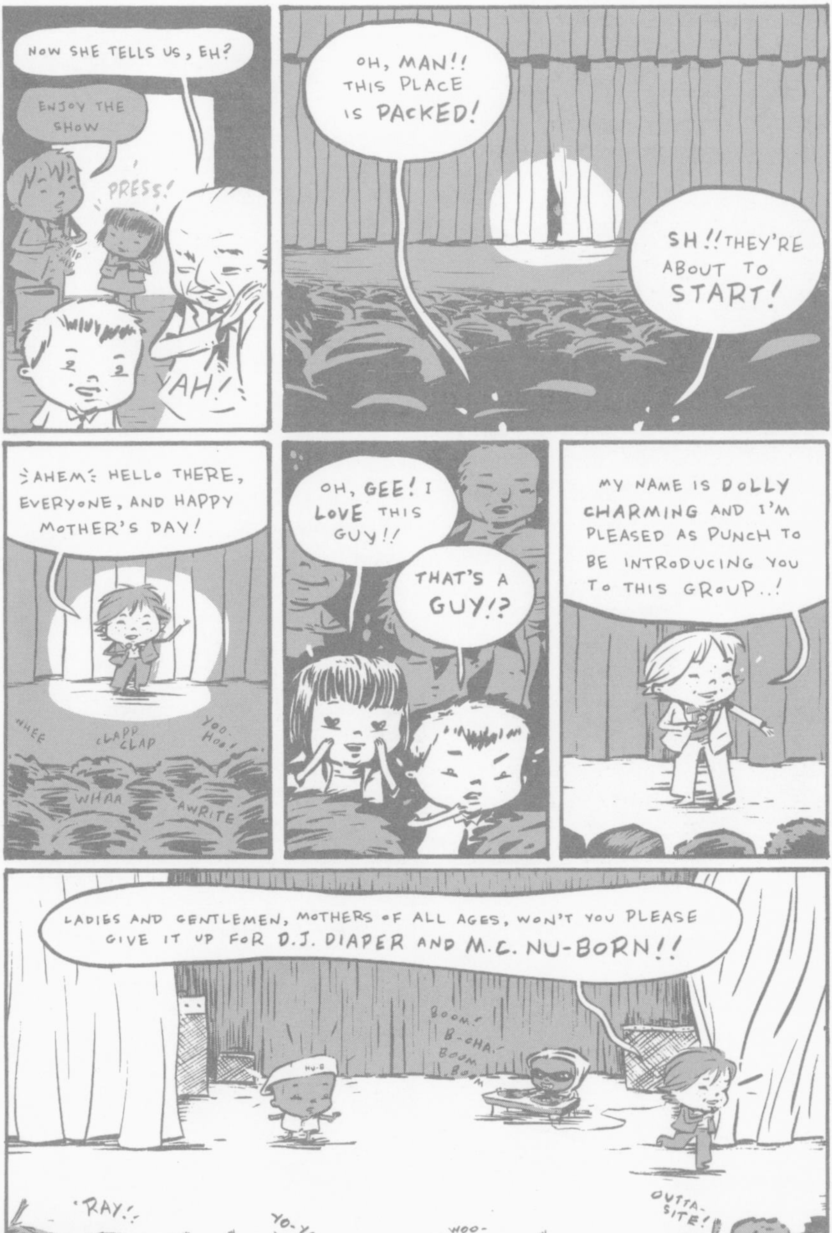
NOW SHE TELLS US, EH?
ENJOY THE SHOW
PRESS!
YAH!
OH, MAN!! THIS PLACE IS PACKED!
SH!! THEY'RE ABOUT TO START!
AHEM HELLO THERE, EVERYONE, AND HAPPY MOTHER'S DAY!
WHEE
CLAPP CLAP
YOO-HOO!
WHAA
AWRITE
OH, GEE! I LOVE THIS GUY!!
THAT'S A GUY!?
MY NAME IS DOLLY CHARMING AND I'M PLEASED AS PUNCH TO BE INTRODUCING YOU TO THIS GROUP..!
LADIES AND GENTLEMEN, MOTHERS OF ALL AGES, WON'T YOU PLEASE GIVE IT UP FOR D.J. DIAPER AND M.C. NU-BORN!!
BOOM! B-CHA-BOOM BOOM
'RAY!
YO-YO YO!!
WOO-WOO!
GO D.J.
OUTTA-SITE!
3

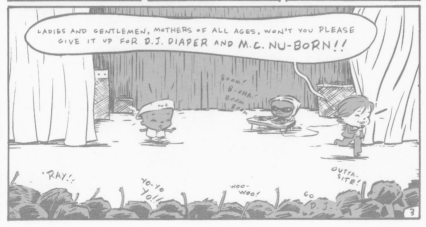

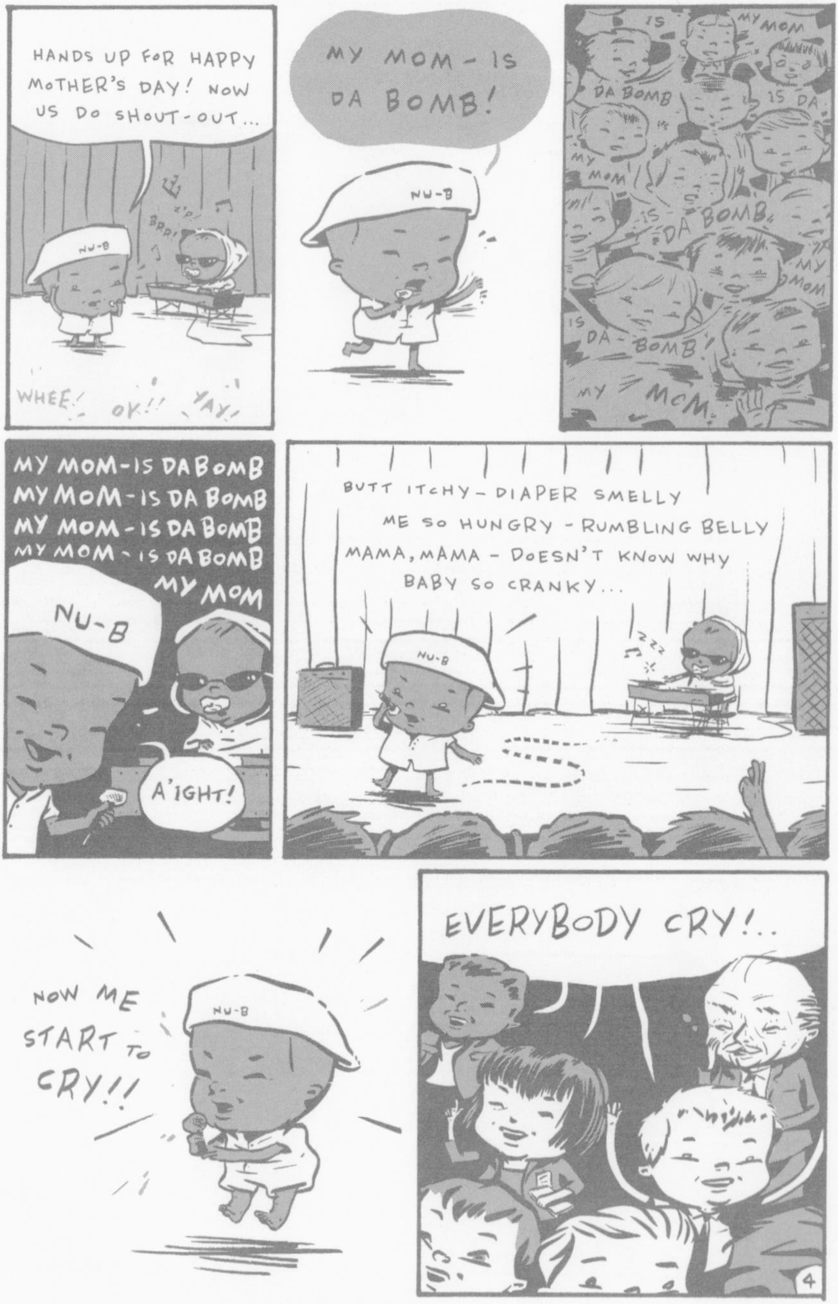
HANDS UP FOR HAPPY MOTHER'S DAY! NOW US DO SHOUT-OUT...
NU-B
WHEE! OK!! YAY!
MY MOM - IS DA BOMB!
NU-B
IS
MY MOM
DA BOMB
IS DA
MY MOM
IS DA BOMB
MY MOM
IS
DA - BOMB!
MY MOM
MY MOM - IS DA BOMB
MY MOM - IS DA BOMB
MY MOM - IS DA BOMB
MY MOM - IS DA BOMB
MY MOM
NU-B
A'IGHT!
BUTT ITCHY - DIAPER SMELLY
ME SO HUNGRY - RUMBLING BELLY
MAMA, MAMA - DOESN'T KNOW WHY
BABY SO CRANKY...
NU-B
NOW ME START TO CRY!!
NU-B
EVERYBODY CRY!..
4

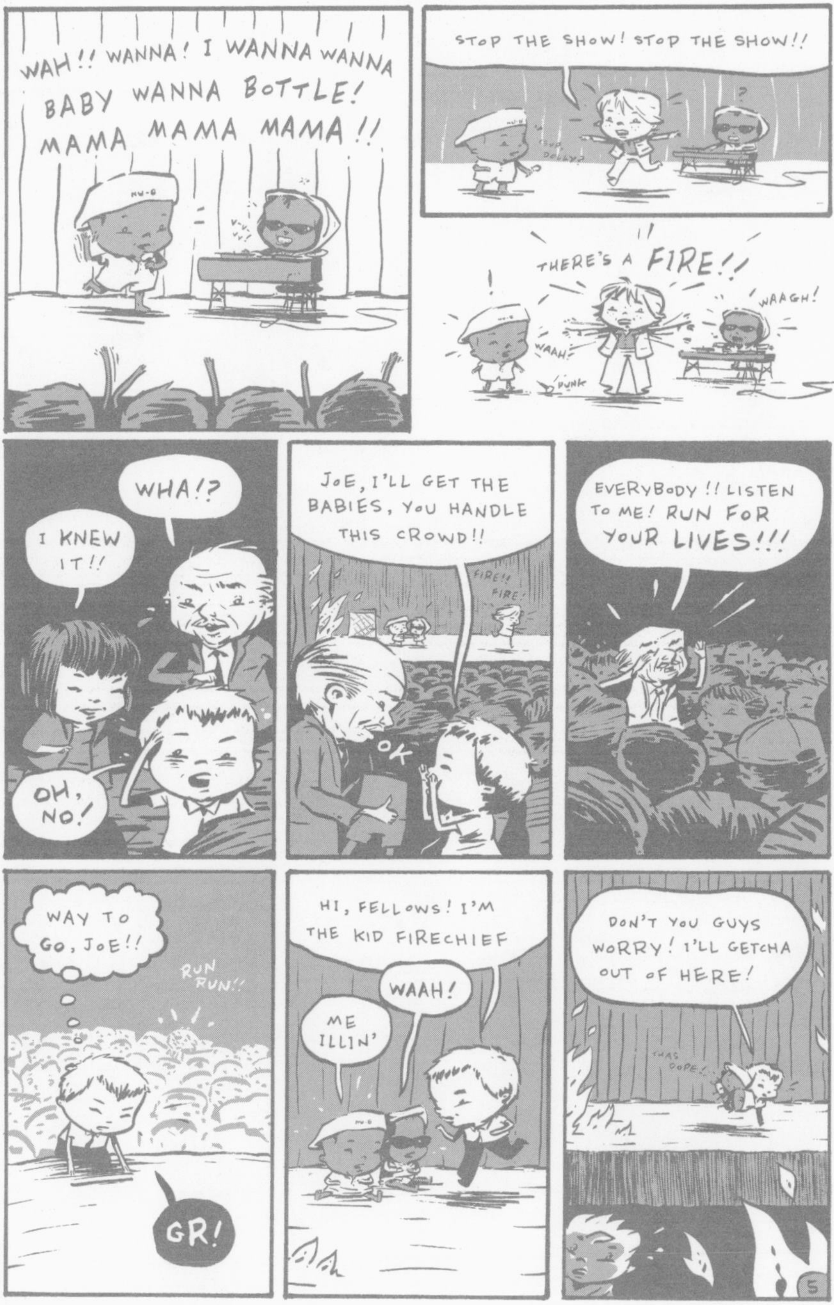

WAH!! WANNA! I WANNA WANNA BABY WANNA BOTTLE! MAMA MAMA MAMA!!
STOP THE SHOW! STOP THE SHOW!!
?
THERE'S A FIRE!!
WAAH!
WAAGH!
DUNK
WHA!?
I KNEW IT!!
OH, NO!
JOE, I'LL GET THE BABIES, YOU HANDLE THIS CROWD!!
FIRE!! FIRE!
OK
EVERYBODY!! LISTEN TO ME! RUN FOR YOUR LIVES!!!
WAY TO GO, JOE!!
RUN RUN!!
GR!
HI, FELLOWS! I'M THE KID FIRECHIEF
WAAH!
ME ILLIN'
DON'T YOU GUYS WORRY! I'LL GETCHA OUT OF HERE!
THAS DOPE!
5

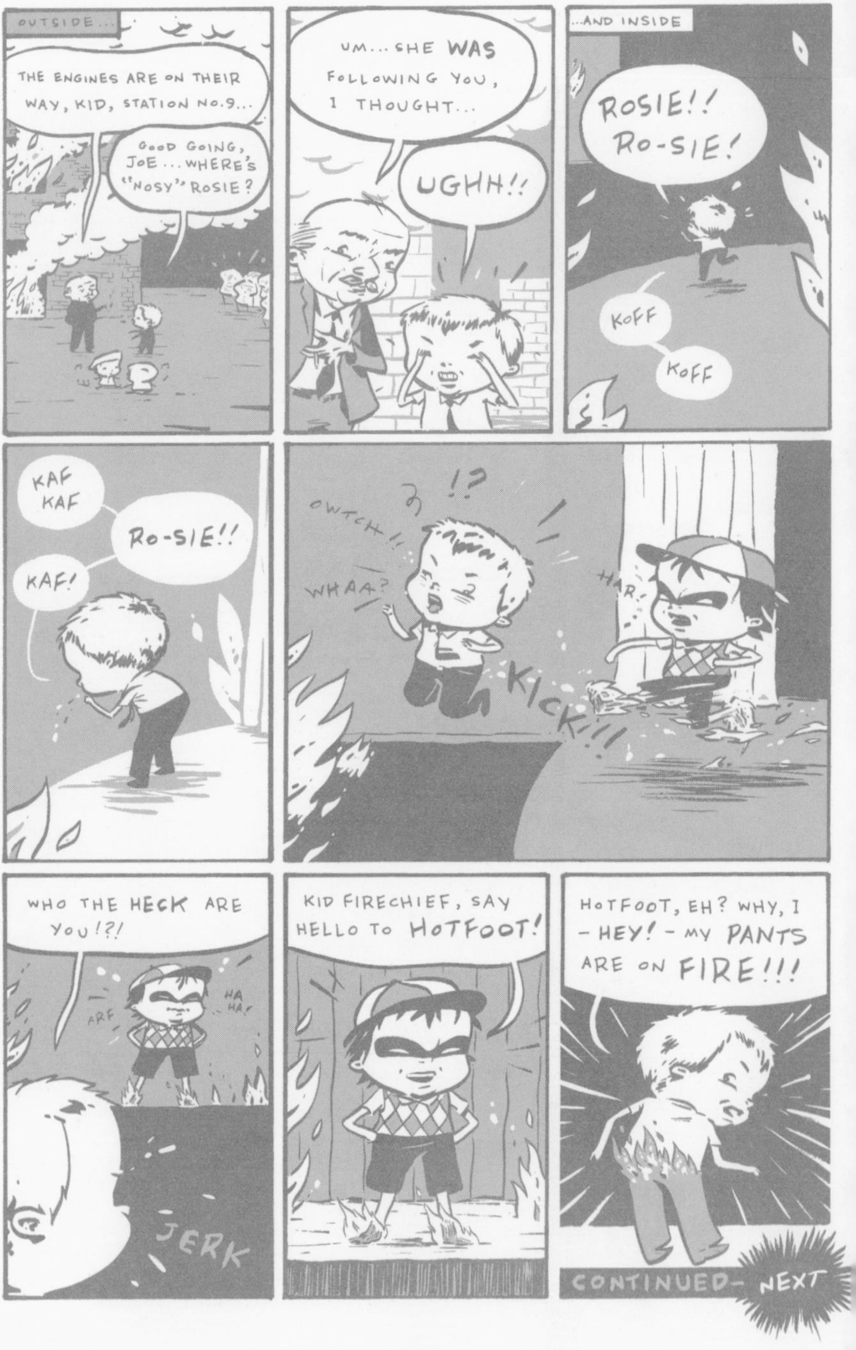
OUTSIDE...
THE ENGINES ARE ON THEIR WAY, KID, STATION No.9...
GOOD GOING, JOE... WHERE'S "NOSY" ROSIE?
UM... SHE WAS FOLLOWING YOU, I THOUGHT...
UGHH!!
...AND INSIDE
ROSIE!! RO-SIE!
KOFF
KOFF
KAF KAF
RO-SIE!!
KAF!
OWTCH!!
!?
WHAA?
HAR
KICK!!!
WHO THE HECK ARE YOU!?!
ARF
HA HA!
JERK
KID FIRECHIEF, SAY HELLO TO HOTFOOT!
HOTFOOT, EH? WHY, I - HEY! - MY PANTS ARE ON FIRE!!!
CONTINUED- NEXT

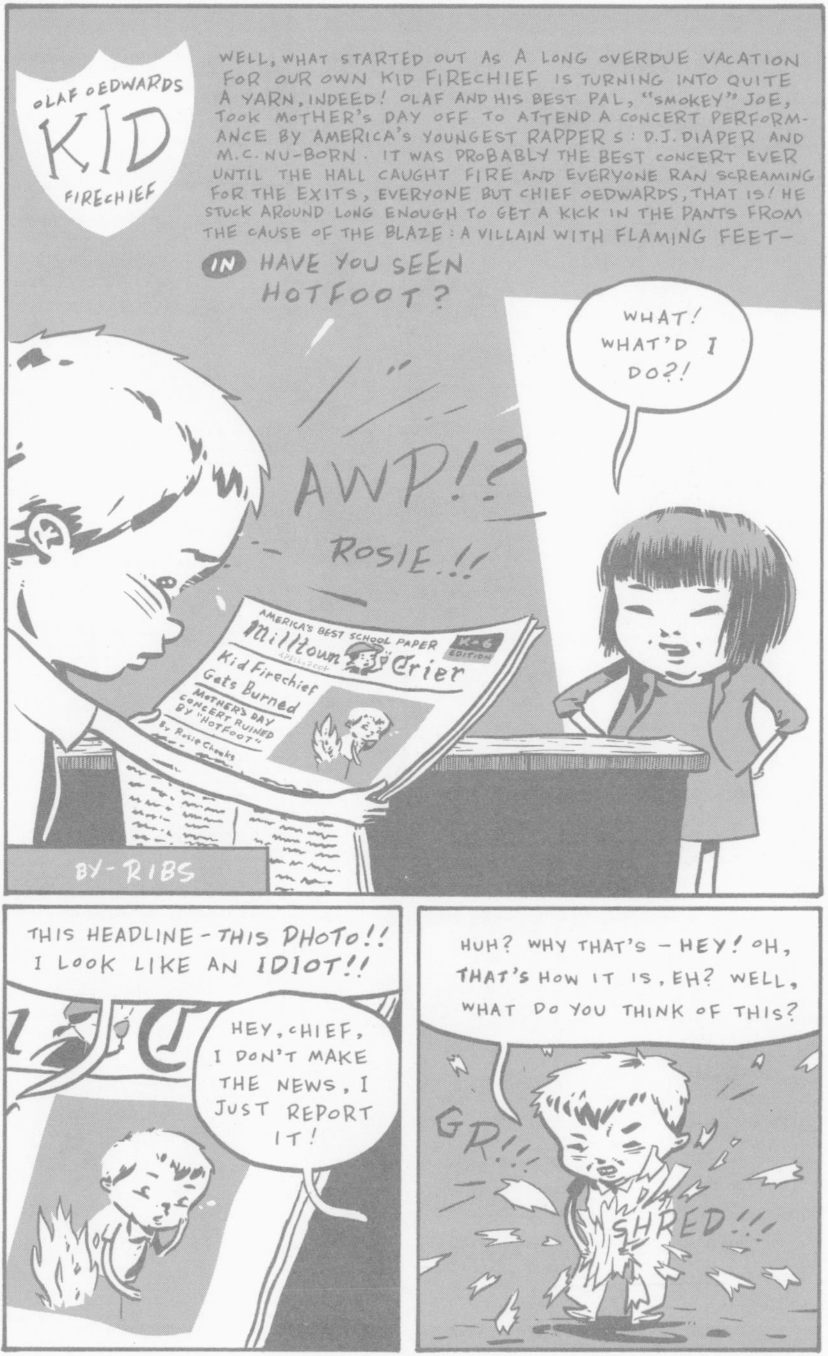
OLAF OEDWARDS
KID
FIRECHIEF
WELL, WHAT STARTED OUT AS A LONG OVERDUE VACATION FOR OUR OWN KID FIRECHIEF IS TURNING INTO QUITE A YARN, INDEED! OLAF AND HIS BEST PAL, "SMOKEY" JOE, TOOK MOTHER'S DAY OFF TO ATTEND A CONCERT PERFORMANCE BY AMERICA'S YOUNGEST RAPPERS: D.J. DIAPER AND M.C. NU-BORN. IT WAS PROBABLY THE BEST CONCERT EVER UNTIL THE HALL CAUGHT FIRE AND EVERYONE RAN SCREAMING FOR THE EXITS, EVERYONE BUT CHIEF OEDWARDS, THAT IS! HE STUCK AROUND LONG ENOUGH TO GET A KICK IN THE PANTS FROM THE CAUSE OF THE BLAZE: A VILLAIN WITH FLAMING FEET—
IN HAVE YOU SEEN HOTFOOT?
AWP!?
ROSIE..!!
WHAT! WHAT'D I DO?!
AMERICA'S BEST SCHOOL PAPER
Milltown Crier
K-6 EDITION
Kid Firechief Gets Burned
MOTHER'S DAY CONCERT RUINED BY "HOTFOOT"
By Rosie Cheeks
BY-RIBS
THIS HEADLINE - THIS PHOTO!! I LOOK LIKE AN IDIOT!!
HEY, CHIEF, I DON'T MAKE THE NEWS, I JUST REPORT IT!
HUH? WHY THAT'S - HEY! OH, THAT'S HOW IT IS, EH? WELL, WHAT DO YOU THINK OF THIS?
GR!!
SHRED!!!

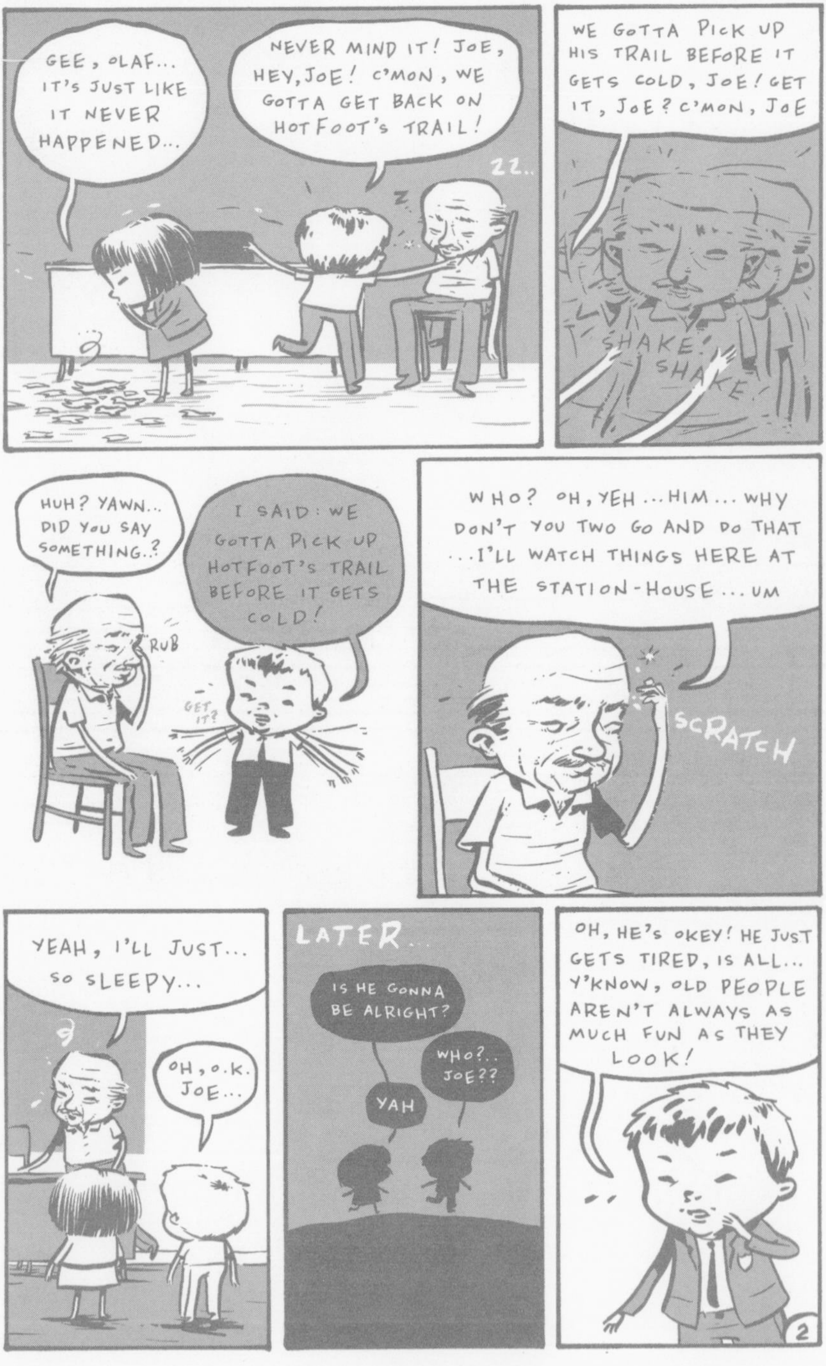

GEE, OLAF... IT'S JUST LIKE IT NEVER HAPPENED...
NEVER MIND IT! JOE, HEY, JOE! C'MON, WE GOTTA GET BACK ON HOTFOOT'S TRAIL!
Z
ZZ..
WE GOTTA PICK UP HIS TRAIL BEFORE IT GETS COLD, JOE! GET IT, JOE? C'MON, JOE
SHAKE SHAKE
HUH? YAWN... DID YOU SAY SOMETHING..?
I SAID: WE GOTTA PICK UP HOTFOOT'S TRAIL BEFORE IT GETS COLD!
RUB
GET IT?
WHO? OH, YEH ...HIM... WHY DON'T YOU TWO GO AND DO THAT ...I'LL WATCH THINGS HERE AT THE STATION-HOUSE ...UM
SCRATCH
YEAH, I'LL JUST... SO SLEEPY...
OH, O.K. JOE...
LATER...
IS HE GONNA BE ALRIGHT?
WHO?.. JOE??
YAH
OH, HE'S OKEY! HE JUST GETS TIRED, IS ALL... Y'KNOW, OLD PEOPLE AREN'T ALWAYS AS MUCH FUN AS THEY LOOK!
2

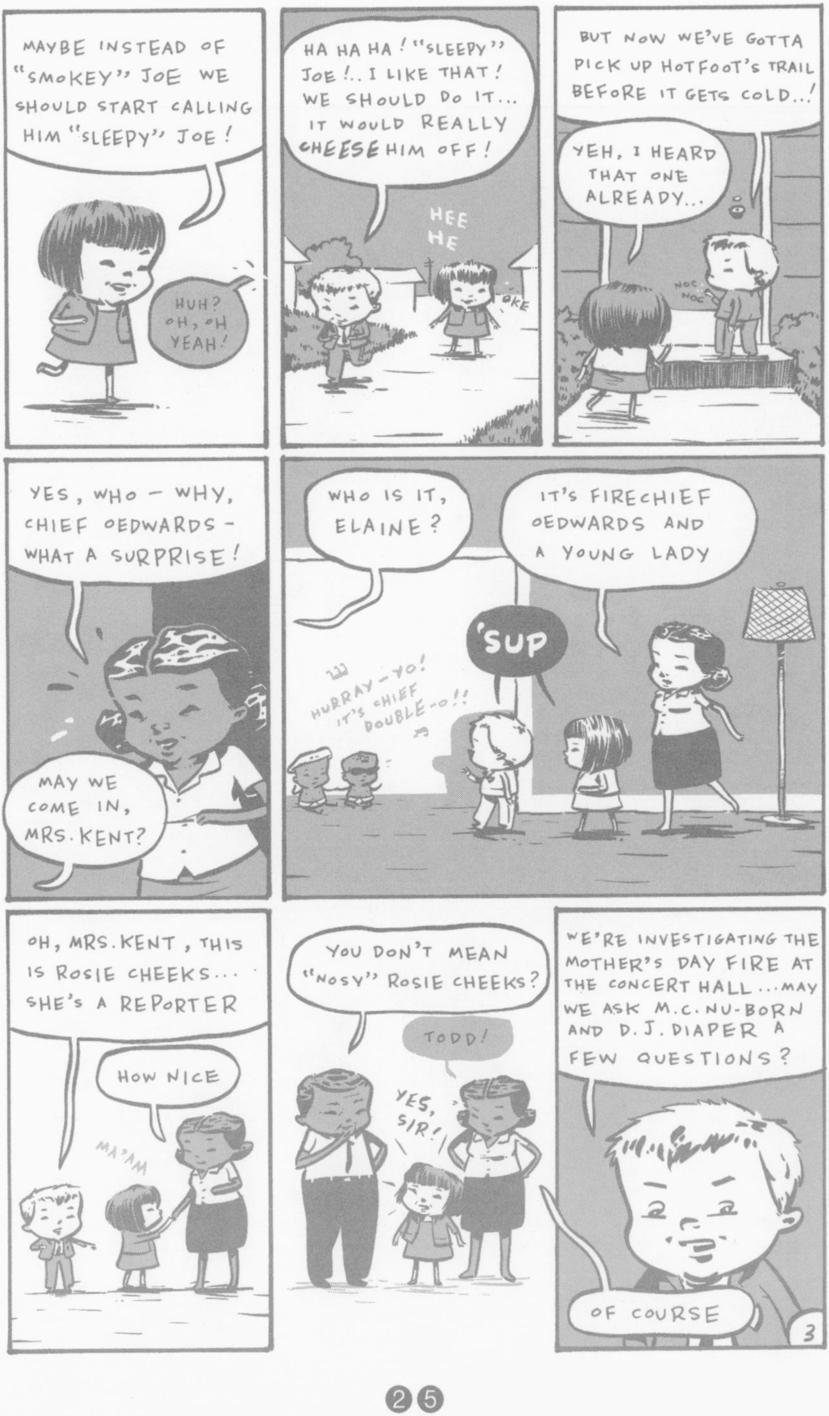
MAYBE INSTEAD OF "SMOKEY" JOE WE SHOULD START CALLING HIM "SLEEPY" JOE!
HUH? OH, OH YEAH!
HA HA HA! "SLEEPY" JOE!.. I LIKE THAT! WE SHOULD DO IT... IT WOULD REALLY CHEESE HIM OFF!
HEE HE
BUT NOW WE'VE GOTTA PICK UP HOTFOOT'S TRAIL BEFORE IT GETS COLD..!
YEH, I HEARD THAT ONE ALREADY...
YES, WHO - WHY, CHIEF OEDWARDS - WHAT A SURPRISE!
MAY WE COME IN, MRS. KENT?
WHO IS IT, ELAINE?
IT'S FIRECHIEF OEDWARDS AND A YOUNG LADY
'SUP
HURRAY-YO! IT'S CHIEF DOUBLE-O!!
OH, MRS. KENT, THIS IS ROSIE CHEEKS... SHE'S A REPORTER
HOW NICE
MA'AM
YOU DON'T MEAN "NOSY" ROSIE CHEEKS?
TODD!
YES, SIR!
WE'RE INVESTIGATING THE MOTHER'S DAY FIRE AT THE CONCERT HALL... MAY WE ASK M.C. NU-BORN AND D.J. DIAPER A FEW QUESTIONS?
OF COURSE
3

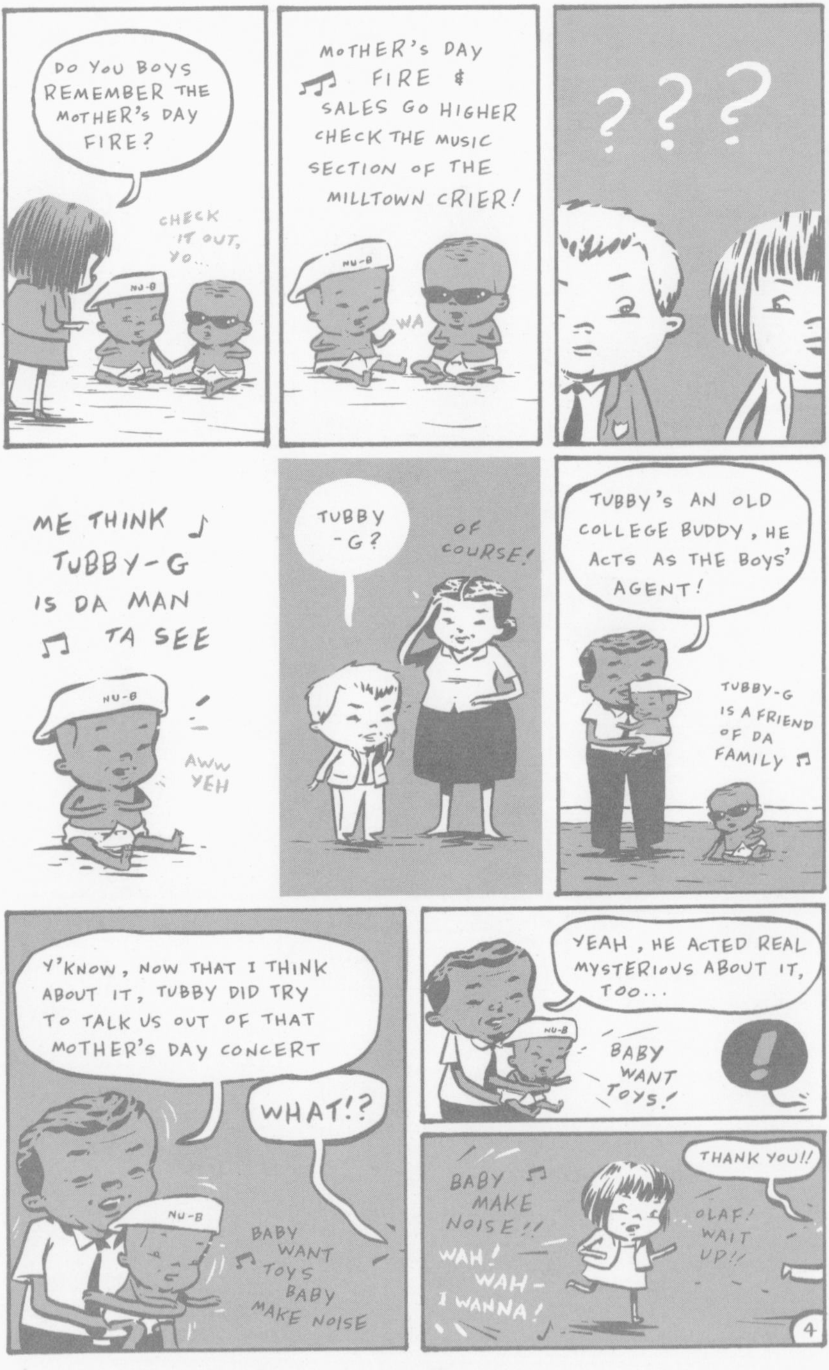
DO YOU BOYS REMEMBER THE MOTHER'S DAY FIRE?
CHECK IT OUT, YO...
MOTHER'S DAY FIRE & SALES GO HIGHER CHECK THE MUSIC SECTION OF THE MILLTOWN CRIER!
NU-B
WA
???
ME THINK TUBBY-G IS DA MAN TA SEE
AWW YEH
TUBBY -G?
OF COURSE!
TUBBY'S AN OLD COLLEGE BUDDY, HE ACTS AS THE BOYS' AGENT!
TUBBY-G IS A FRIEND OF DA FAMILY
Y'KNOW, NOW THAT I THINK ABOUT IT, TUBBY DID TRY TO TALK US OUT OF THAT MOTHER'S DAY CONCERT
WHAT!?
BABY WANT TOYS BABY MAKE NOISE
YEAH, HE ACTED REAL MYSTERIOUS ABOUT IT, TOO...
BABY WANT TOYS!
!
THANK YOU!!
BABY MAKE NOISE!!
WAH! WAH- I WANNA!
OLAF! WAIT UP!!
4

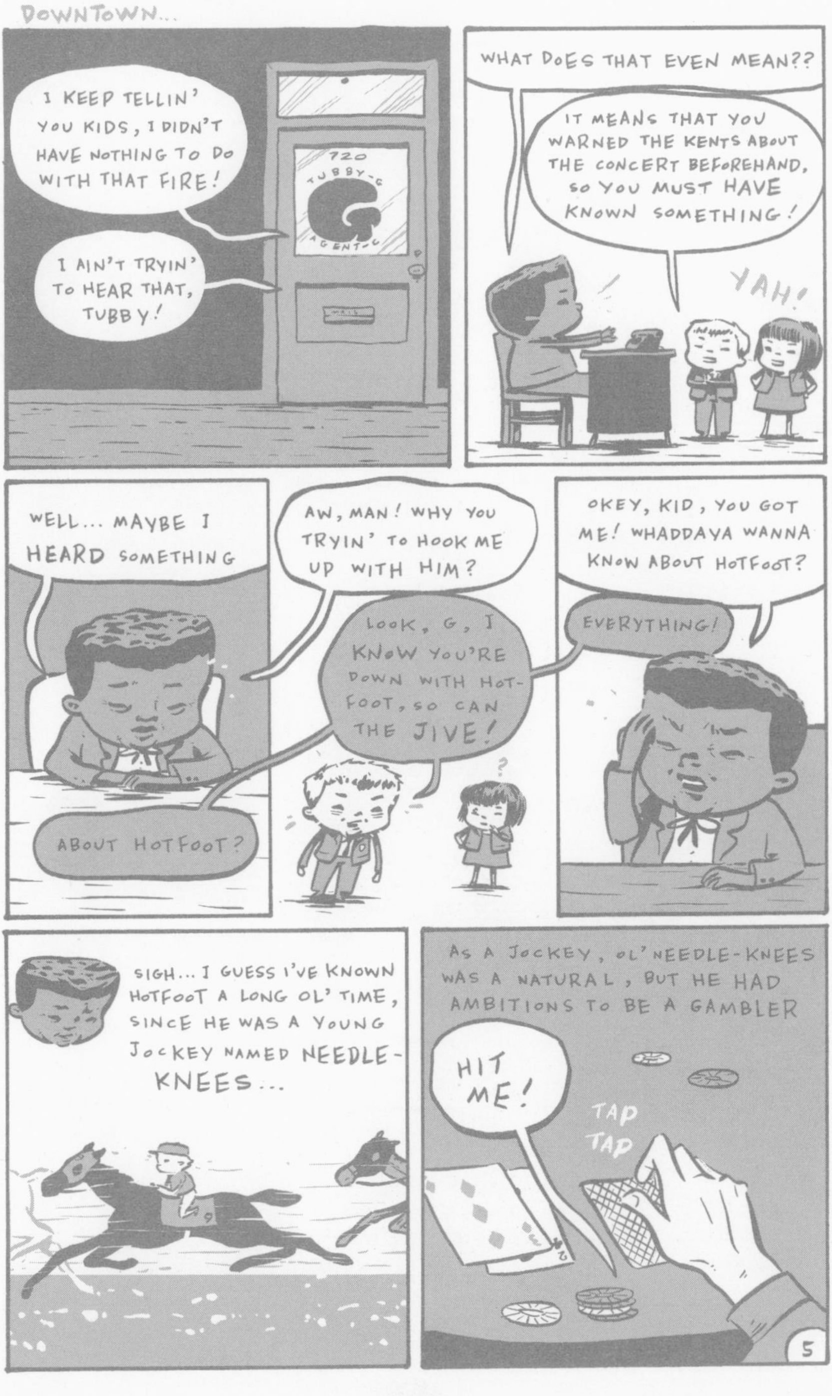
DOWNTOWN...
I KEEP TELLIN' YOU KIDS, I DIDN'T HAVE NOTHING TO DO WITH THAT FIRE!
I AIN'T TRYIN' TO HEAR THAT, TUBBY!
720 TUBBY-G AGENT-C
WHAT DOES THAT EVEN MEAN??
IT MEANS THAT YOU WARNED THE KENTS ABOUT THE CONCERT BEFOREHAND, SO YOU MUST HAVE KNOWN SOMETHING!
YAH!
WELL... MAYBE I HEARD SOMETHING
ABOUT HOTFOOT?
AW, MAN! WHY YOU TRYIN' TO HOOK ME UP WITH HIM?
LOOK, G, I KNOW YOU'RE DOWN WITH HOT-FOOT, SO CAN THE JIVE!
OKEY, KID, YOU GOT ME! WHADDAYA WANNA KNOW ABOUT HOTFOOT?
EVERYTHING!
SIGH... I GUESS I'VE KNOWN HOTFOOT A LONG OL' TIME, SINCE HE WAS A YOUNG JOCKEY NAMED NEEDLE-KNEES...
AS A JOCKEY, OL' NEEDLE-KNEES WAS A NATURAL, BUT HE HAD AMBITIONS TO BE A GAMBLER
HIT ME!
TAP TAP
5

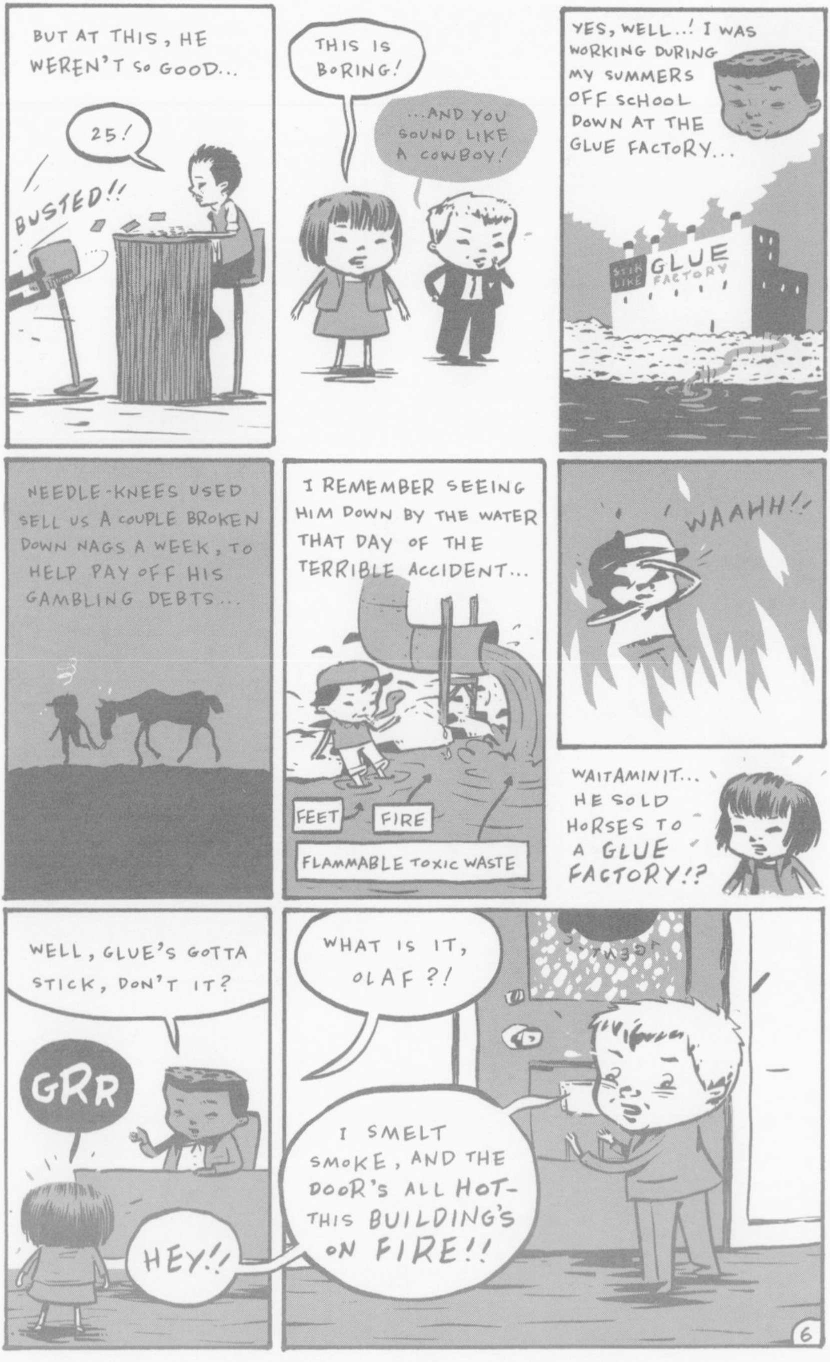

BUT AT THIS, HE WEREN'T SO GOOD...
25!
BUSTED!!
THIS IS BORING!
...AND YOU SOUND LIKE A COWBOY!
YES, WELL...! I WAS WORKING DURING MY SUMMERS OFF SCHOOL DOWN AT THE GLUE FACTORY...
STIK LIKE GLUE FACTORY
NEEDLE-KNEES USED SELL US A COUPLE BROKEN DOWN NAGS A WEEK, TO HELP PAY OFF HIS GAMBLING DEBTS...
I REMEMBER SEEING HIM DOWN BY THE WATER THAT DAY OF THE TERRIBLE ACCIDENT...
FEET
FIRE
FLAMMABLE TOXIC WASTE
WAAHH!!
WAITAMINIT... HE SOLD HORSES TO A GLUE FACTORY!?
WELL, GLUE'S GOTTA STICK, DON'T IT?
GRR
HEY!!
WHAT IS IT, OLAF?!
I SMELT SMOKE, AND THE DOOR'S ALL HOT- THIS BUILDING'S ON FIRE!!
6

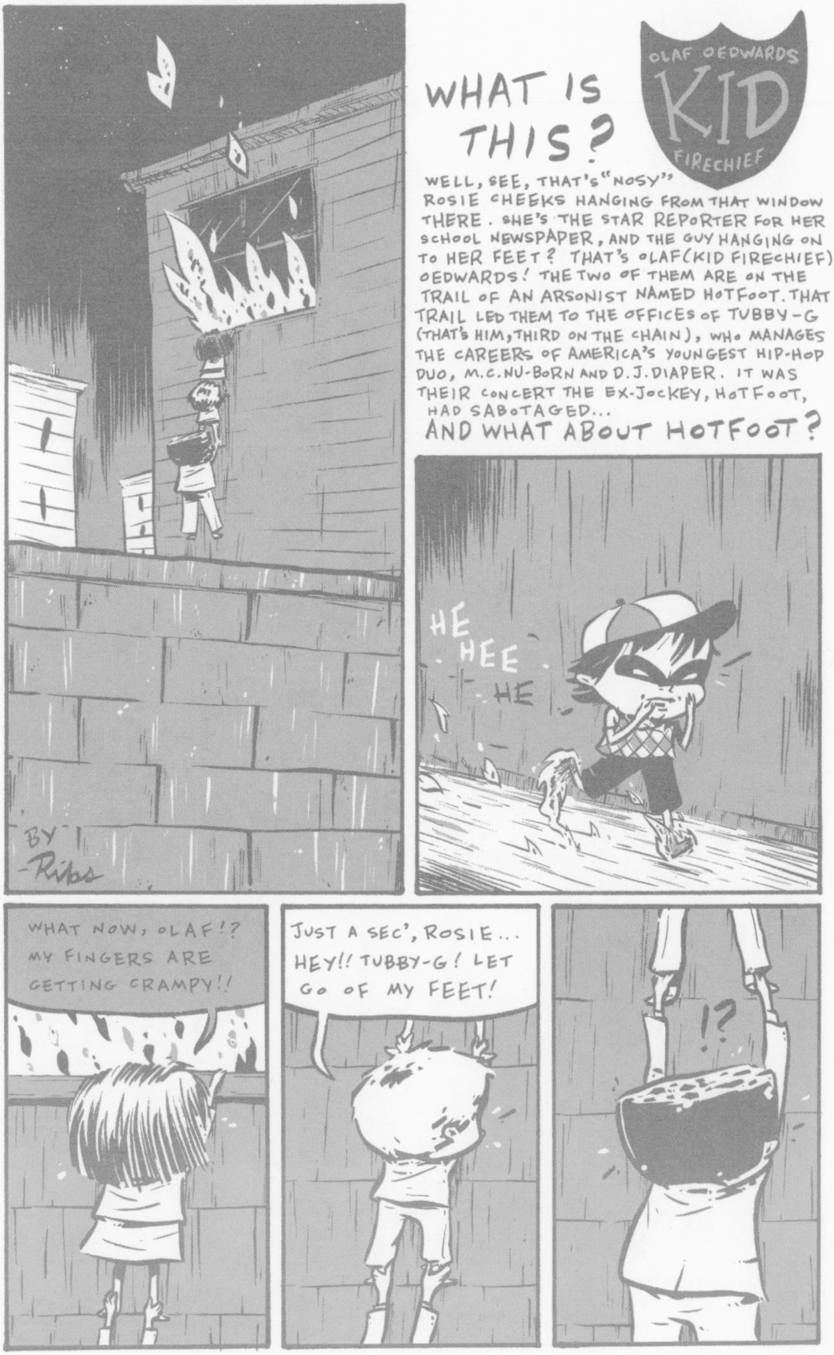
OLAF OEDWARDS
KID
FIRECHIEF
WHAT IS THIS?
WELL, SEE, THAT'S "NOSY" ROSIE CHEEKS HANGING FROM THAT WINDOW THERE. SHE'S THE STAR REPORTER FOR HER SCHOOL NEWSPAPER, AND THE GUY HANGING ON TO HER FEET? THAT'S OLAF (KID FIRECHIEF) OEDWARDS! THE TWO OF THEM ARE ON THE TRAIL OF AN ARSONIST NAMED HOTFOOT. THAT TRAIL LED THEM TO THE OFFICES OF TUBBY-G (THAT'S HIM, THIRD ON THE CHAIN), WHO MANAGES THE CAREERS OF AMERICA'S YOUNGEST HIP-HOP DUO, M.C. NU-BORN AND D.J. DIAPER. IT WAS THEIR CONCERT THE EX-JOCKEY, HOTFOOT, HAD SABOTAGED...
AND WHAT ABOUT HOTFOOT?
BY -Ribs
HE HEE HE
WHAT NOW, OLAF!? MY FINGERS ARE GETTING CRAMPY!!
JUST A SEC', ROSIE... HEY!! TUBBY-G! LET GO OF MY FEET!
!?

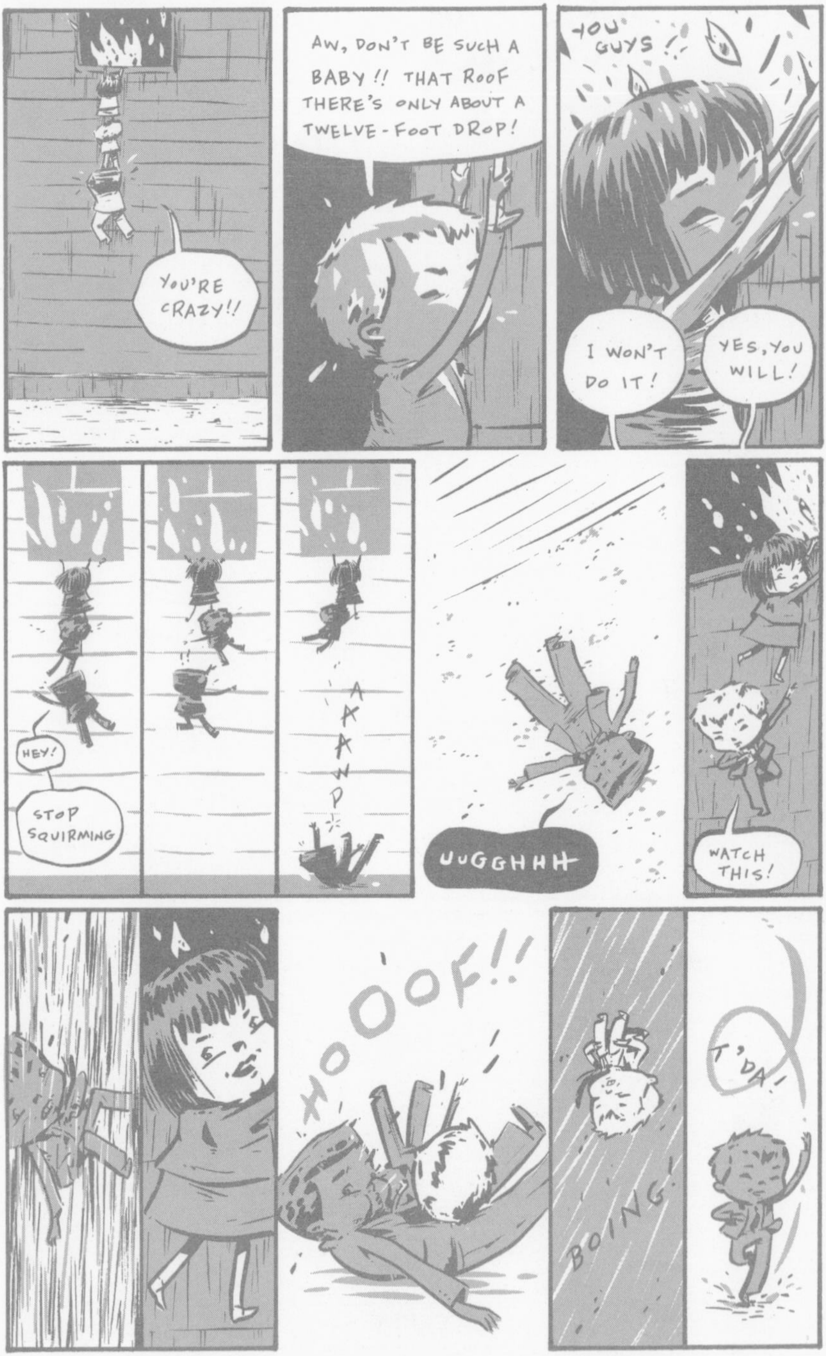
YOU'RE CRAZY!!
AW, DON'T BE SUCH A BABY!! THAT ROOF THERE'S ONLY ABOUT A TWELVE-FOOT DROP!
YOU GUYS!
I WON'T DO IT!
YES, YOU WILL!
HEY!
STOP SQUIRMING
AAAAND
UUGGHHH
WATCH THIS!
HOOOF!!
BOING!
T'DA!

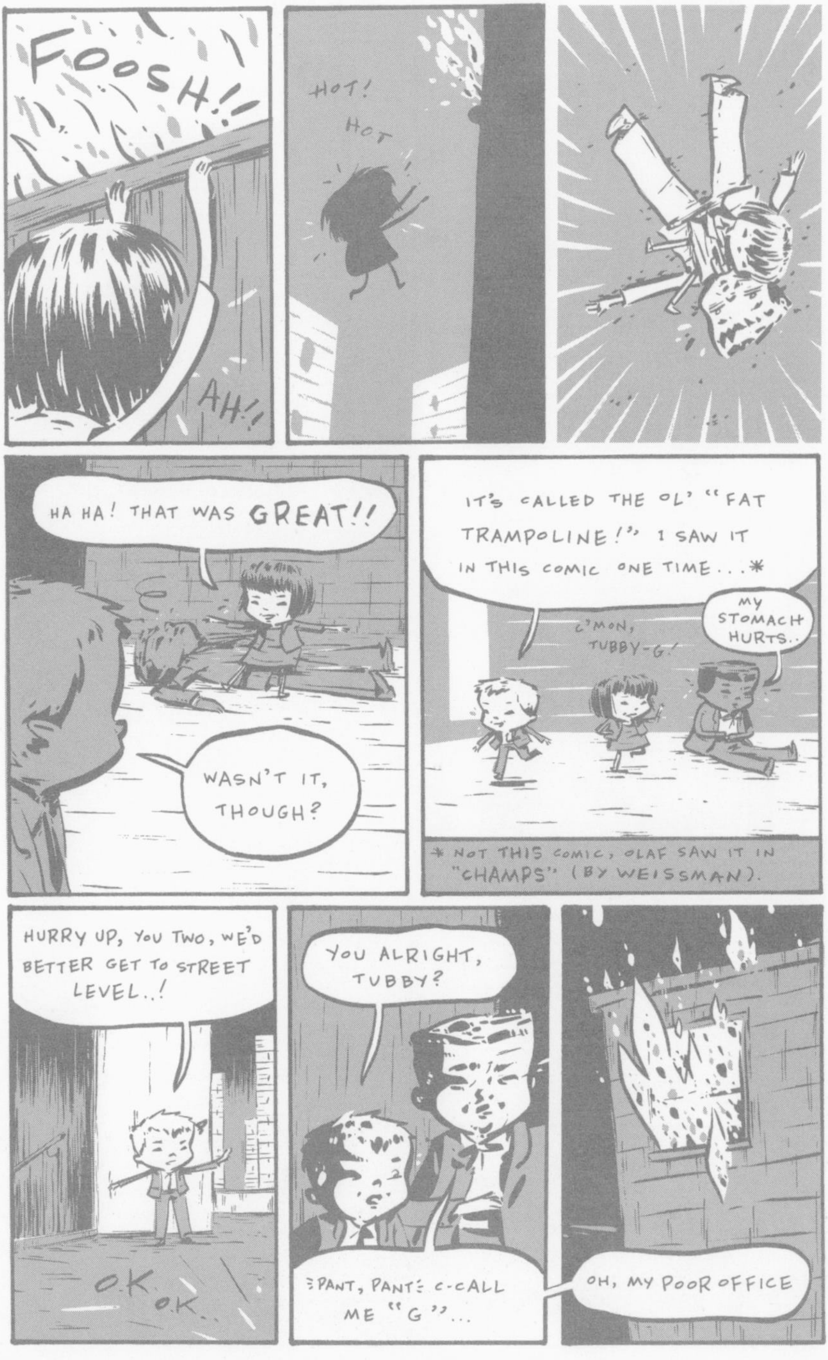
FOOSH!!
AH!!
HOT!
HOT
HA HA! THAT WAS GREAT!!
WASN'T IT, THOUGH?
IT'S CALLED THE OL' "FAT TRAMPOLINE!" I SAW IT IN THIS COMIC ONE TIME...*
C'MON, TUBBY-G!
MY STOMACH HURTS..
* NOT THIS COMIC, OLAF SAW IT IN "CHAMPS" (BY WEISSMAN).
HURRY UP, YOU TWO, WE'D BETTER GET TO STREET LEVEL..!
O.K.
O.K.
YOU ALRIGHT, TUBBY?
=PANT, PANT= C-CALL ME "G"...
OH, MY POOR OFFICE

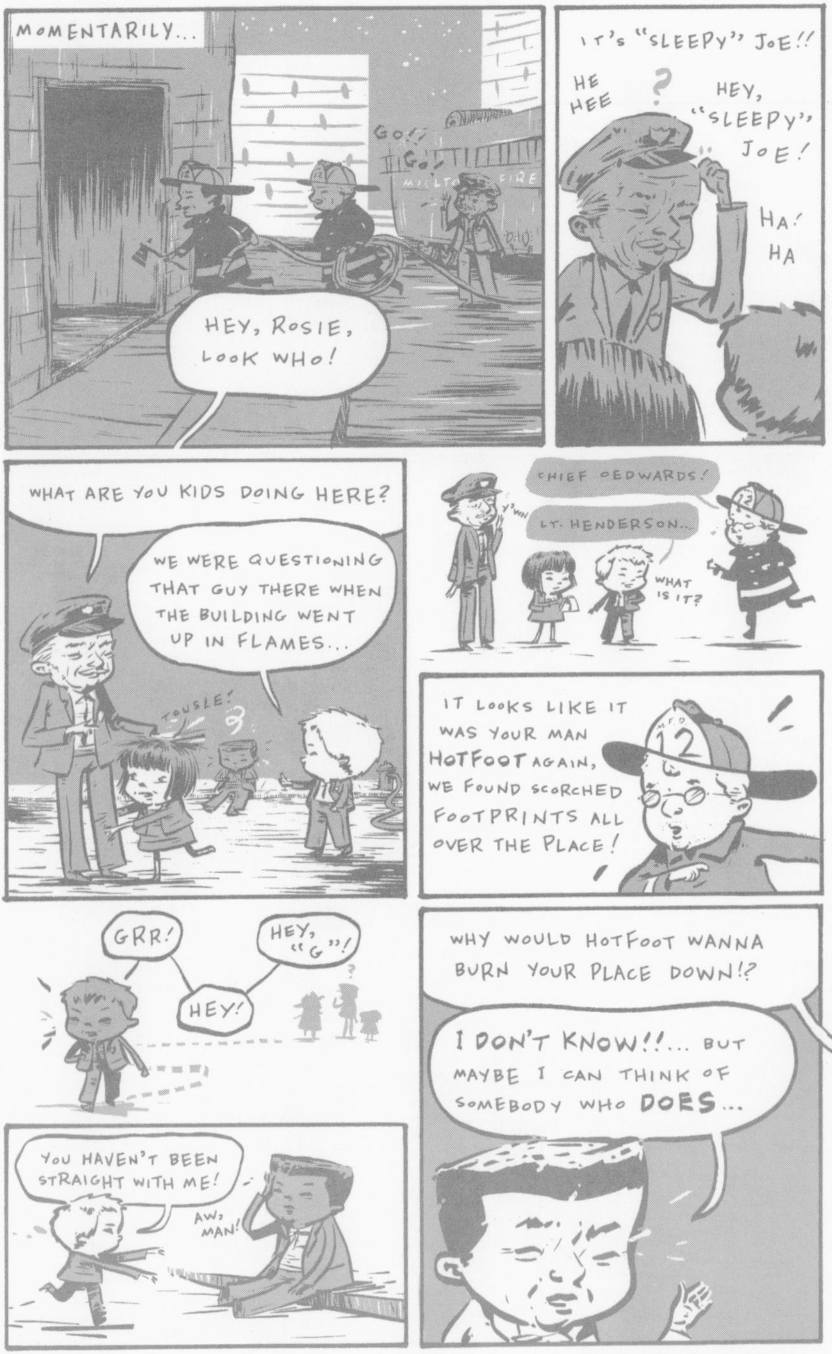
MOMENTARILY...
GO!!
GO!!
HEY, ROSIE, LOOK WHO!
IT'S "SLEEPY" JOE!!
HE HEE
?
HEY, "SLEEPY" JOE!
HA! HA
WHAT ARE YOU KIDS DOING HERE?
WE WERE QUESTIONING THAT GUY THERE WHEN THE BUILDING WENT UP IN FLAMES...
TOUSLE!
CHIEF OEDWARDS!
LT. HENDERSON...
WHAT IS IT?
IT LOOKS LIKE IT WAS YOUR MAN HOTFOOT AGAIN, WE FOUND SCORCHED FOOTPRINTS ALL OVER THE PLACE!
GRR!
HEY, "G"!
HEY!
YOU HAVEN'T BEEN STRAIGHT WITH ME!
AW, MAN!
WHY WOULD HOTFOOT WANNA BURN YOUR PLACE DOWN!?
I DON'T KNOW!!... BUT MAYBE I CAN THINK OF SOMEBODY WHO DOES...

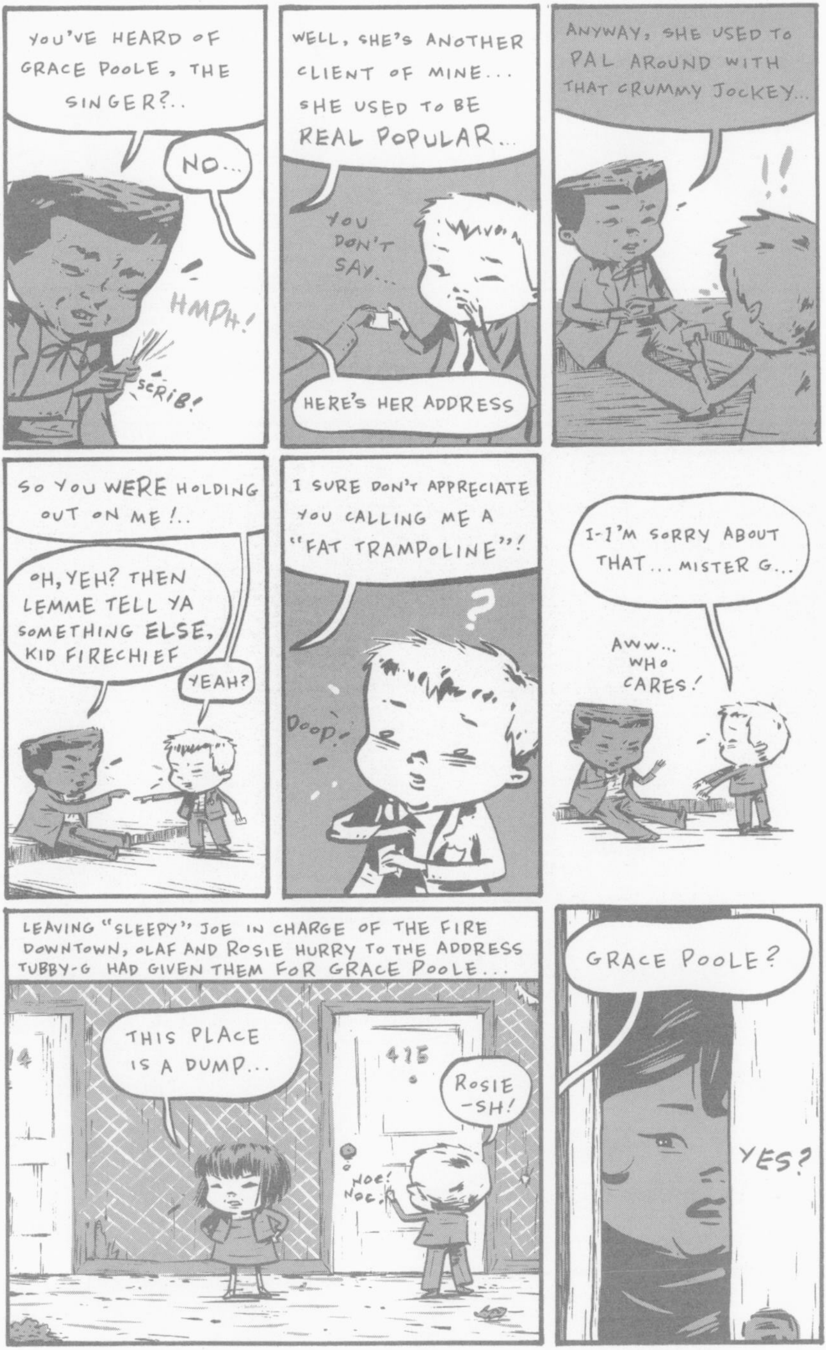

YOU'VE HEARD OF GRACE POOLE, THE SINGER?..
NO...
HMPH!
SCRIB!
WELL, SHE'S ANOTHER CLIENT OF MINE... SHE USED TO BE REAL POPULAR...
YOU DON'T SAY...
HERE'S HER ADDRESS
ANYWAY, SHE USED TO PAL AROUND WITH THAT CRUMMY JOCKEY...
!!
SO YOU WERE HOLDING OUT ON ME!..
OH, YEH? THEN LEMME TELL YA SOMETHING ELSE, KID FIRECHIEF
YEAH?
I SURE DON'T APPRECIATE YOU CALLING ME A "FAT TRAMPOLINE"!
?
DOOP
I-I'M SORRY ABOUT THAT... MISTER G...
AWW... WHO CARES!
LEAVING "SLEEPY" JOE IN CHARGE OF THE FIRE DOWNTOWN, OLAF AND ROSIE HURRY TO THE ADDRESS TUBBY-G HAD GIVEN THEM FOR GRACE POOLE...
THIS PLACE IS A DUMP...
415
ROSIE -SH!
NOC! NOC.
GRACE POOLE?
YES?

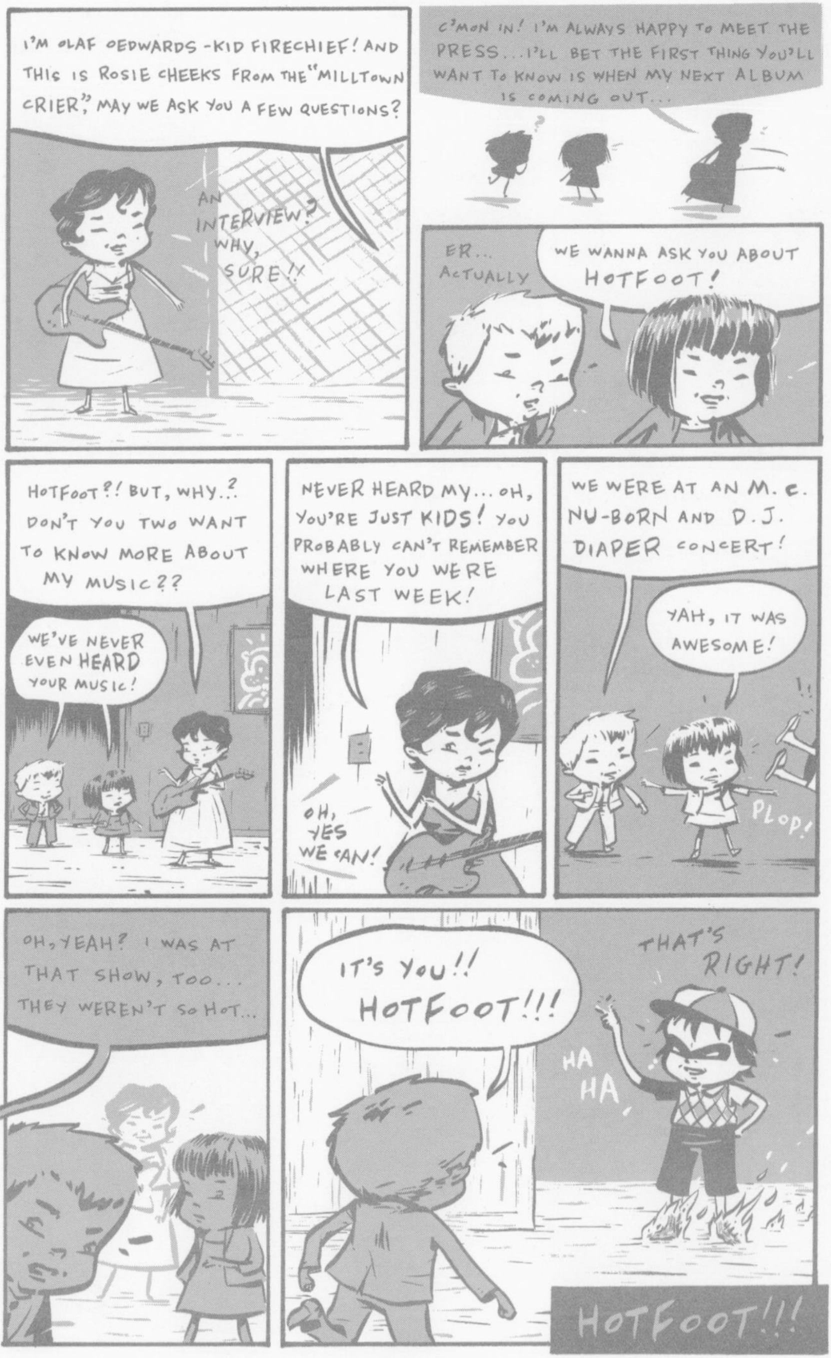
I'M OLAF OEDWARDS - KID FIRECHIEF! AND THIS IS ROSIE CHEEKS FROM THE "MILLTOWN CRIER," MAY WE ASK YOU A FEW QUESTIONS?
AN INTERVIEW? WHY, SURE!!
C'MON IN! I'M ALWAYS HAPPY TO MEET THE PRESS... I'LL BET THE FIRST THING YOU'LL WANT TO KNOW IS WHEN MY NEXT ALBUM IS COMING OUT...
ER... ACTUALLY
WE WANNA ASK YOU ABOUT HOTFOOT!
HOTFOOT?! BUT, WHY..? DON'T YOU TWO WANT TO KNOW MORE ABOUT MY MUSIC??
WE'VE NEVER EVEN HEARD YOUR MUSIC!
NEVER HEARD MY... OH, YOU'RE JUST KIDS! YOU PROBABLY CAN'T REMEMBER WHERE YOU WERE LAST WEEK!
OH, YES WE CAN!
WE WERE AT AN M.C. NU-BORN AND D.J. DIAPER CONCERT!
YAH, IT WAS AWESOME!
PLOP!
OH, YEAH? I WAS AT THAT SHOW, TOO... THEY WEREN'T SO HOT...
IT'S YOU!! HOTFOOT!!!
THAT'S RIGHT!
HA HA
HOTFOOT!!!

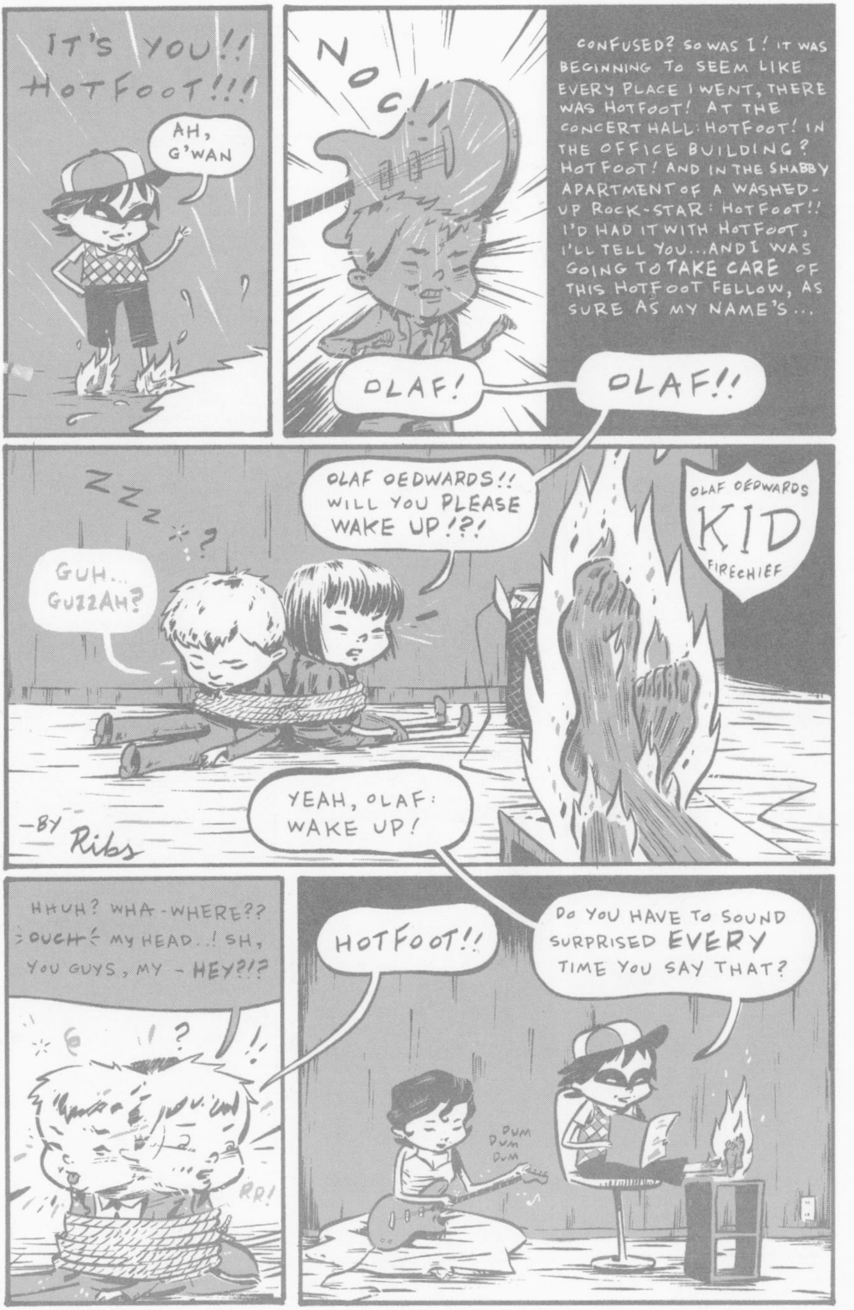
IT'S YOU!! HOTFOOT!!!
AH, G'WAN
NOC!
CONFUSED? SO WAS I! IT WAS BEGINNING TO SEEM LIKE EVERY PLACE I WENT, THERE WAS HOTFOOT! AT THE CONCERT HALL: HOTFOOT! IN THE OFFICE BUILDING? HOTFOOT! AND IN THE SHABBY APARTMENT OF A WASHED-UP ROCK-STAR: HOTFOOT!! I'D HAD IT WITH HOTFOOT, I'LL TELL YOU... AND I WAS GOING TO TAKE CARE OF THIS HOTFOOT FELLOW, AS SURE AS MY NAME'S...
OLAF!
OLAF!!
ZZZ
OLAF OEDWARDS!! WILL YOU PLEASE WAKE UP!?!
OLAF OEDWARDS KID FIRECHIEF
GUH... GUZZAH?
YEAH, OLAF: WAKE UP!
—BY Ribs
HHUH? WHA-WHERE?? OUCH MY HEAD..! SH, YOU GUYS, MY - HEY?!?
HOTFOOT!!
DO YOU HAVE TO SOUND SURPRISED EVERY TIME YOU SAY THAT?
DUM DUM DUM
RR!

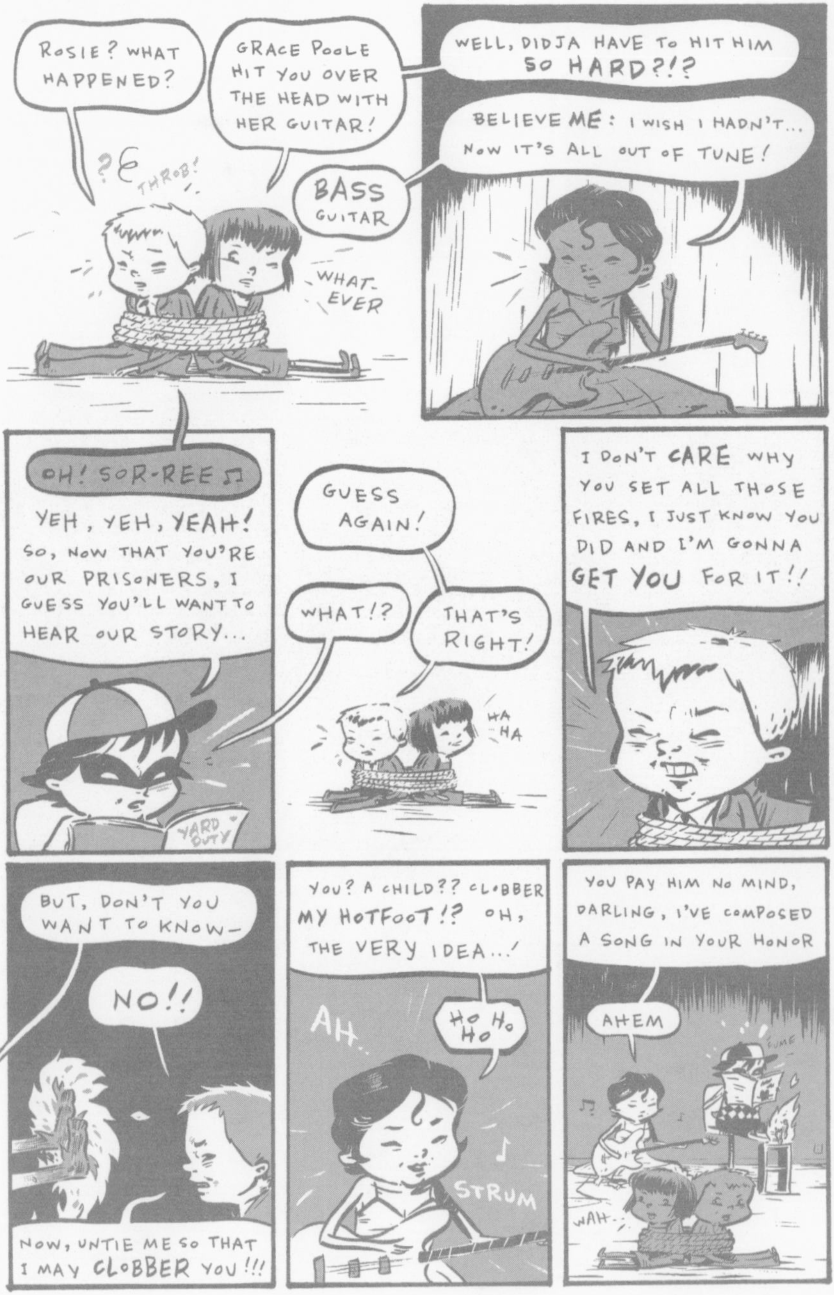
ROSIE? WHAT HAPPENED?
GRACE POOLE HIT YOU OVER THE HEAD WITH HER GUITAR!
?E THROB!
BASS GUITAR
WHAT-EVER
WELL, DIDJA HAVE TO HIT HIM SO HARD?!?
BELIEVE ME: I WISH I HADN'T... NOW IT'S ALL OUT OF TUNE!
OH! SOR-REE ♫
YEH, YEH, YEAH! SO, NOW THAT YOU'RE OUR PRISONERS, I GUESS YOU'LL WANT TO HEAR OUR STORY...
YARD DUTY
GUESS AGAIN!
WHAT!?
THAT'S RIGHT!
HA HA
I DON'T CARE WHY YOU SET ALL THOSE FIRES, I JUST KNOW YOU DID AND I'M GONNA GET YOU FOR IT!!
BUT, DON'T YOU WANT TO KNOW—
NO!!
NOW, UNTIE ME SO THAT I MAY CLOBBER YOU!!!
YOU? A CHILD?? CLOBBER MY HOTFOOT!? OH, THE VERY IDEA...!
AH..
HO HO HO
STRUM
YOU PAY HIM NO MIND, DARLING, I'VE COMPOSED A SONG IN YOUR HONOR
AHEM
FUME
WAH..

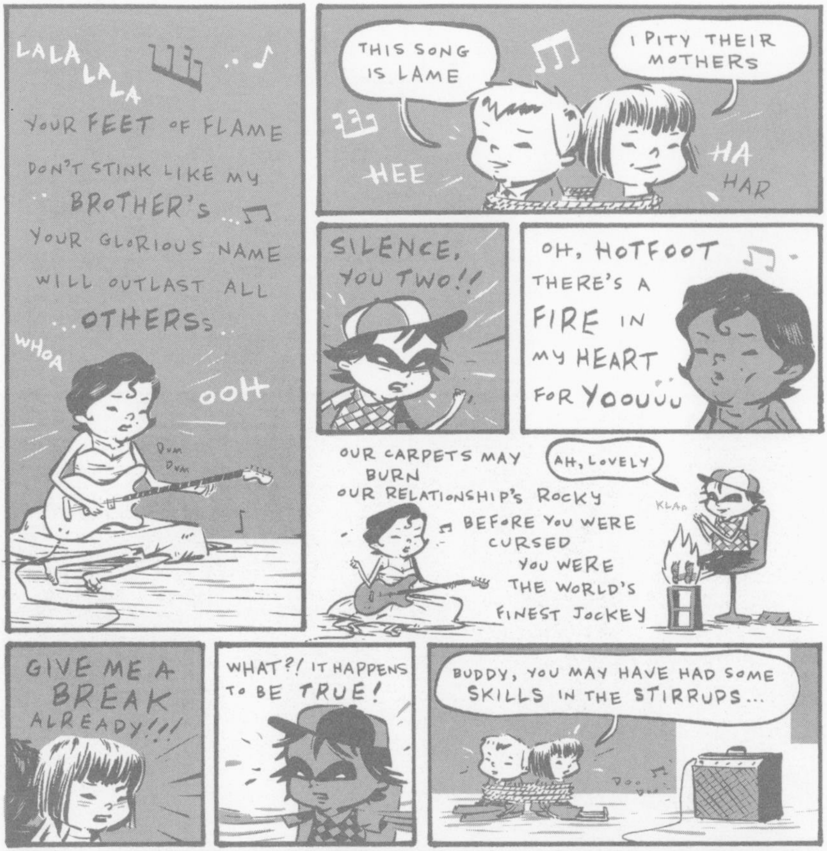
LALA LA LA
YOUR FEET OF FLAME
DON'T STINK LIKE MY
... BROTHER'S ...
YOUR GLORIOUS NAME
WILL OUTLAST ALL
... OTHERSs ..
WHOA
OOH
DUM DUM
THIS SONG IS LAME
I PITY THEIR MOTHERS
HEE
HA HAR
SILENCE, YOU TWO!!
OH, HOTFOOT THERE'S A FIRE IN MY HEART FOR YOOUUU
OUR CARPETS MAY BURN
AH, LOVELY
OUR RELATIONSHIP'S ROCKY
KLAP
BEFORE YOU WERE CURSED YOU WERE THE WORLD'S FINEST JOCKEY
GIVE ME A BREAK ALREADY!!!
WHAT?! IT HAPPENS TO BE TRUE!
BUDDY, YOU MAY HAVE HAD SOME SKILLS IN THE STIRRUPS...
...BUT NO ONE WHO SOLD HORSES TO THE GLUE FACTORY CAN EVER BE CALLED THE "WORLD'S FINEST JOCKEY"!
GASP!!
HOTFOOT! IS THIS TRUE!?
OH, COME ON... YOU KNEW ALL ABOUT THAT...
FIEND!! I NEVER
GRACE! BABY, I—
CHOKE!
THUNK!

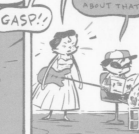

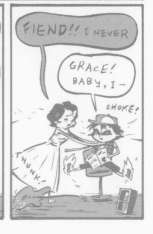

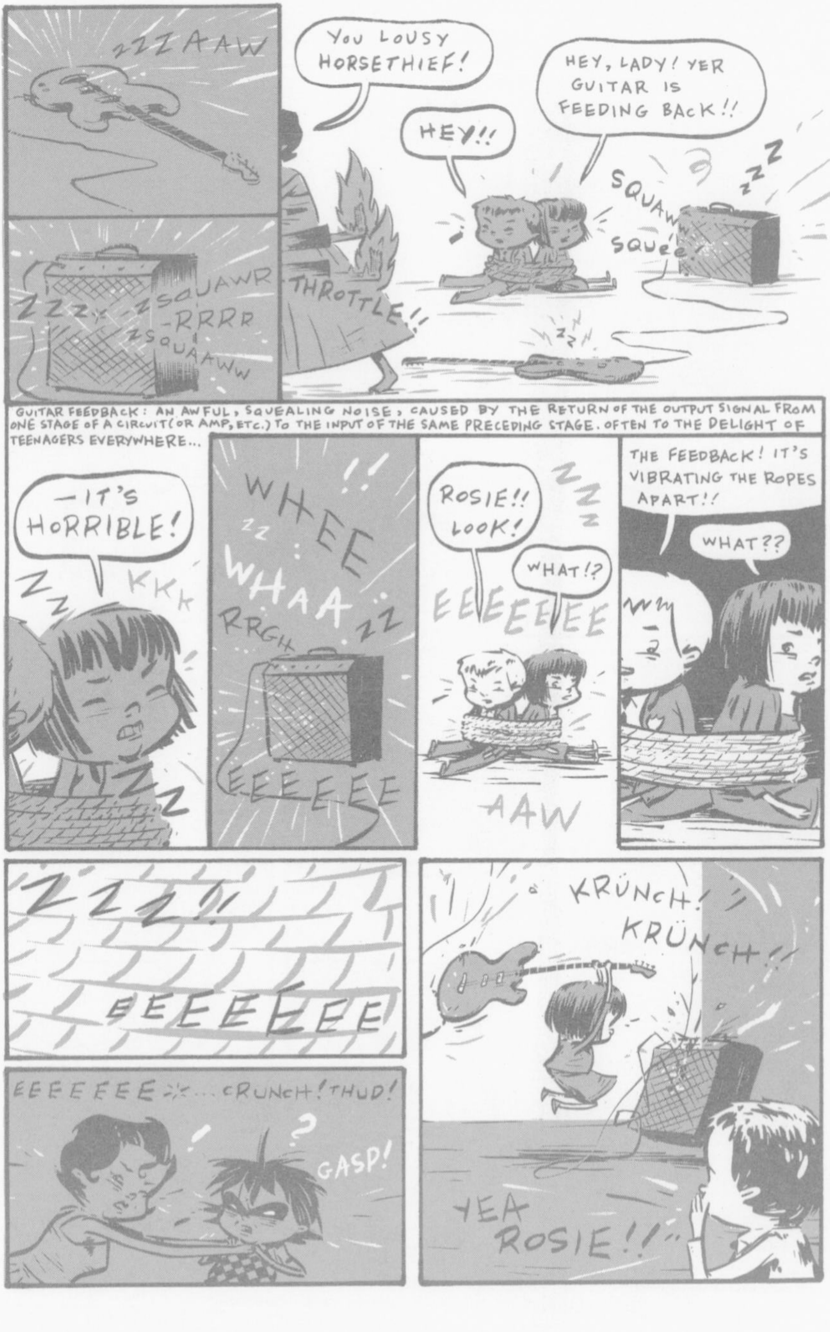
ZZZAAAW
You lousy horsethief!
HEY!!
Hey, lady! Yer guitar is feeding back!!
SQUAWW
SQUEE
ZZZ
ZZZZ-ZSQUAWR-RRRR ZSQUAAWW
THROTTLE!!
GUITAR FEEDBACK: AN AWFUL, SQUEALING NOISE, CAUSED BY THE RETURN OF THE OUTPUT SIGNAL FROM ONE STAGE OF A CIRCUIT (OR AMP, ETC.) TO THE INPUT OF THE SAME PRECEDING STAGE. OFTEN TO THE DELIGHT OF TEENAGERS EVERYWHERE...
—It's horrible!
KKK
WHEE
WHAA
RRGH
EEEEEEE
Rosie!! Look!
WHAT!?
EEEEEEEE
AAW
The feedback! It's vibrating the ropes apart!!
WHAT??
ZZZ!!
EEEEEEEE
EEEEEEE... CRUNCH! THUD!
GASP!
KRÜNCH! KRÜNCH!!
YEA ROSIE!!

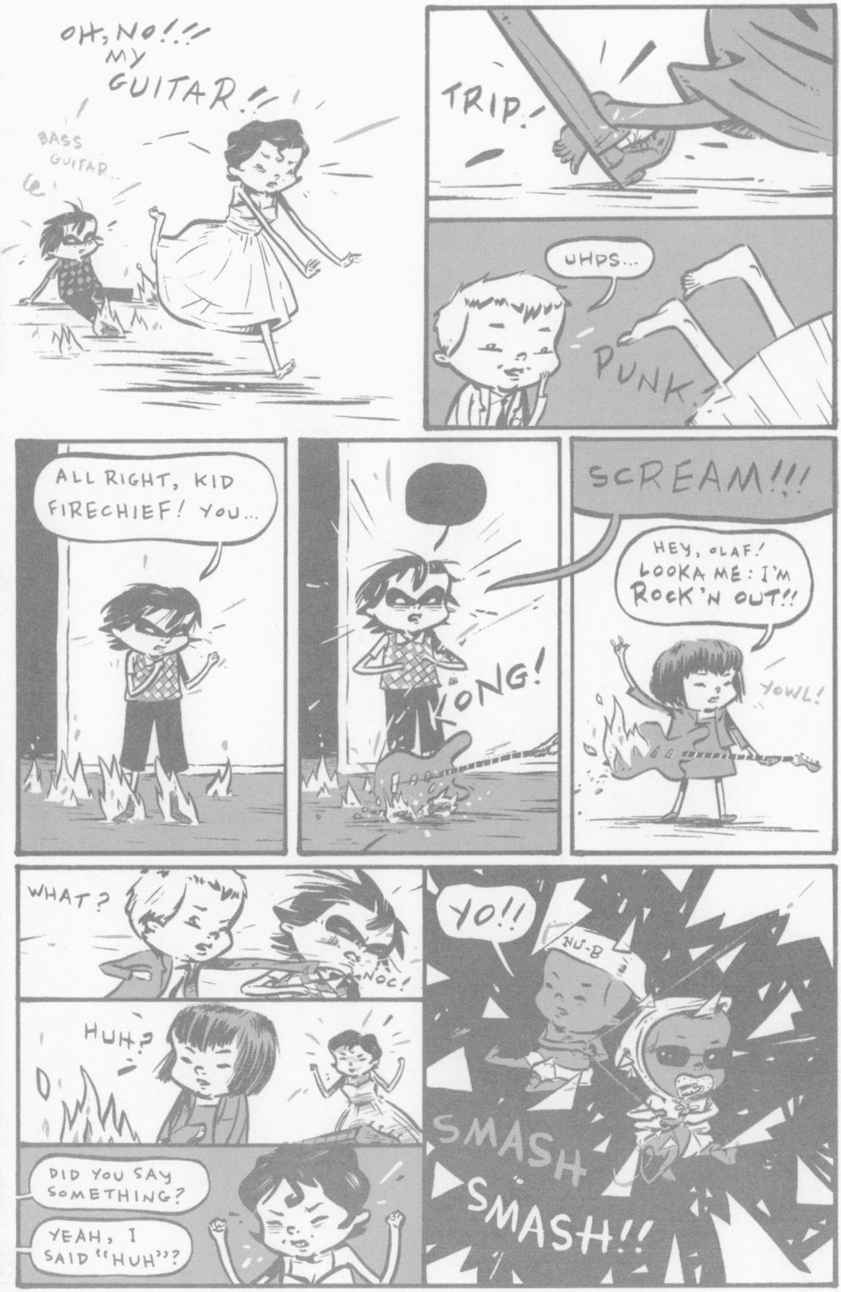

OH, NO!!! MY GUITAR!!
BASS GUITAR..
TRIP.
UHPS...
PUNK.
ALL RIGHT, KID FIRECHIEF! YOU...
KONG!
SCREAM!!!
HEY, OLAF! LOOKA ME: I'M ROCK'N OUT!!
YOWL!
WHAT?
NOC!
HUH?
DID YOU SAY SOMETHING?
YEAH, I SAID "HUH"?
YO!!
NU-B
SMASH
SMASH!!

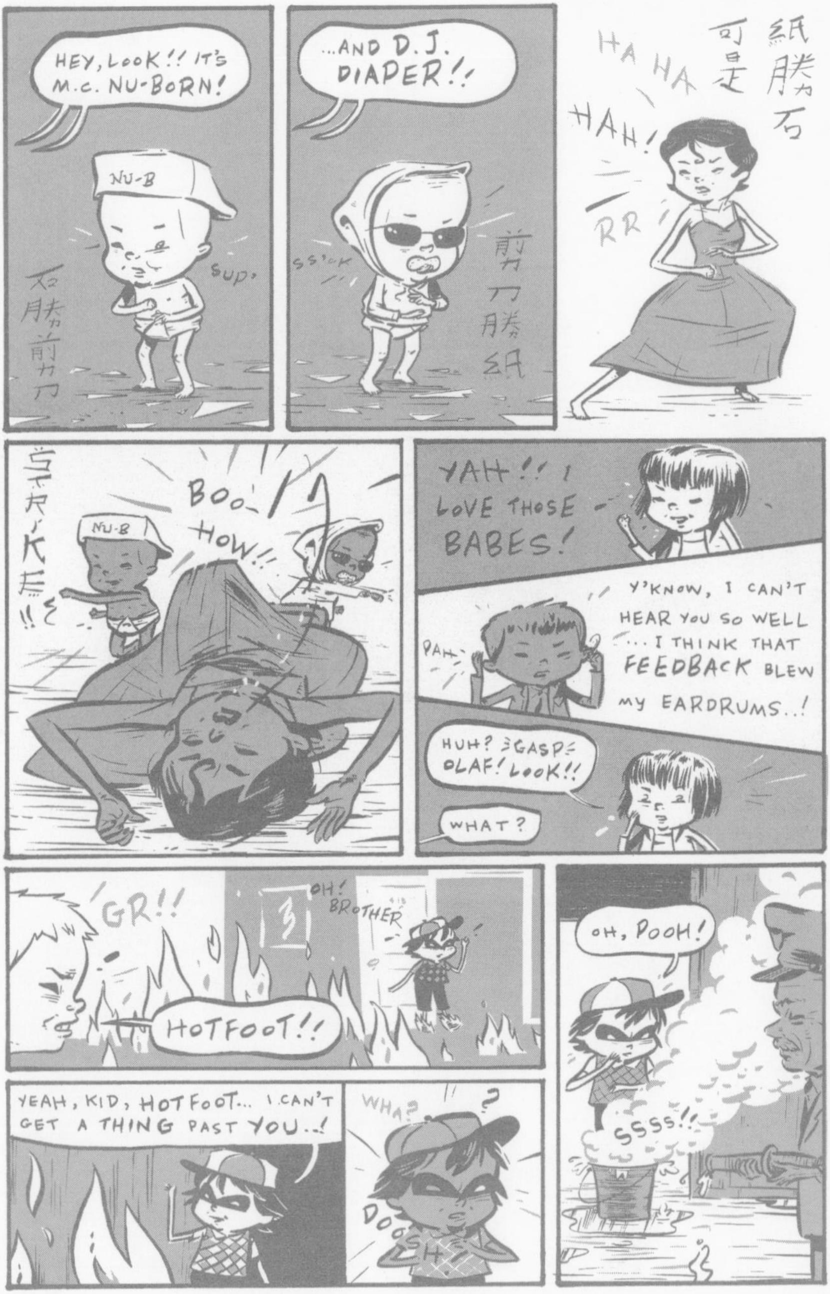
HEY, LOOK!! IT'S M.C. NU-BORN!
NU-B
SUP.
石勝剪刀
...AND D.J. DIAPER!!
SS'UK
剪刀勝紙
HA HA HA HAH!
紙勝石
可是
RR
BOO HOO HOW!!
NU-B
STRIKE!!
YAH!! I LOVE THOSE BABES!
Y'KNOW, I CAN'T HEAR YOU SO WELL ...I THINK THAT FEEDBACK BLEW MY EARDRUMS..!
PAH
HUH? GASP OLAF! LOOK!!
WHAT?
GR!!
OH! BROTHER
HOTFOOT!!
OH, POOH!
SSSS!!
YEAH, KID, HOTFOOT... I CAN'T GET A THING PAST YOU..!
WHA?
?
DOOSH

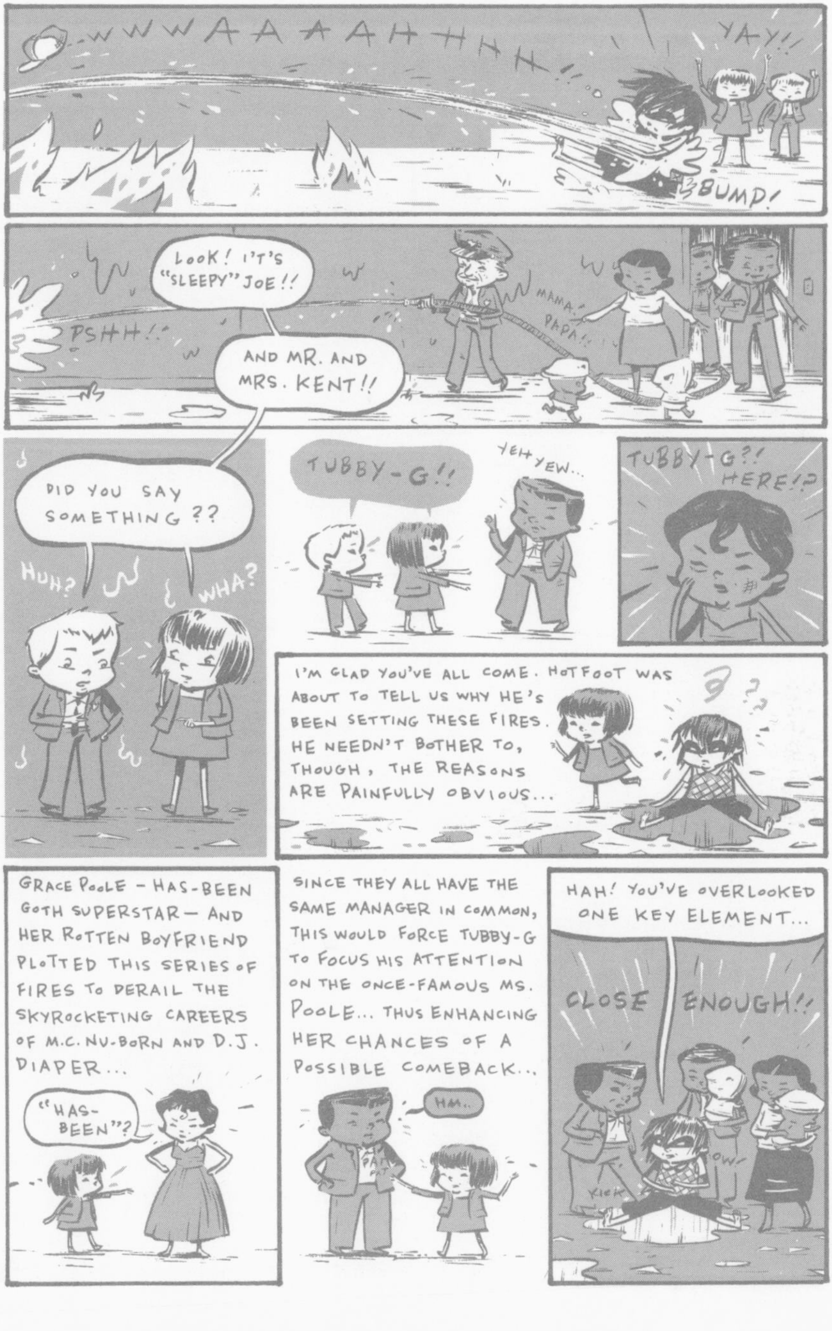
WWWAAAAHHHHH
YAY!!
BUMP!
LOOK! IT'S "SLEEPY" JOE!!
PSHH!!
AND MR. AND MRS. KENT!!
MAMA! PAPA!!
DID YOU SAY SOMETHING??
HUH?
WHA?
TUBBY-G!!
YEH YEW...
TUBBY-G?! HERE!?
I'M GLAD YOU'VE ALL COME. HOTFOOT WAS ABOUT TO TELL US WHY HE'S BEEN SETTING THESE FIRES. HE NEEDN'T BOTHER TO, THOUGH, THE REASONS ARE PAINFULLY OBVIOUS...
GRACE POOLE - HAS-BEEN GOTH SUPERSTAR - AND HER ROTTEN BOYFRIEND PLOTTED THIS SERIES OF FIRES TO DERAIL THE SKYROCKETING CAREERS OF M.C. NU-BORN AND D.J. DIAPER...
"HAS-BEEN"?
SINCE THEY ALL HAVE THE SAME MANAGER IN COMMON, THIS WOULD FORCE TUBBY-G TO FOCUS HIS ATTENTION ON THE ONCE-FAMOUS MS. POOLE... THUS ENHANCING HER CHANCES OF A POSSIBLE COMEBACK...
HM..
HAH! YOU'VE OVERLOOKED ONE KEY ELEMENT...
CLOSE ENOUGH!!
OW!
KICK

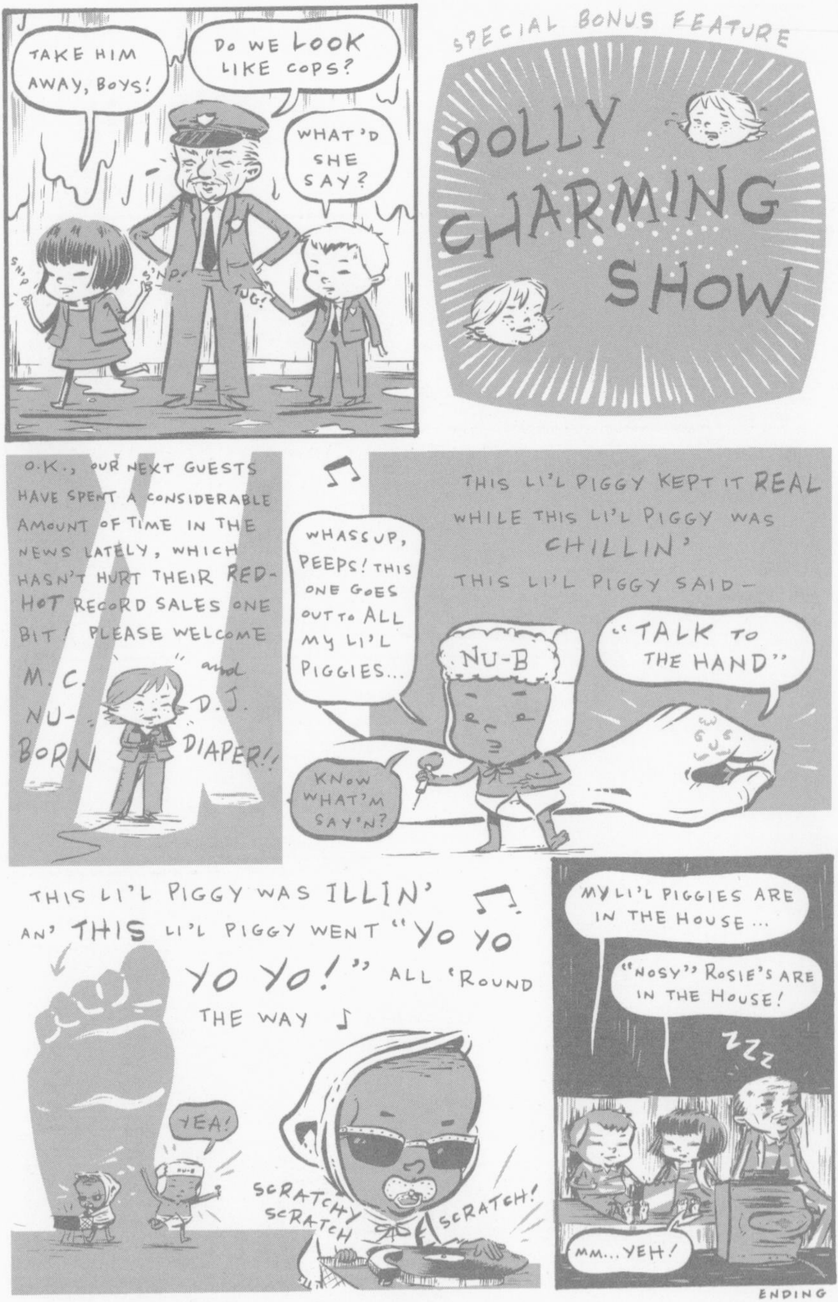

TAKE HIM AWAY, BOYS!
DO WE LOOK LIKE COPS?
WHAT'D SHE SAY?
SNIP
SNIP
TUG!
SPECIAL BONUS FEATURE
DOLLY CHARMING SHOW
O.K., OUR NEXT GUESTS HAVE SPENT A CONSIDERABLE AMOUNT OF TIME IN THE NEWS LATELY, WHICH HASN'T HURT THEIR RED-HOT RECORD SALES ONE BIT! PLEASE WELCOME
M.C. NU-BORN and D.J. DIAPER!!
THIS LI'L PIGGY KEPT IT REAL WHILE THIS LI'L PIGGY WAS CHILLIN' THIS LI'L PIGGY SAID—
WHASSUP, PEEPS! THIS ONE GOES OUT TO ALL MY LI'L PIGGIES...
NU-B
"TALK TO THE HAND"
KNOW WHAT'M SAY'N?
THIS LI'L PIGGY WAS ILLIN' AN' THIS LI'L PIGGY WENT "YO YO YO YO!" ALL 'ROUND THE WAY
YEA!
NU-B
SCRATCHY SCRATCH
SCRATCH!
MY LI'L PIGGIES ARE IN THE HOUSE...
"NOSY" ROSIE'S ARE IN THE HOUSE!
ZZZ
MM...YEH!
ENDING

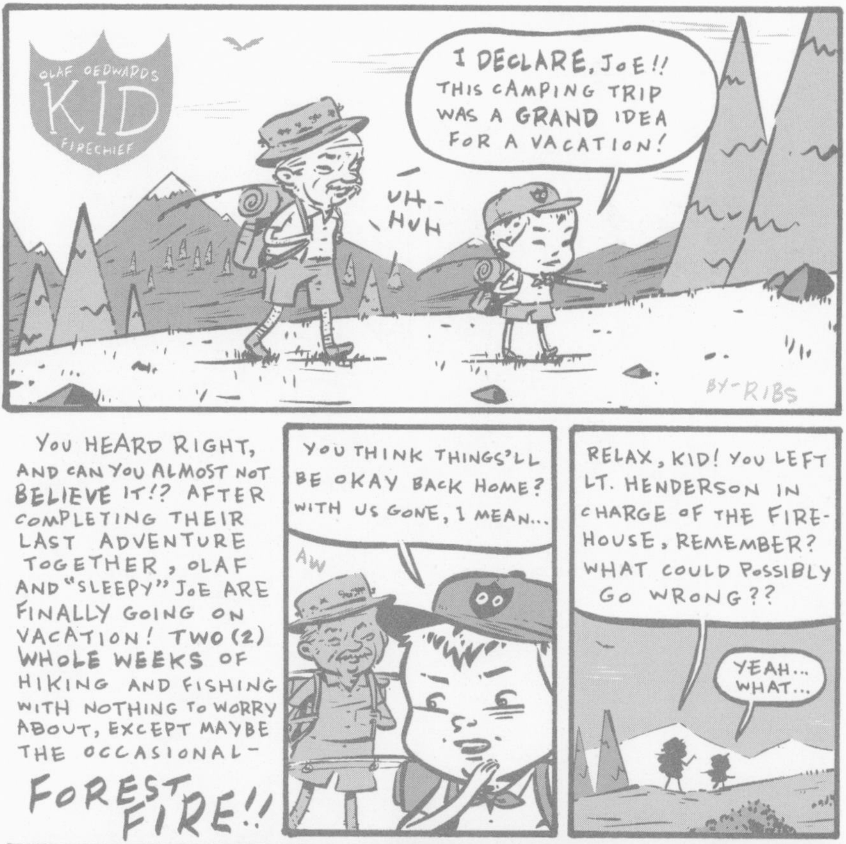
OLAF OEDWARDS
KID
FIRECHIEF
I DECLARE, JOE!! THIS CAMPING TRIP WAS A GRAND IDEA FOR A VACATION!
UH-HUH
BY-RIBS
YOU HEARD RIGHT, AND CAN YOU ALMOST NOT BELIEVE IT!? AFTER COMPLETING THEIR LAST ADVENTURE TOGETHER, OLAF AND "SLEEPY" JOE ARE FINALLY GOING ON VACATION! TWO (2) WHOLE WEEKS OF HIKING AND FISHING WITH NOTHING TO WORRY ABOUT, EXCEPT MAYBE THE OCCASIONAL-
FOREST FIRE!!
YOU THINK THINGS'LL BE OKAY BACK HOME? WITH US GONE, I MEAN...
AW
RELAX, KID! YOU LEFT LT. HENDERSON IN CHARGE OF THE FIRE-HOUSE, REMEMBER? WHAT COULD POSSIBLY GO WRONG??
YEAH... WHAT...
MEANWHILE
RING! RING! RING!!!
CHIEF
Back in 5 Minutes
SOON
THERE! THAT WASN'T TOO HARD, EH?
WHEO

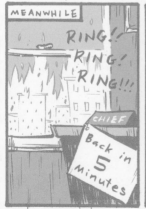

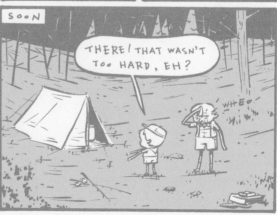

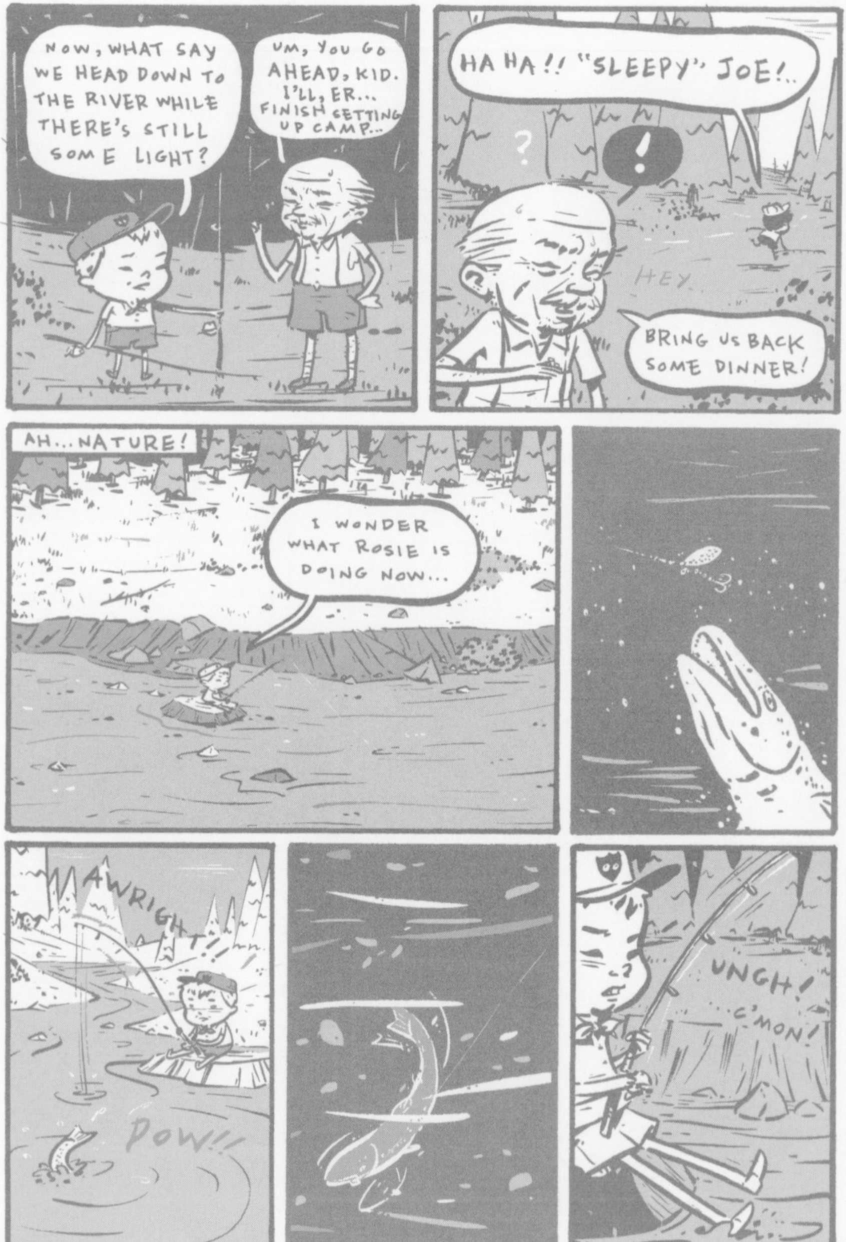
NOW, WHAT SAY WE HEAD DOWN TO THE RIVER WHILE THERE'S STILL SOME LIGHT?
UM, YOU GO AHEAD, KID. I'LL, ER... FINISH SETTING UP CAMP...
HA HA!! "SLEEPY" JOE!..
?
!
HEY
BRING US BACK SOME DINNER!
AH... NATURE!
I WONDER WHAT ROSIE IS DOING NOW...
AWRIGHT
POW!!
UNGH!
C'MON!

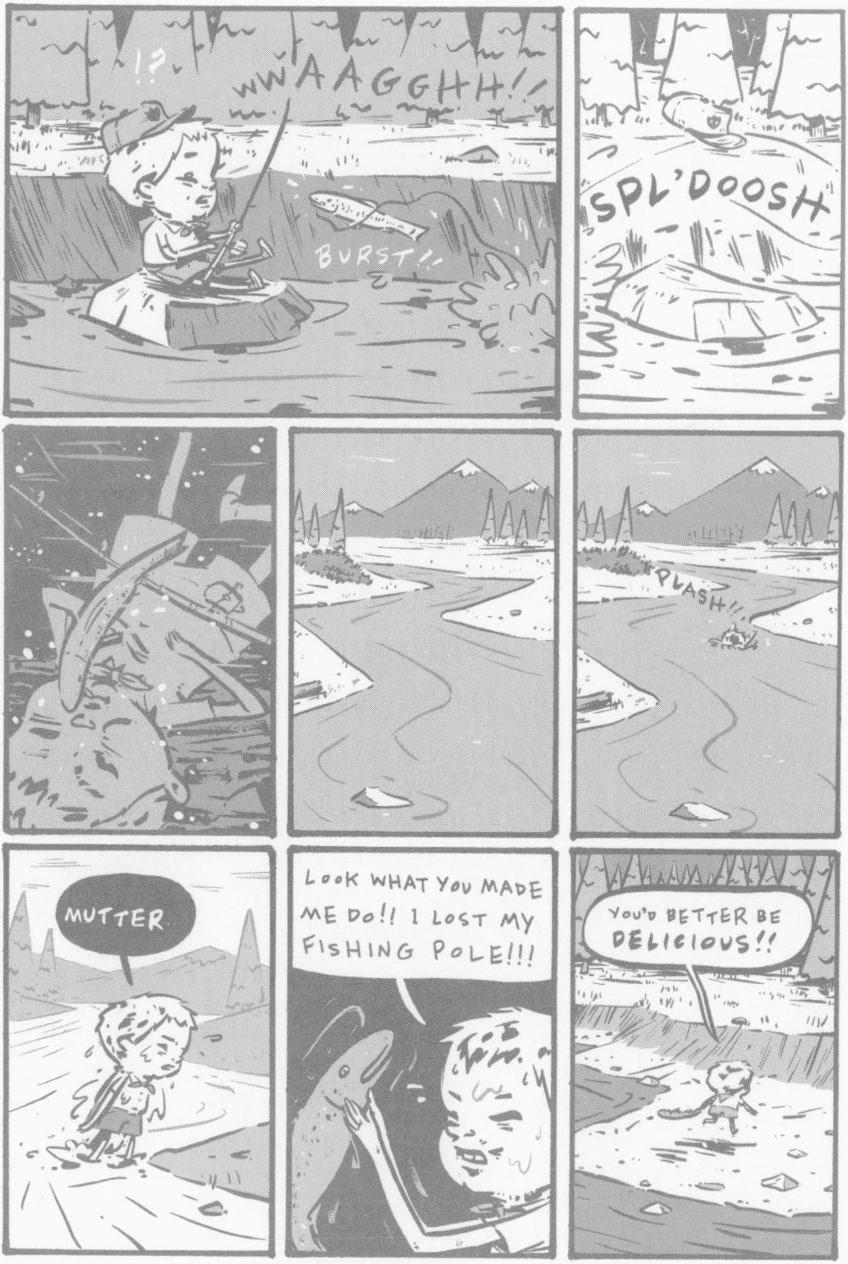
!?
WWAAGGHH!!
BURST!!
SPL'DOOSH
PLASH!!
MUTTER
LOOK WHAT YOU MADE ME DO!! I LOST MY FISHING POLE!!!
YOU'D BETTER BE DELICIOUS!!

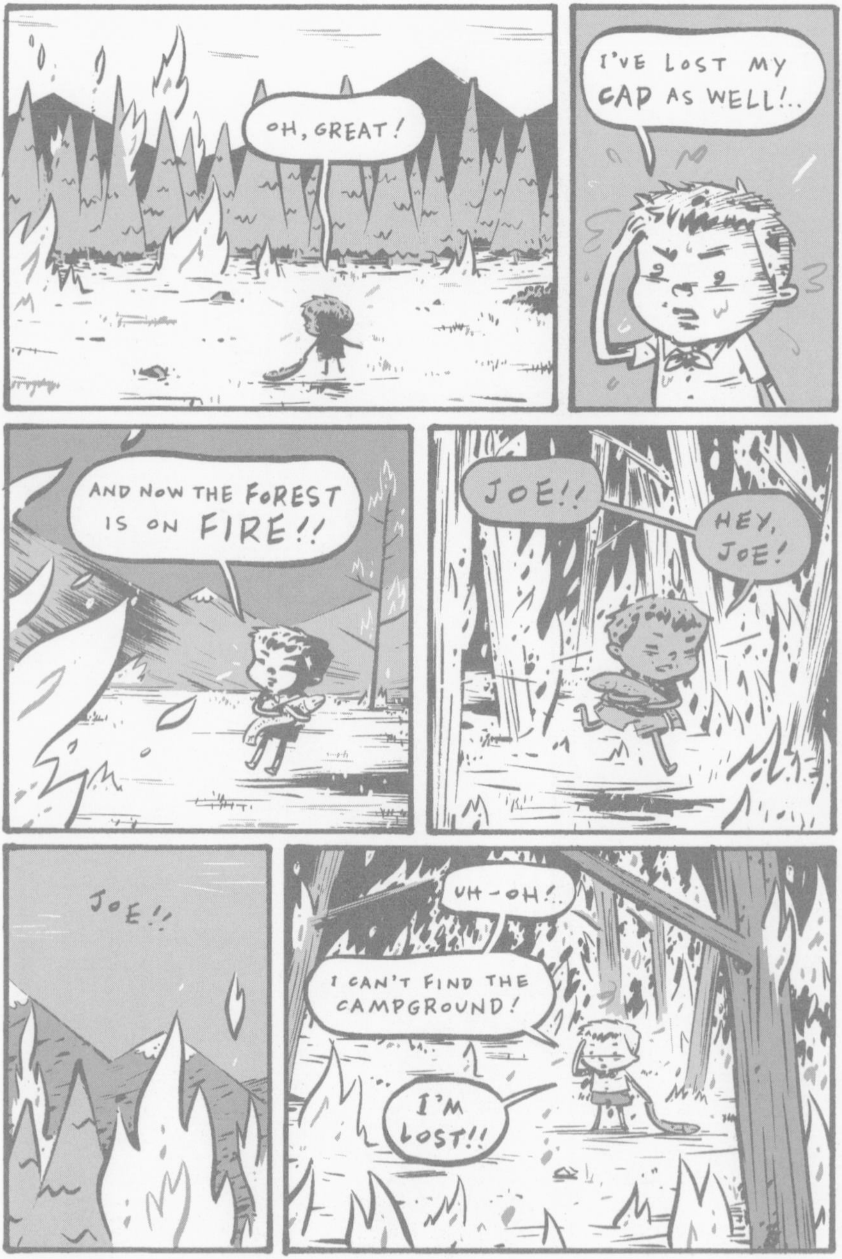
OH, GREAT!
I'VE LOST MY CAP AS WELL!..
AND NOW THE FOREST IS ON FIRE!!
JOE!!
HEY, JOE!
JOE!!
UH-OH!..
I CAN'T FIND THE CAMPGROUND!
I'M LOST!!

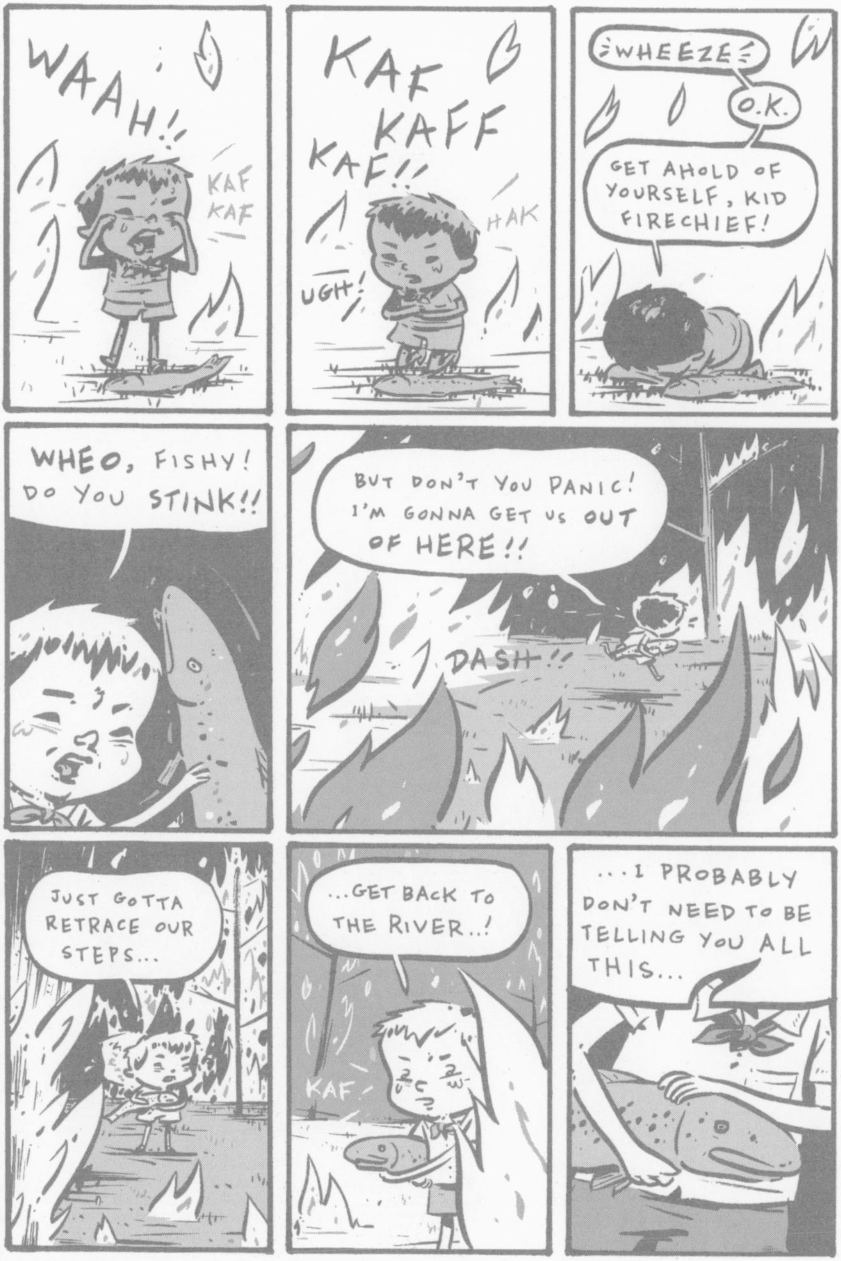
WAAH!
KAF KAF
KAF KAFF KAF!!
HAK
UGH!
WHEEZE
O.K.
GET AHOLD OF YOURSELF, KID FIRECHIEF!
WHEO, FISHY! DO YOU STINK!!
BUT DON'T YOU PANIC! I'M GONNA GET US OUT OF HERE!!
DASH
JUST GOTTA RETRACE OUR STEPS...
...GET BACK TO THE RIVER..!
KAF
...I PROBABLY DON'T NEED TO BE TELLING YOU ALL THIS...

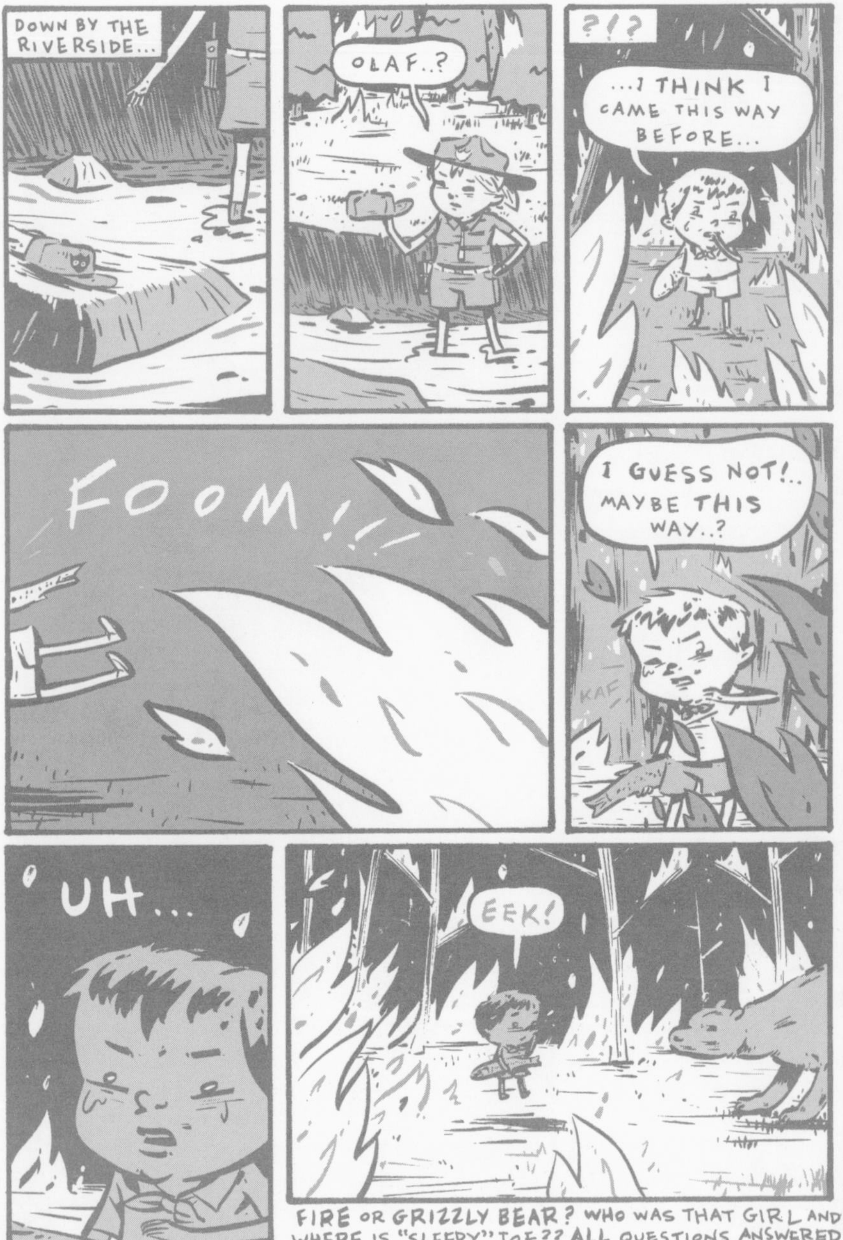
DOWN BY THE RIVERSIDE...
OLAF..?
?!?
...I THINK I CAME THIS WAY BEFORE...
FOOM!!
I GUESS NOT!.. MAYBE THIS WAY..?
KAF
UH...
EEK!

FIRE OR GRIZZLY BEAR? WHO WAS THAT GIRL AND WHERE IS "SLEEPY" JOE?? ALL QUESTIONS ANSWERED NEXT!

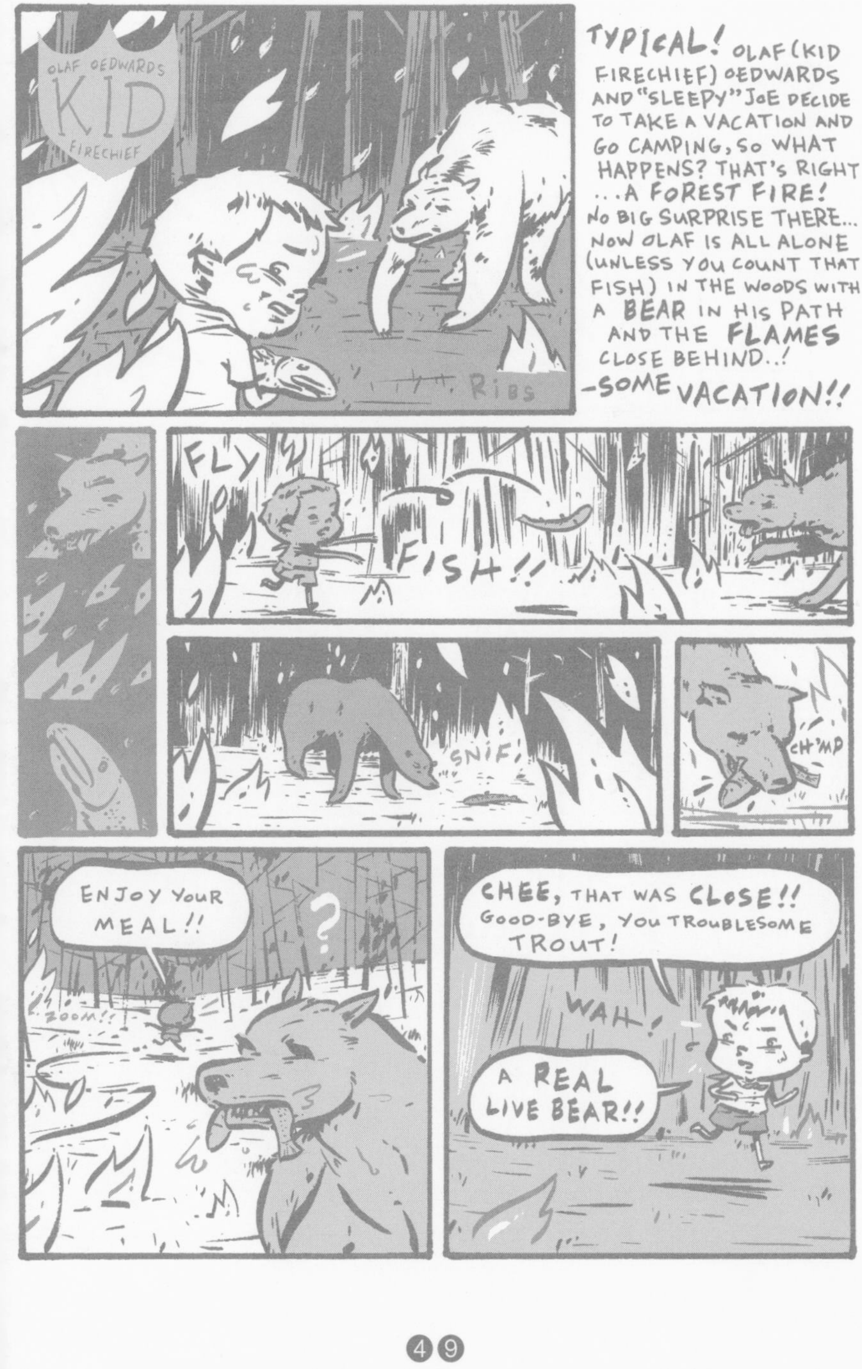
OLAF OEDWARDS
KID
FIRECHIEF
TYPICAL! OLAF (KID FIRECHIEF) OEDWARDS AND "SLEEPY" JOE DECIDE TO TAKE A VACATION AND GO CAMPING, SO WHAT HAPPENS? THAT'S RIGHT ...A FOREST FIRE! NO BIG SURPRISE THERE... NOW OLAF IS ALL ALONE (UNLESS YOU COUNT THAT FISH) IN THE WOODS WITH A BEAR IN HIS PATH AND THE FLAMES CLOSE BEHIND..! -SOME VACATION!!
RIBS
FLY
FISH!!
SNIF
CH'MP
ENJOY YOUR MEAL!!
?
ZOOM!!
CHEE, THAT WAS CLOSE!! GOOD-BYE, YOU TROUBLESOME TROUT!
WAH!
A REAL LIVE BEAR!!

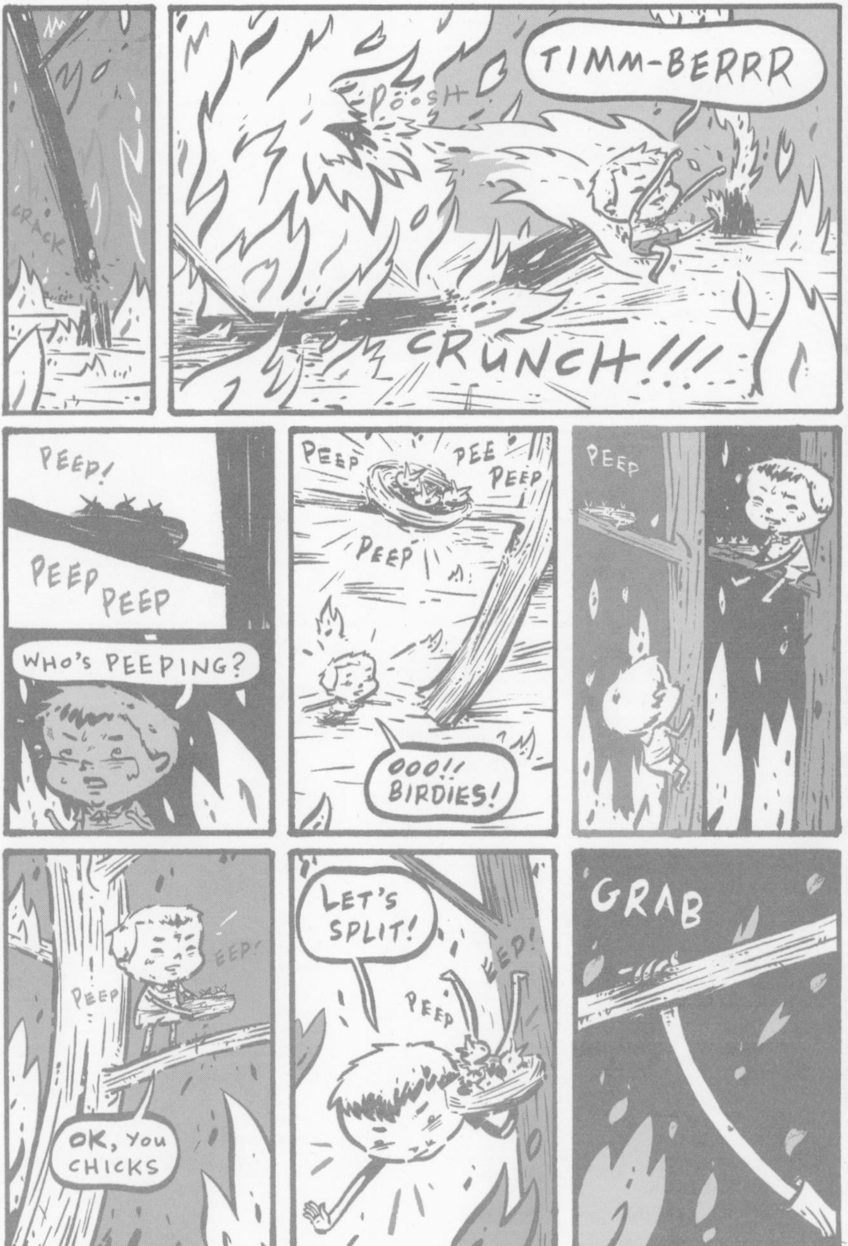
CRACK
POOSH
TIMM-BERRR
CRUNCH!!!
PEEP!
PEEP PEEP
WHO'S PEEPING?
PEEP
PEE PEEP
PEEP
OOO!! BIRDIES!
PEEP
PEEP
EEP!
OK, YOU CHICKS
LET'S SPLIT!
PEEP
EEP!
GRAB

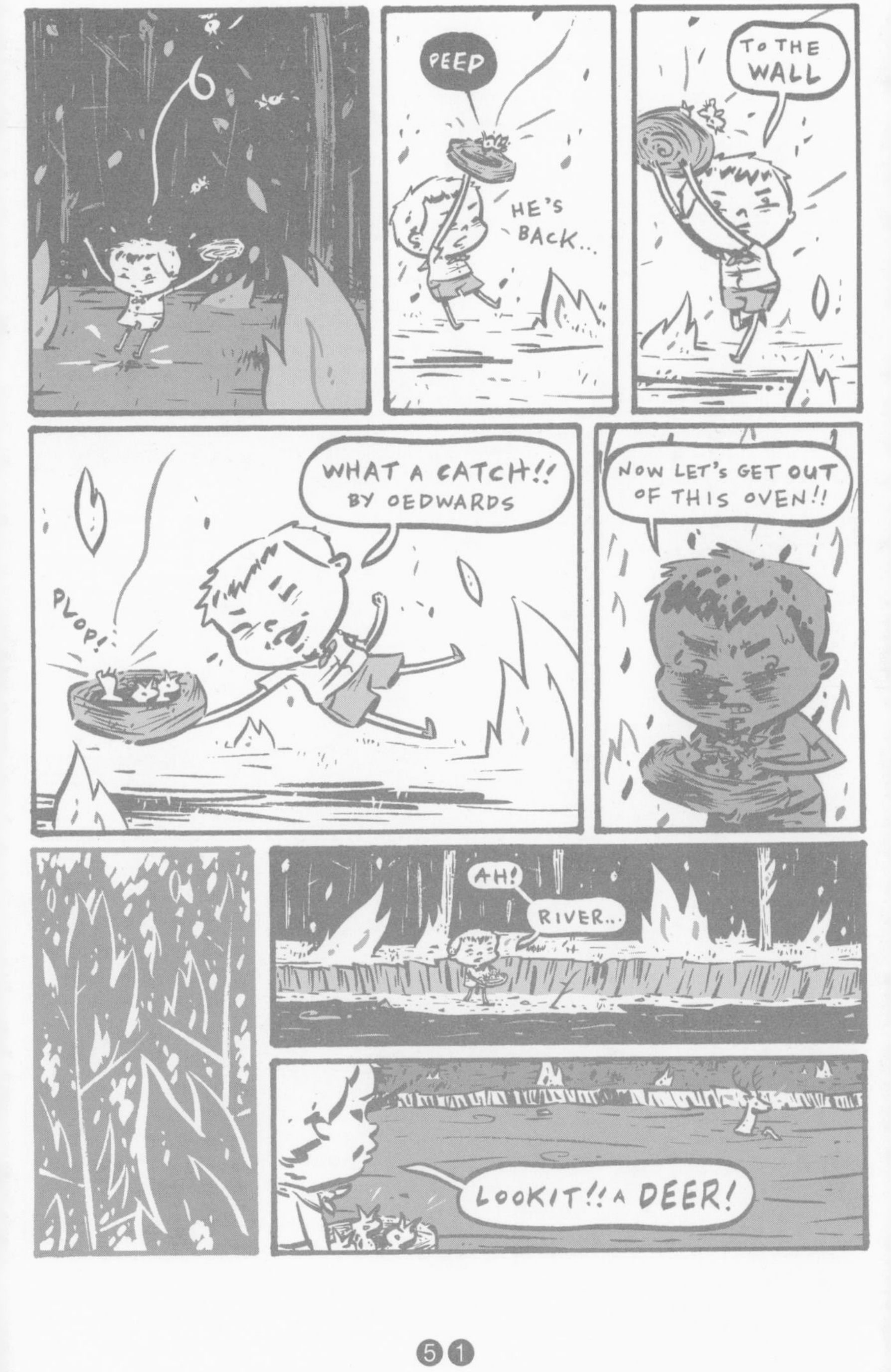
PEEP
HE'S BACK...
TO THE WALL
WHAT A CATCH!! BY OEDWARDS
PLOP!
NOW LET'S GET OUT OF THIS OVEN!!
AH!
RIVER...
LOOKIT!! A DEER!

ISN'T NATURE WONDERFUL?

BAAAAWWW

ALL RIGHT, YOU THREE! THE CURRENT'S PRETTY SWIFT HERE, SO HANG ON (WITH YOUR FEET)!..

PEEP.

PEEP

PEEP.

PEEP

BR!

WAH!!

TOO SWIFT!

BAAAAAAWWWWW

OH, WOULD YA LOOK AT THIS!

PEEP.

OLAF

WATERFALL

ROCKS

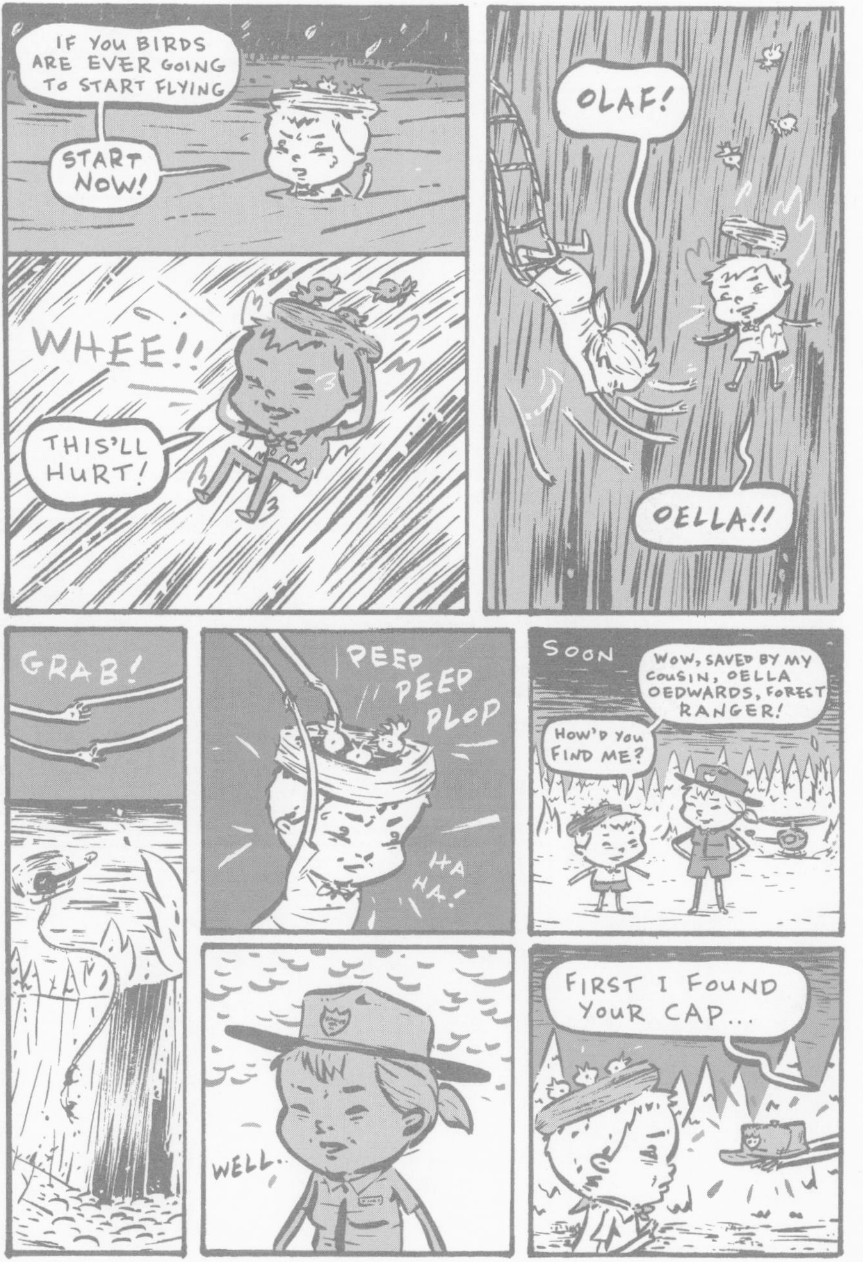
IF YOU BIRDS ARE EVER GOING TO START FLYING
START NOW!
OLAF!
WHEE!!
THIS'LL HURT!
OELLA!!
GRAB!
PEEP PEEP PLOP
HA HA!
SOON
WOW, SAVED BY MY COUSIN, OELLA OEDWARDS, FOREST RANGER!
HOW'D YOU FIND ME?
WELL..
FIRST I FOUND YOUR CAP...

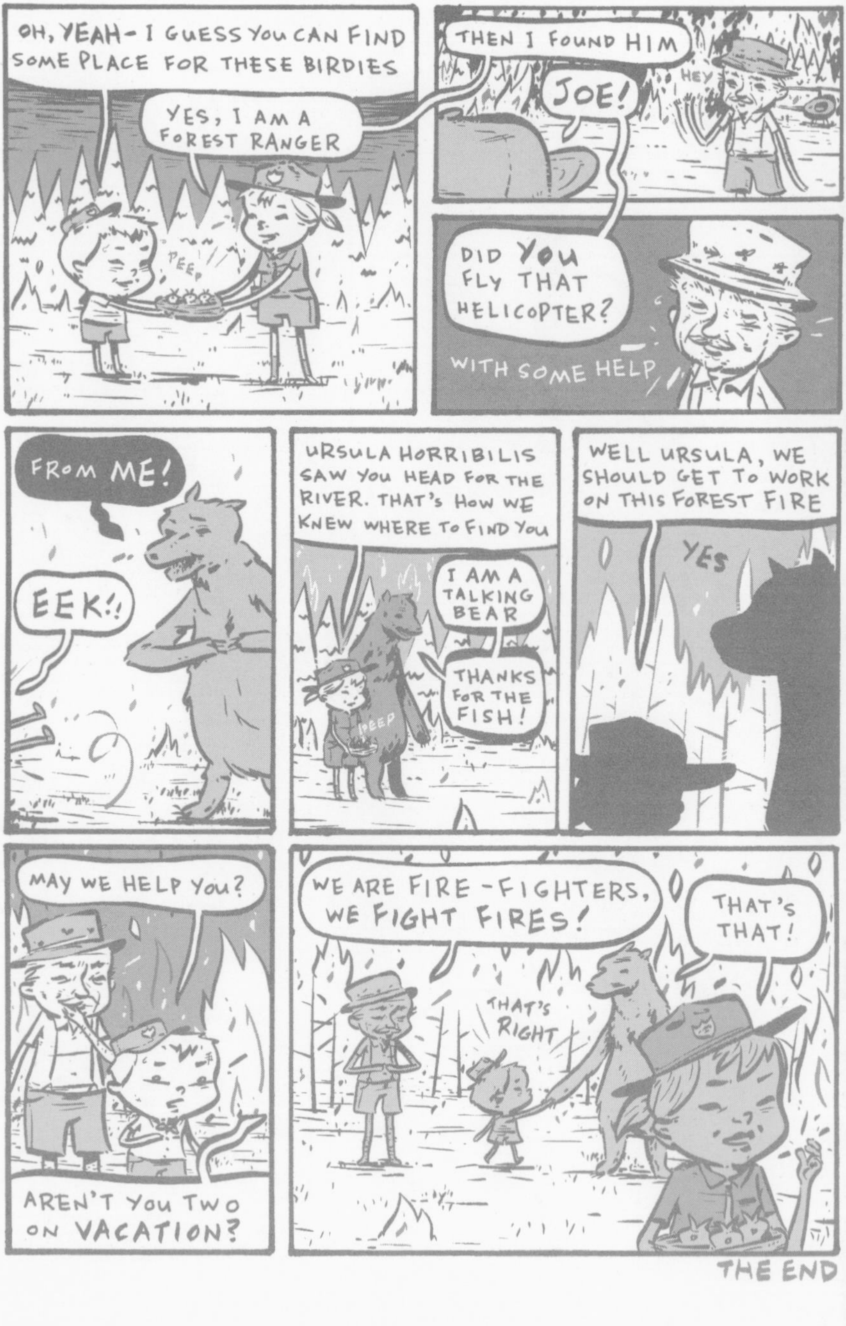
OH, YEAH- I GUESS YOU CAN FIND SOME PLACE FOR THESE BIRDIES
YES, I AM A FOREST RANGER
PEEP
THEN I FOUND HIM
JOE!
HEY
DID YOU FLY THAT HELICOPTER?
WITH SOME HELP
FROM ME!
EEK!!
URSULA HORRIBILIS SAW YOU HEAD FOR THE RIVER. THAT'S HOW WE KNEW WHERE TO FIND YOU
I AM A TALKING BEAR
THANKS FOR THE FISH!
PEEP
WELL URSULA, WE SHOULD GET TO WORK ON THIS FOREST FIRE
YES
MAY WE HELP YOU?
AREN'T YOU TWO ON VACATION?
WE ARE FIRE-FIGHTERS, WE FIGHT FIRES!
THAT'S THAT!
THAT'S RIGHT
THE END

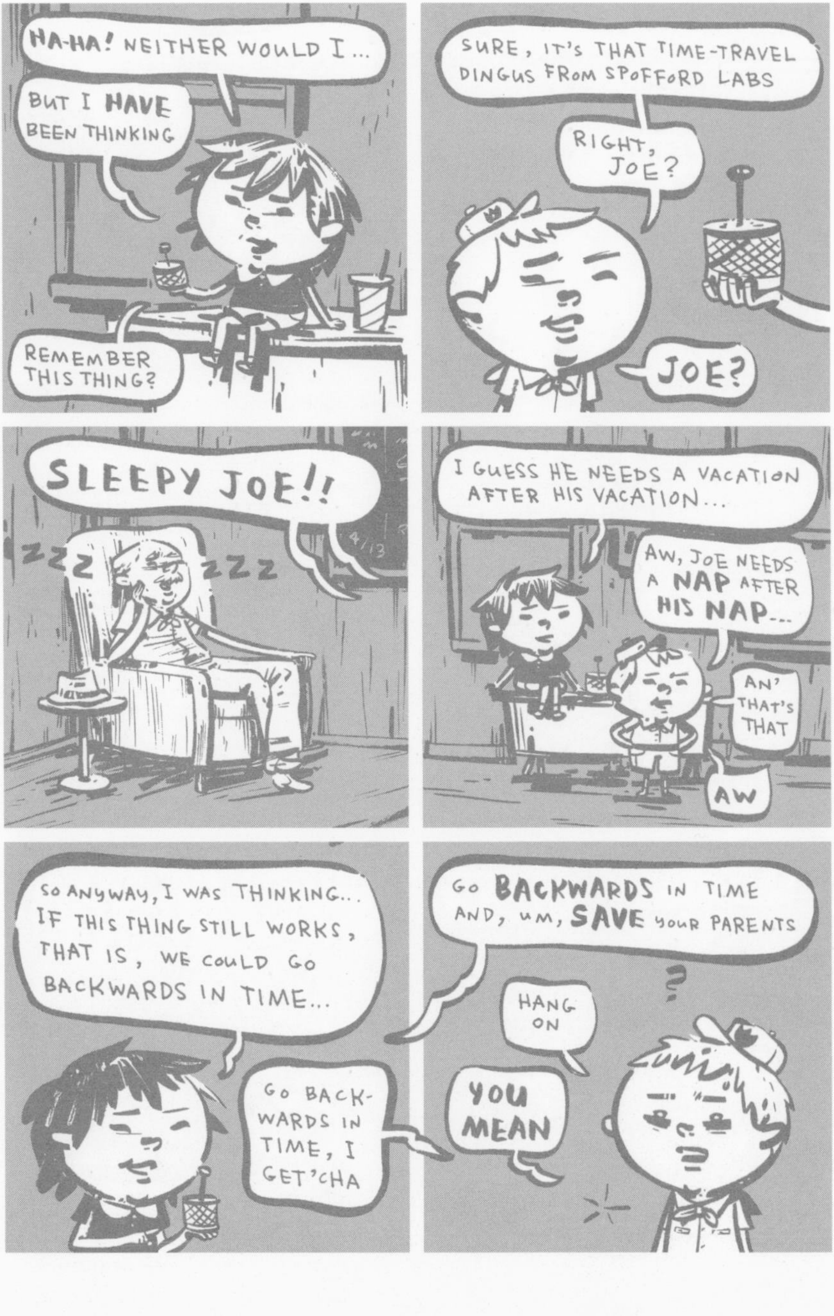
HA-HA! NEITHER WOULD I...
BUT I HAVE BEEN THINKING
REMEMBER THIS THING?
SURE, IT'S THAT TIME-TRAVEL DINGUS FROM SPOFFORD LABS
RIGHT, JOE?
JOE?
SLEEPY JOE!!
ZZZ ZZZ
I GUESS HE NEEDS A VACATION AFTER HIS VACATION...
AW, JOE NEEDS A NAP AFTER HIS NAP...
AN' THAT'S THAT
AW
SO ANYWAY, I WAS THINKING... IF THIS THING STILL WORKS, THAT IS, WE COULD GO BACKWARDS IN TIME...
GO BACKWARDS IN TIME, I GET'CHA
GO BACKWARDS IN TIME AND, UM, SAVE YOUR PARENTS
?
HANG ON
YOU MEAN

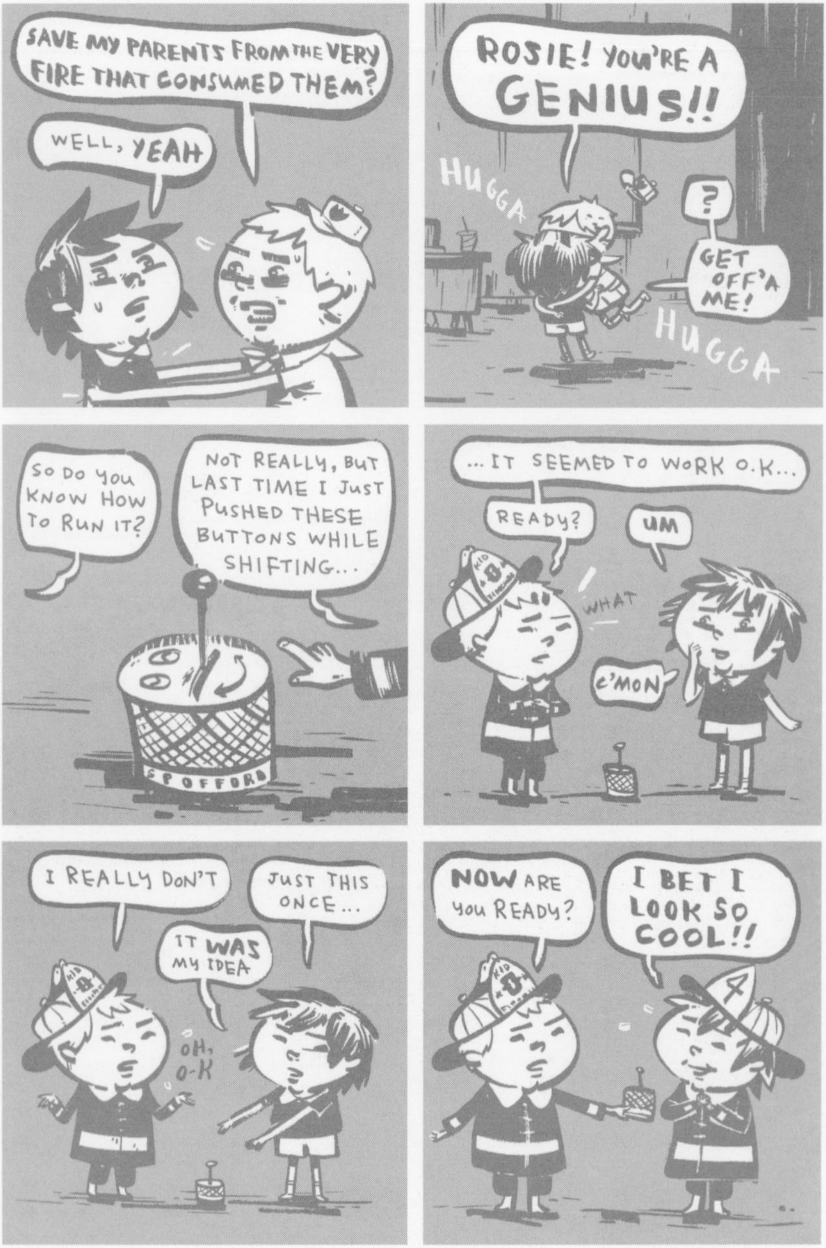
SAVE MY PARENTS FROM THE VERY FIRE THAT CONSUMED THEM?
WELL, YEAH
ROSIE! YOU'RE A GENIUS!!
HUGGA
?
GET OFF'A ME!
HUGGA
SO DO YOU KNOW HOW TO RUN IT?
NOT REALLY, BUT LAST TIME I JUST PUSHED THESE BUTTONS WHILE SHIFTING...
SPOFFORD
...IT SEEMED TO WORK O.K...
READY?
UM
WHAT
C'MON
I REALLY DON'T
JUST THIS ONCE...
IT WAS MY IDEA
OH, O-K
NOW ARE YOU READY?
I BET I LOOK SO COOL!!

WHO CAN BLAME HER?

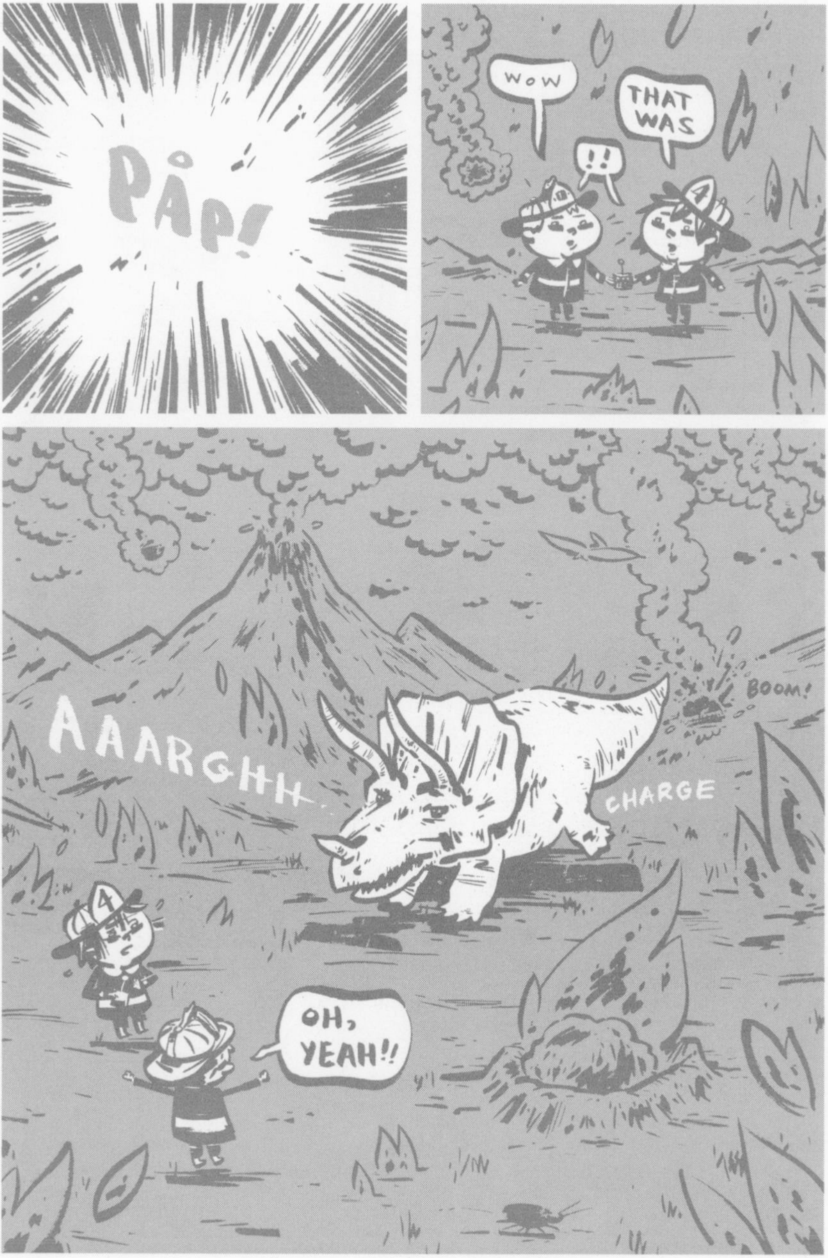
PAP!
WOW
!!
THAT WAS
AAARGHH
CHARGE
BOOM!
OH, YEAH!!

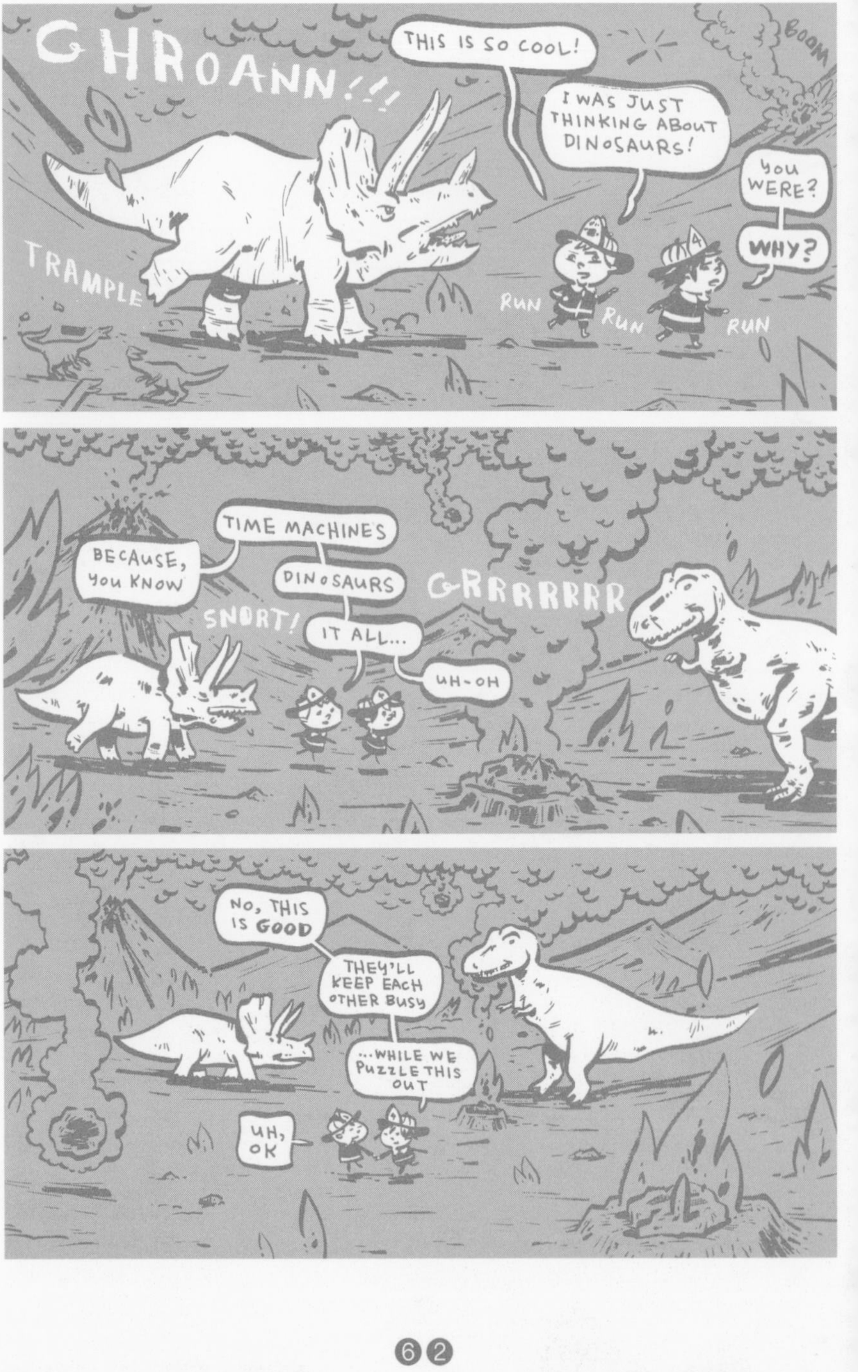
GHROANN!!!
TRAMPLE
THIS IS SO COOL!
I WAS JUST THINKING ABOUT DINOSAURS!
BOOM
YOU WERE?
WHY?
RUN
RUN
RUN
BECAUSE, YOU KNOW
TIME MACHINES
DINOSAURS
IT ALL...
SNORT!
GRRRRRRRR
UH-OH
NO, THIS IS GOOD
THEY'LL KEEP EACH OTHER BUSY
...WHILE WE PUZZLE THIS OUT
UH, OK

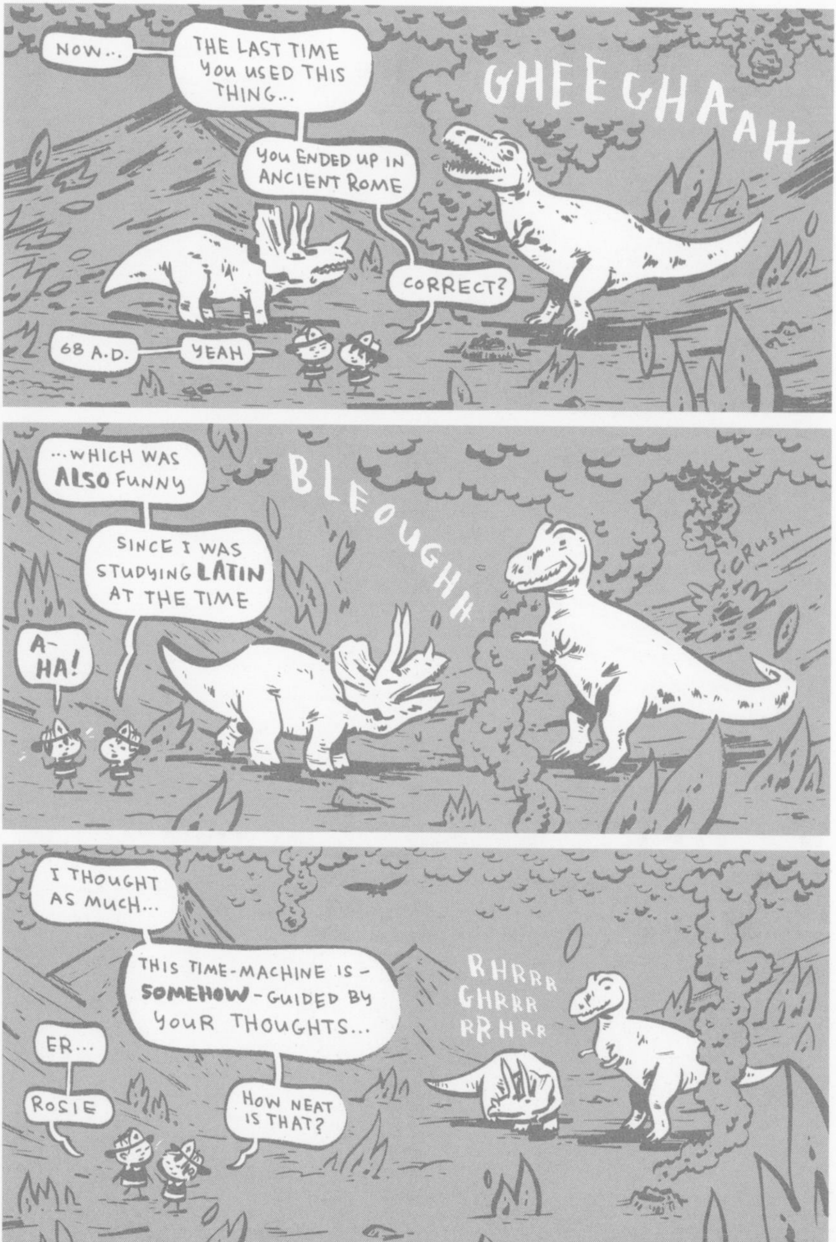
NOW...
THE LAST TIME YOU USED THIS THING...
YOU ENDED UP IN ANCIENT ROME
CORRECT?
GHEEGHAAAH
68 A.D.
YEAH
...WHICH WAS ALSO FUNNY
SINCE I WAS STUDYING LATIN AT THE TIME
BLEOUGHH
CRUSH
A-HA!
I THOUGHT AS MUCH...
THIS TIME-MACHINE IS -SOMEHOW- GUIDED BY YOUR THOUGHTS...
RHRRR GHRRR RRHRR
ER...
ROSIE
HOW NEAT IS THAT?

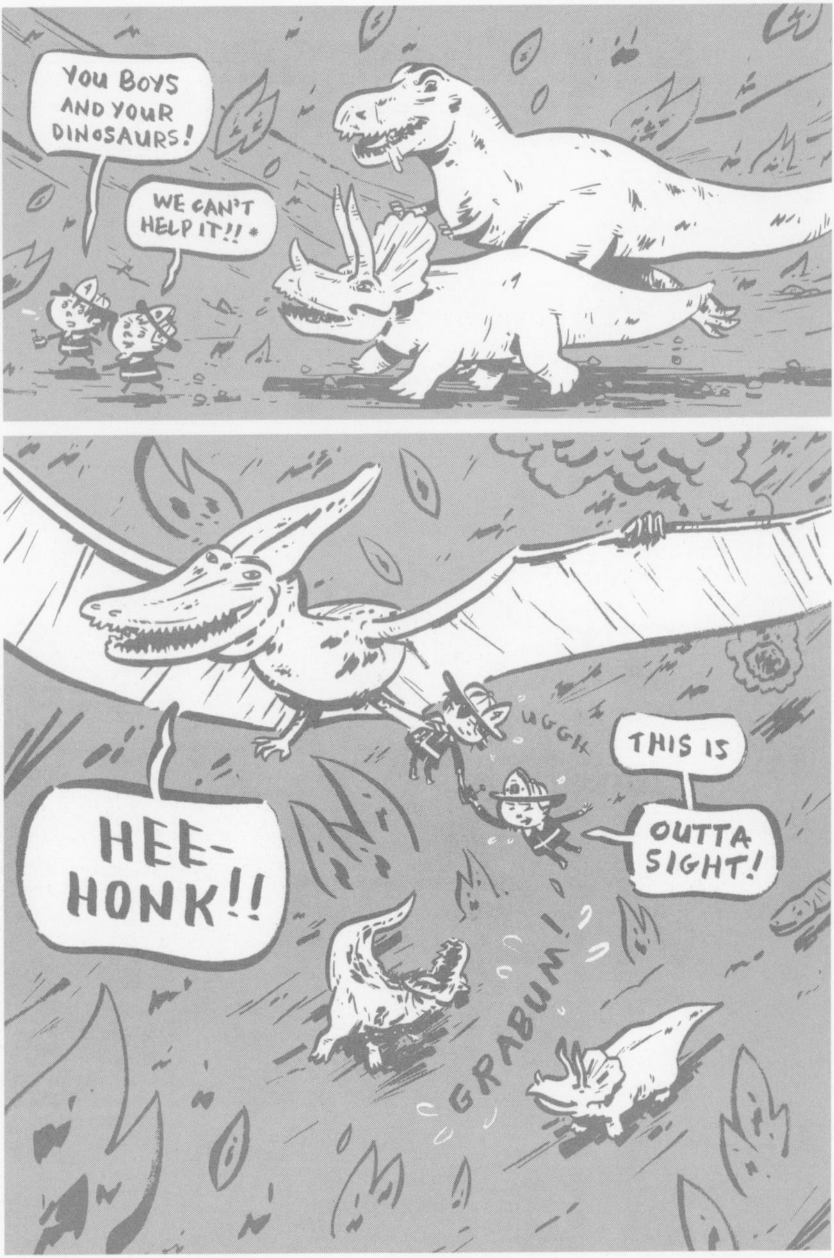
YOU BOYS AND YOUR DINOSAURS!
WE CAN'T HELP IT!! *
HEE-HONK!!
UGGH
THIS IS
OUTTA SIGHT!
GRABUM!

* STUDIES SHOW THAT THE AVERAGE AMERICAN BOY THINKS ABOUT DINOSAURS 39 TIMES PER HOUR.

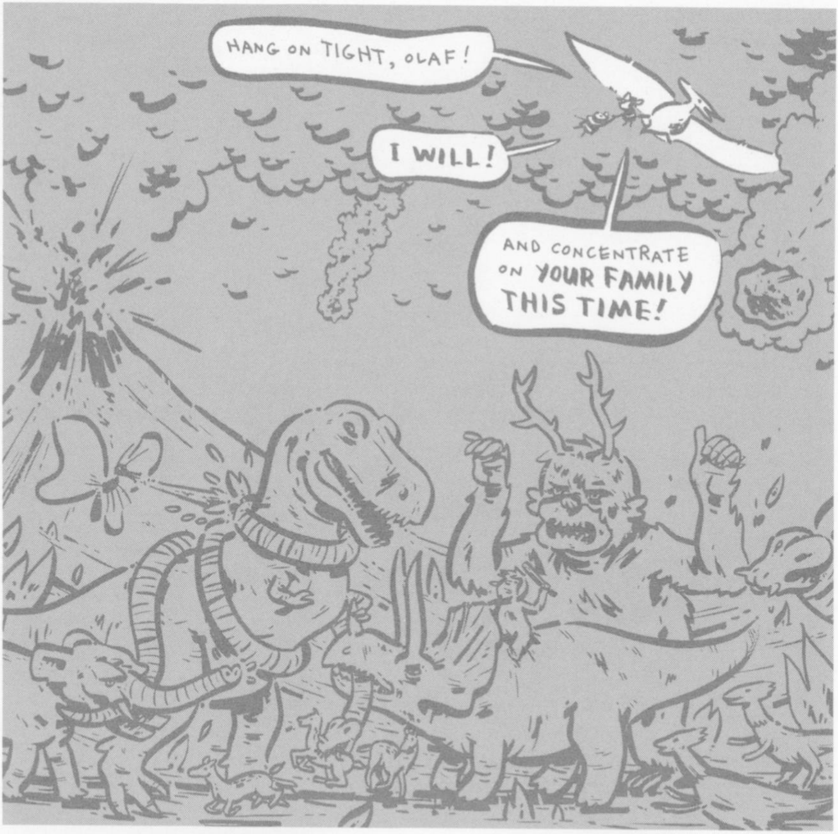
HANG ON TIGHT, OLAF!
I WILL!
AND CONCENTRATE ON YOUR FAMILY THIS TIME!

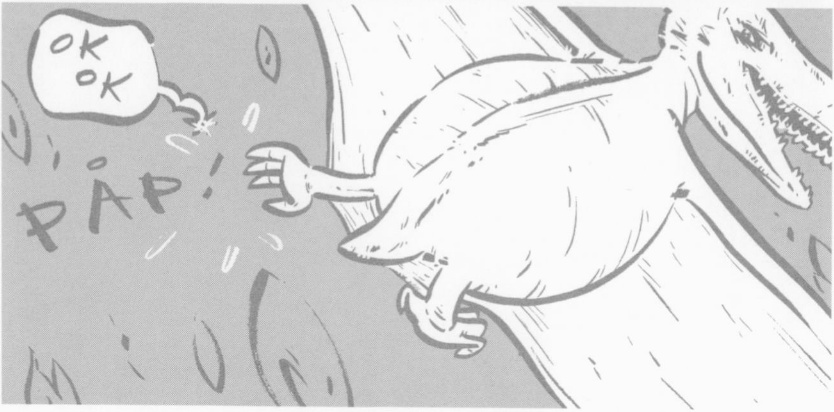
OK OK
PAP!

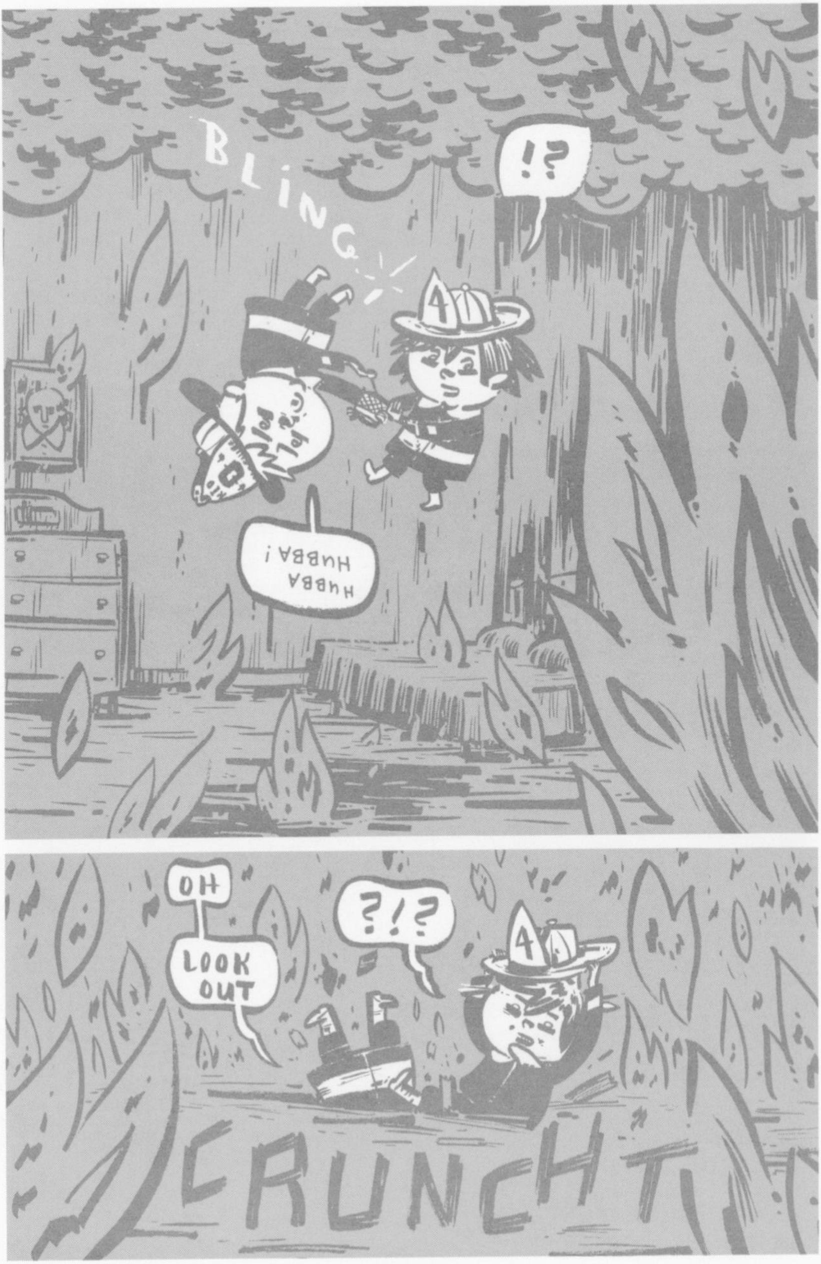
BLING
!?
HUBBA HUBBA!
OH
LOOK OUT
?!?
CRUNCH

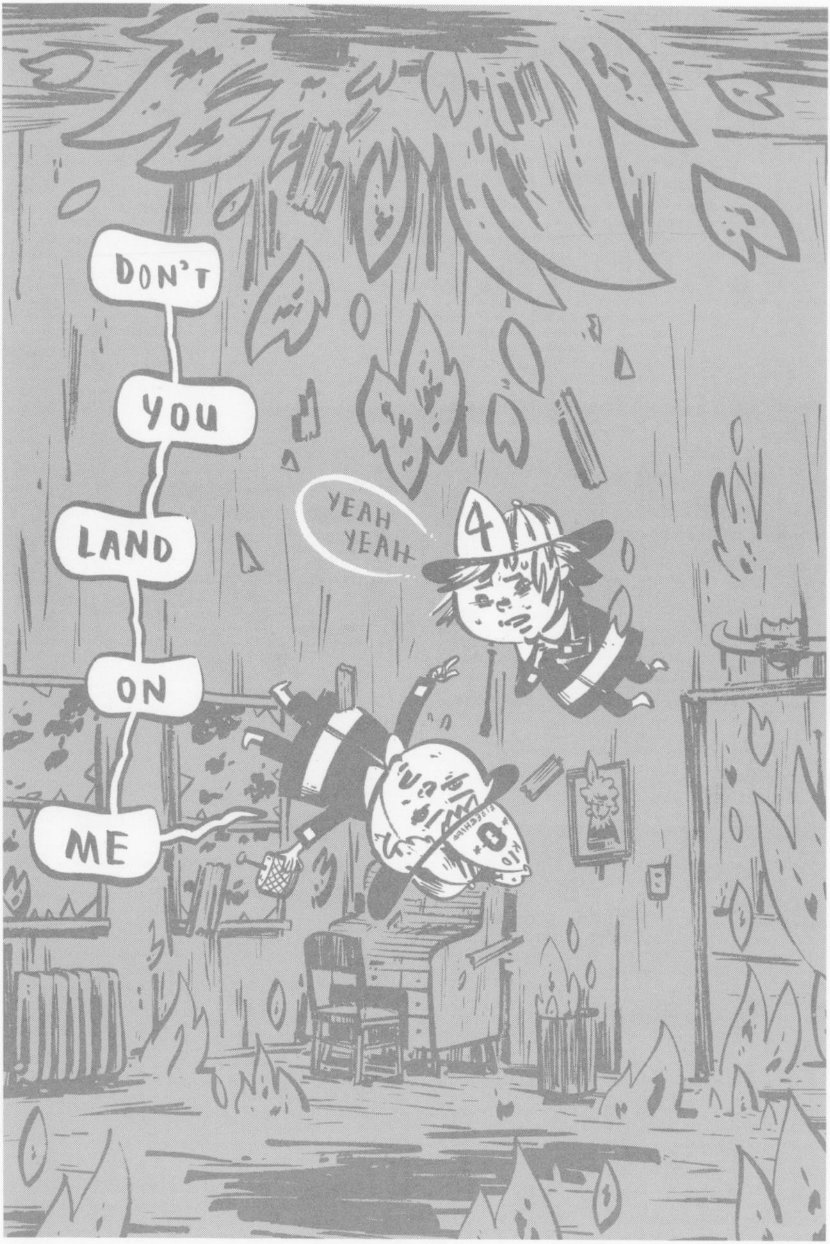
DON'T
YOU
LAND
ON
ME
YEAH YEAH

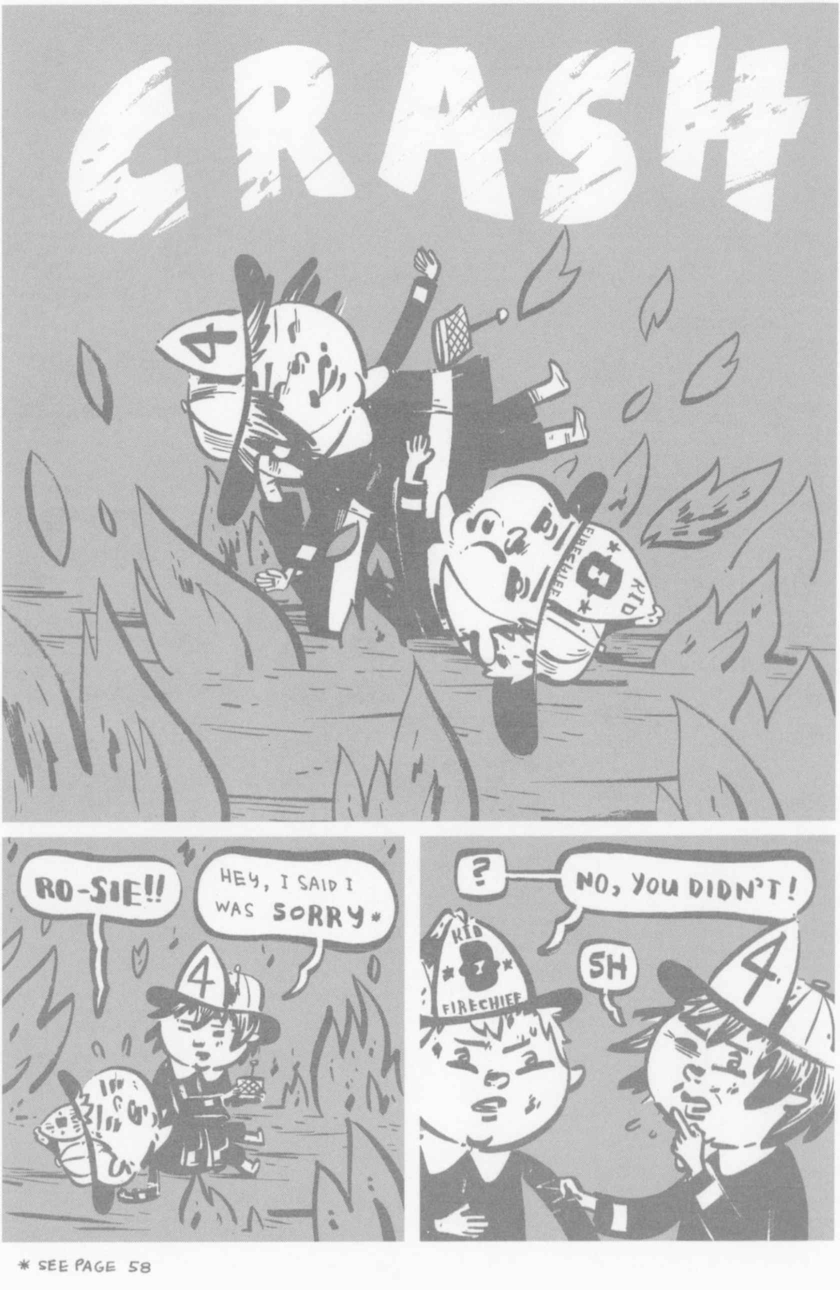
CRASH
RO-SIE!!
HEY, I SAID I WAS SORRY*
?
NO, YOU DIDN'T!
SH

* SEE PAGE 58

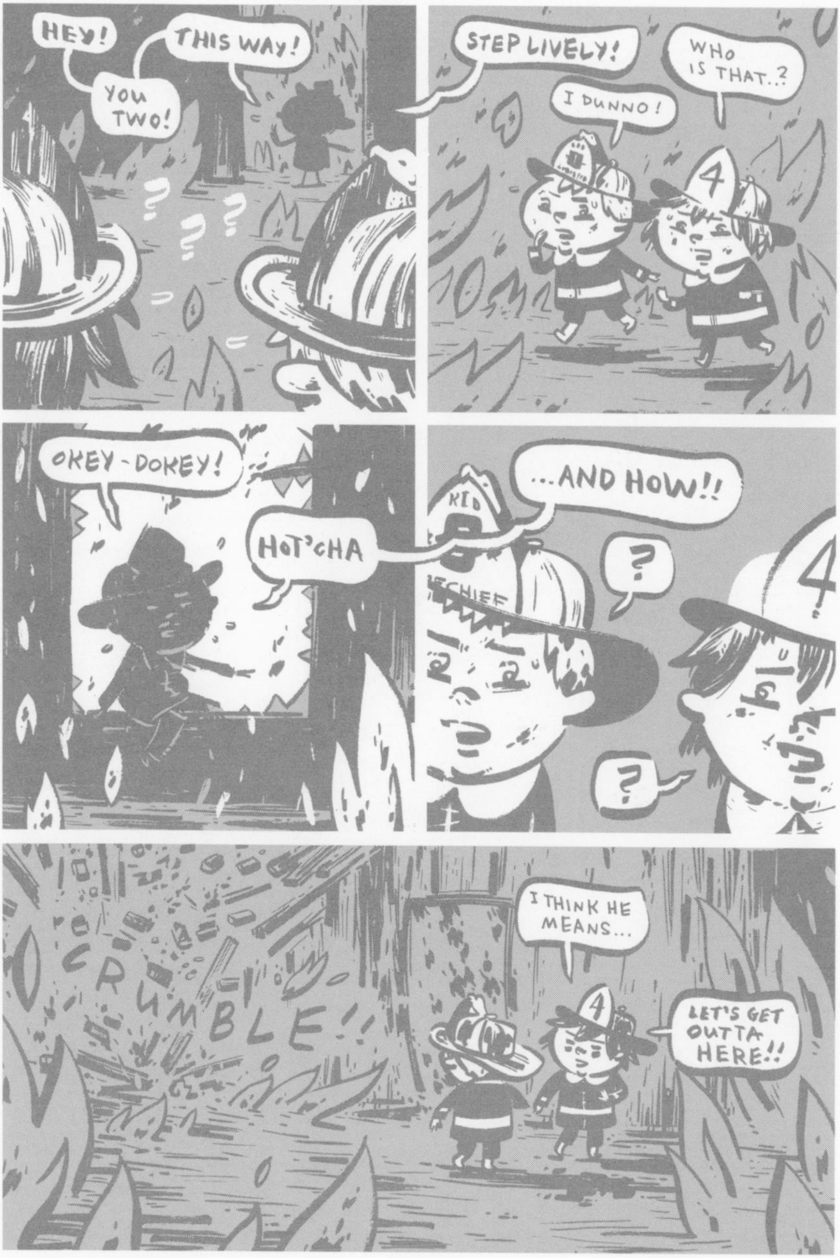
HEY!
YOU TWO!
THIS WAY!
STEP LIVELY!
WHO IS THAT..?
I DUNNO!
OKEY-DOKEY!
HOT'CHA
...AND HOW!!
?
?
CRUMBLE!!
I THINK HE MEANS...
LET'S GET OUTTA HERE!!

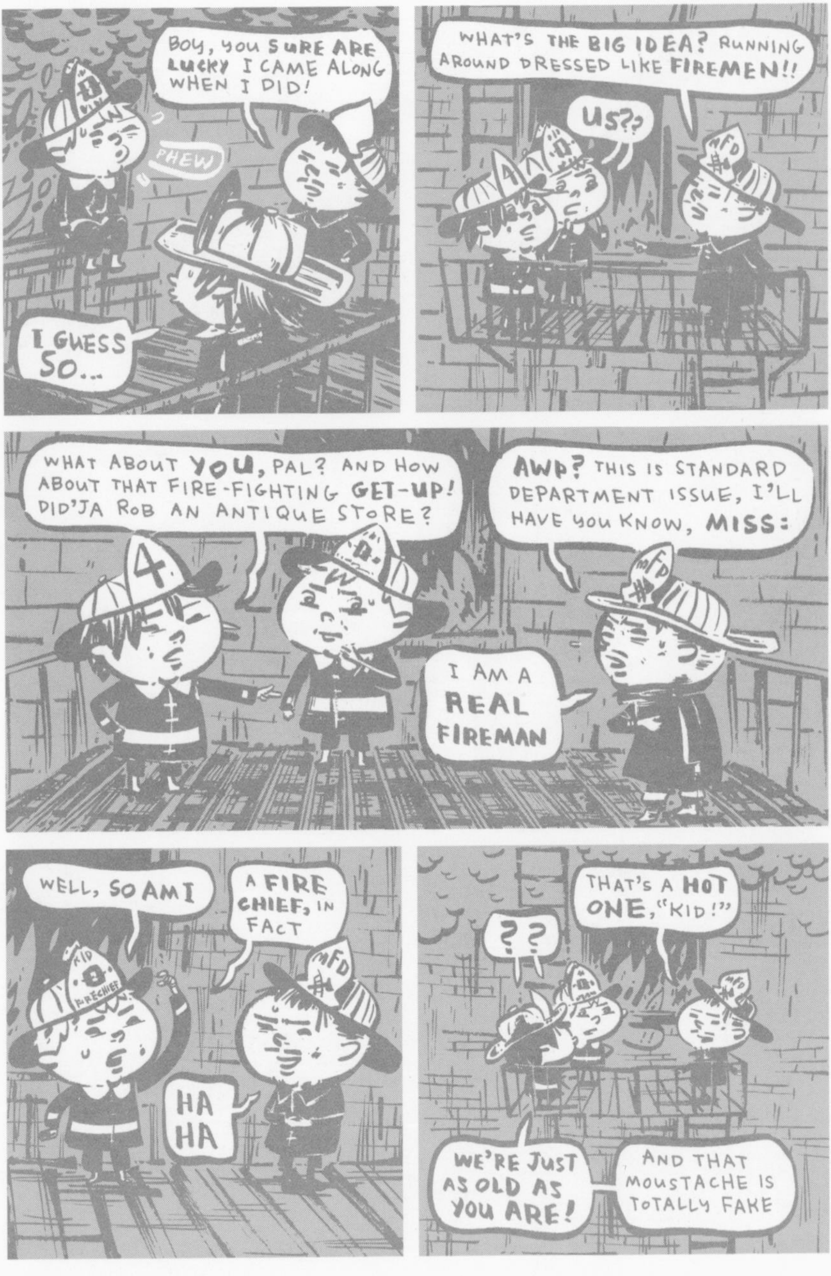
BOY, YOU SURE ARE LUCKY I CAME ALONG WHEN I DID!
PHEW
I GUESS SO...
WHAT'S THE BIG IDEA? RUNNING AROUND DRESSED LIKE FIREMEN!!
US??
WHAT ABOUT YOU, PAL? AND HOW ABOUT THAT FIRE-FIGHTING GET-UP! DID'JA ROB AN ANTIQUE STORE?
AWP? THIS IS STANDARD DEPARTMENT ISSUE, I'LL HAVE YOU KNOW, MISS:
I AM A REAL FIREMAN
WELL, SO AM I
A FIRE CHIEF, IN FACT
HA HA
THAT'S A HOT ONE, "KID!"
??
WE'RE JUST AS OLD AS YOU ARE!
AND THAT MOUSTACHE IS TOTALLY FAKE

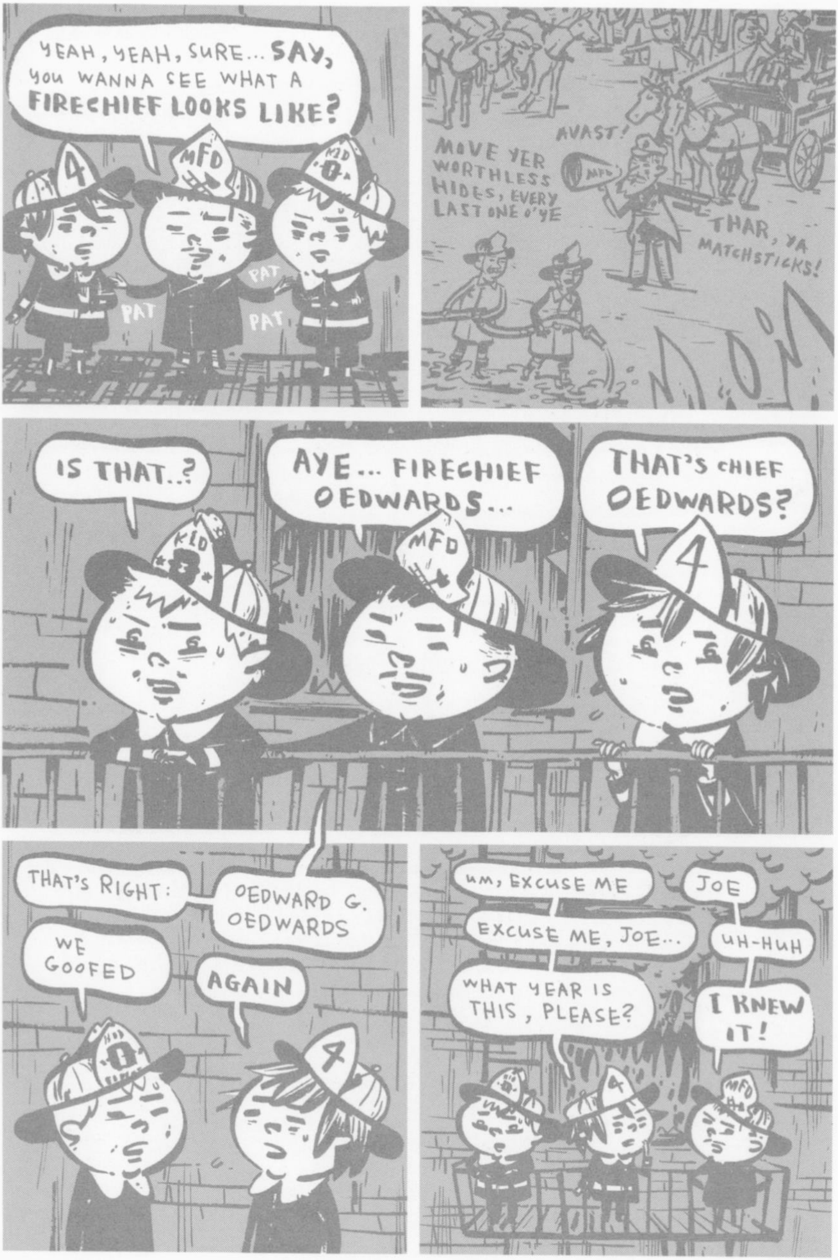
YEAH, YEAH, SURE... SAY, YOU WANNA SEE WHAT A FIRECHIEF LOOKS LIKE?
PAT
PAT
PAT
AVAST!
MOVE YER WORTHLESS HIDES, EVERY LAST ONE O'YE
THAR, YA MATCHSTICKS!
IS THAT..?
AYE... FIRECHIEF OEDWARDS...
THAT'S CHIEF OEDWARDS?
THAT'S RIGHT:
OEDWARD G. OEDWARDS
WE GOOFED
AGAIN
UM, EXCUSE ME
JOE
EXCUSE ME, JOE...
UH-HUH
WHAT YEAR IS THIS, PLEASE?
I KNEW IT!

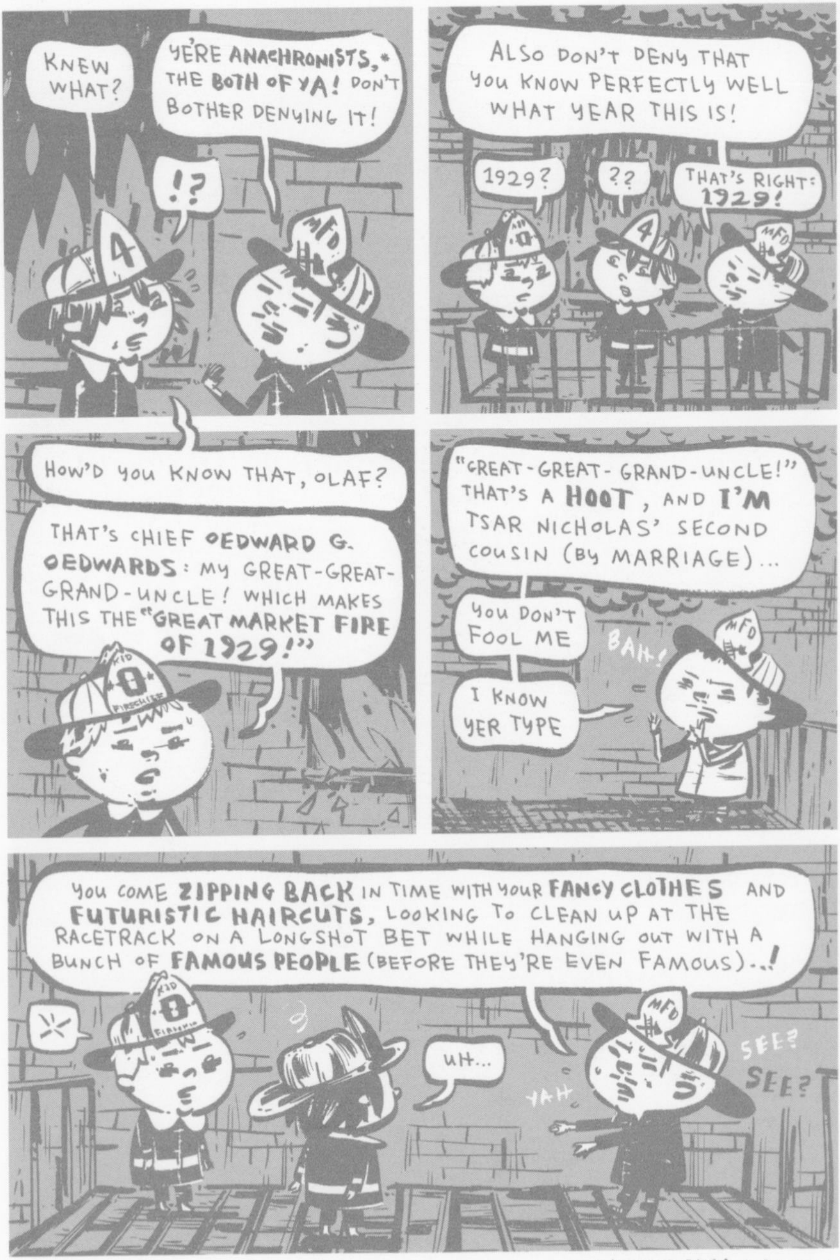
KNEW WHAT?
YE'RE ANACHRONISTS,* THE BOTH OF YA! DON'T BOTHER DENYING IT!
!?
ALSO DON'T DENY THAT YOU KNOW PERFECTLY WELL WHAT YEAR THIS IS!
1929?
??
THAT'S RIGHT: 1929!
HOW'D YOU KNOW THAT, OLAF?
THAT'S CHIEF OEDWARD G. OEDWARDS: MY GREAT-GREAT-GRAND-UNCLE! WHICH MAKES THIS THE "GREAT MARKET FIRE OF 1929!"
"GREAT-GREAT-GRAND-UNCLE!" THAT'S A HOOT, AND I'M TSAR NICHOLAS' SECOND COUSIN (BY MARRIAGE)...
YOU DON'T FOOL ME
BAH!
I KNOW YER TYPE
YOU COME ZIPPING BACK IN TIME WITH YOUR FANCY CLOTHES AND FUTURISTIC HAIRCUTS, LOOKING TO CLEAN UP AT THE RACETRACK ON A LONGSHOT BET WHILE HANGING OUT WITH A BUNCH OF FAMOUS PEOPLE (BEFORE THEY'RE EVEN FAMOUS)..!
UH...
YAH
SEE?
SEE?

* LOOK IT UP, THERE'S NO SUCH WORD

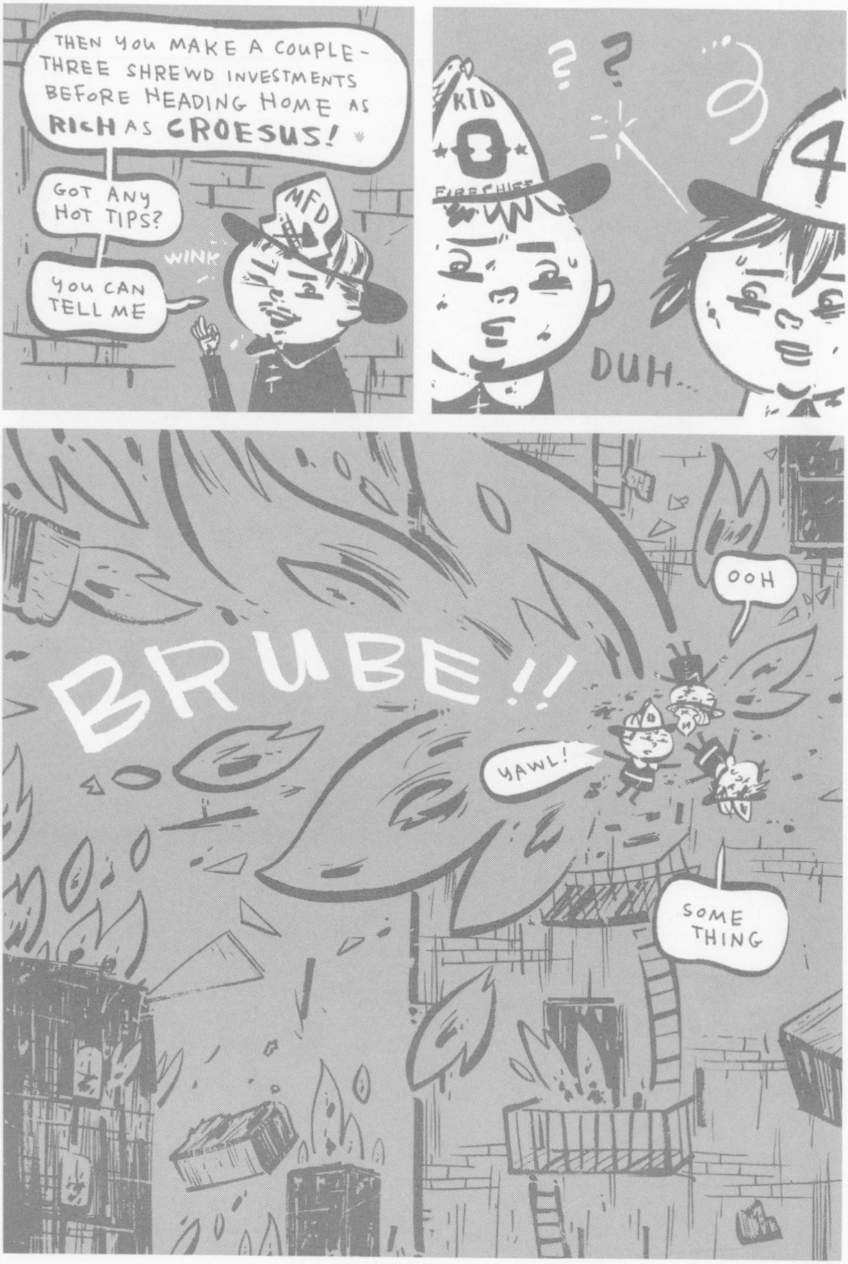
THEN YOU MAKE A COUPLE-THREE SHREWD INVESTMENTS BEFORE HEADING HOME AS RICH AS CROESUS! *
GOT ANY HOT TIPS?
YOU CAN TELL ME
WINK
MFD
KID
0
DUH...
BRUBE!!
OOH
YAWL!
SOME THING

* NOT THE BEST STRATEGY IN 1929

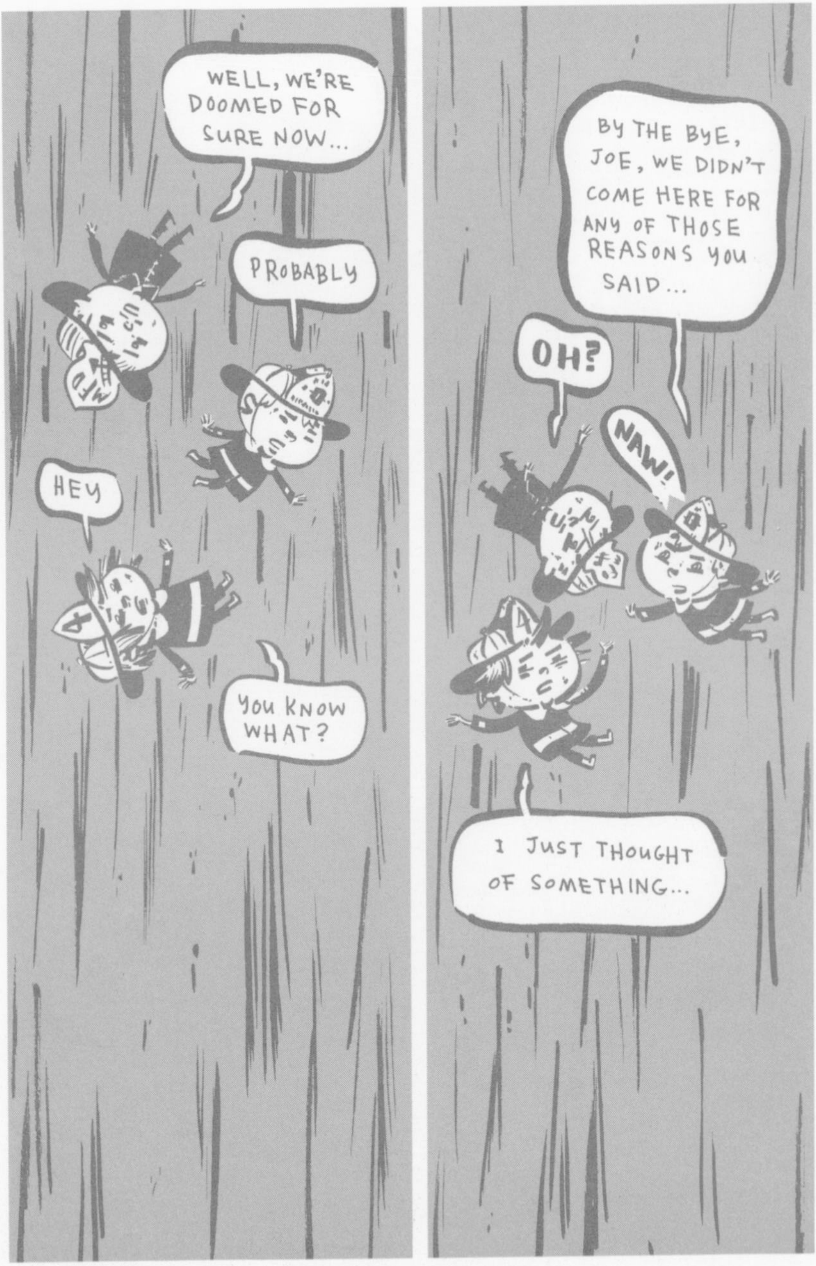
WELL, WE'RE DOOMED FOR SURE NOW...
PROBABLY
HEY
YOU KNOW WHAT?
BY THE BYE, JOE, WE DIDN'T COME HERE FOR ANY OF THOSE REASONS YOU SAID...
OH?
NAW!
I JUST THOUGHT OF SOMETHING...

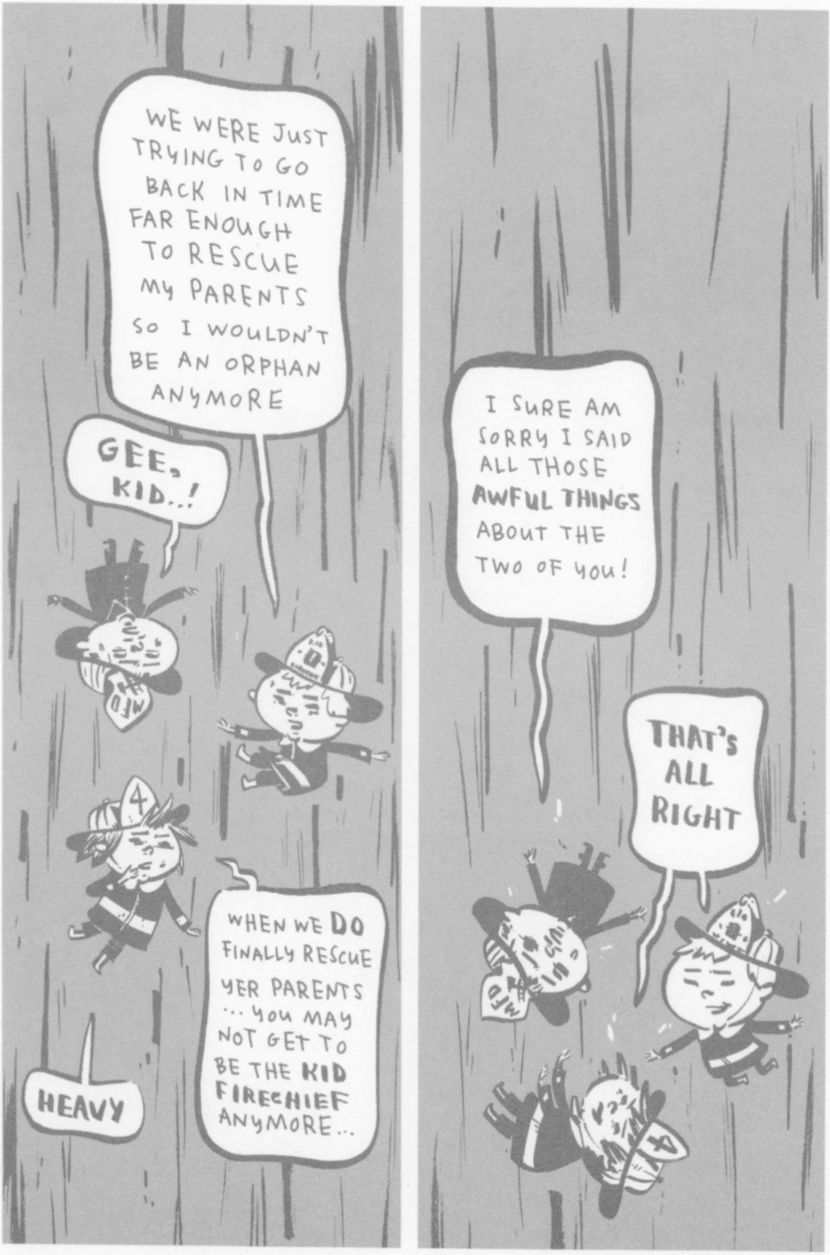
WE WERE JUST TRYING TO GO BACK IN TIME FAR ENOUGH TO RESCUE MY PARENTS SO I WOULDN'T BE AN ORPHAN ANYMORE
GEE, KID..!
WHEN WE DO FINALLY RESCUE YER PARENTS ... YOU MAY NOT GET TO BE THE KID FIRECHIEF ANYMORE...
HEAVY
I SURE AM SORRY I SAID ALL THOSE AWFUL THINGS ABOUT THE TWO OF YOU!
THAT'S ALL RIGHT

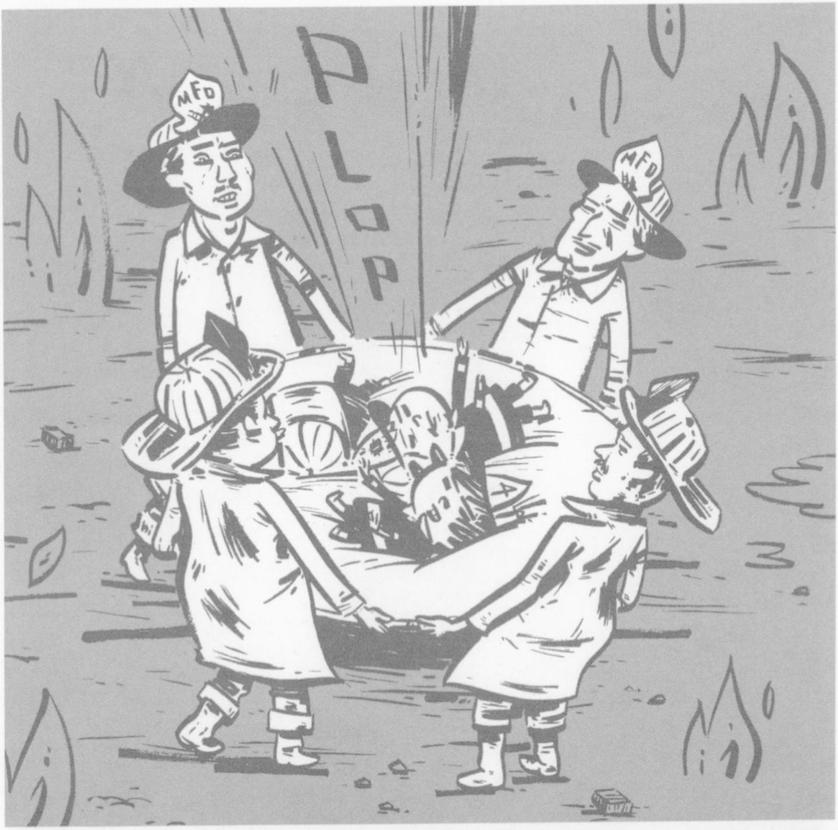
PLOP

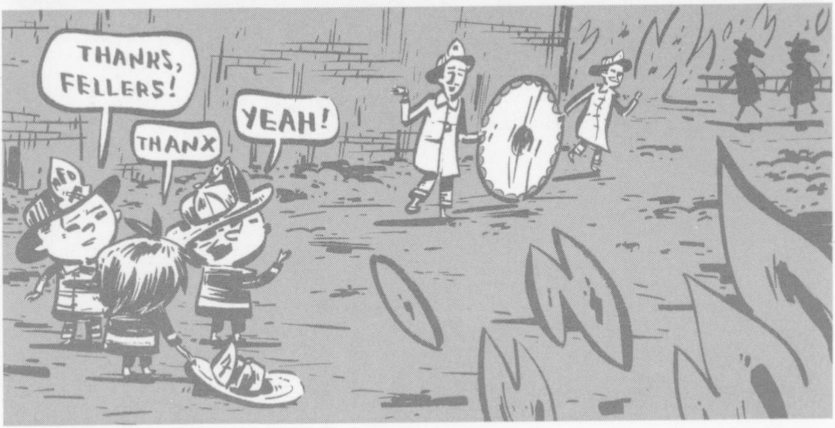
THANKS, FELLERS!
THANX
YEAH!

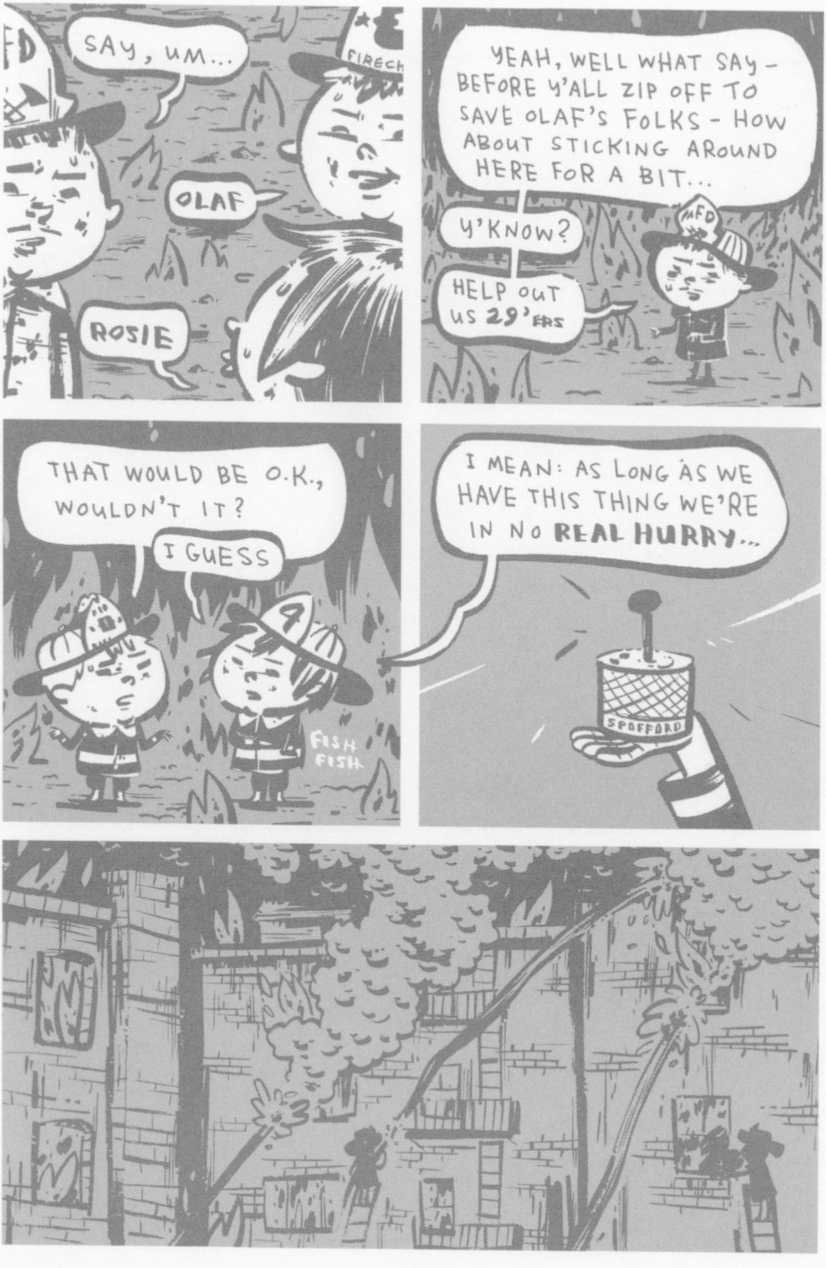
SAY, UM...
OLAF
ROSIE
YEAH, WELL WHAT SAY - BEFORE Y'ALL ZIP OFF TO SAVE OLAF'S FOLKS - HOW ABOUT STICKING AROUND HERE FOR A BIT...
Y'KNOW?
HELP OUT US 29'ERS
THAT WOULD BE O.K., WOULDN'T IT?
I GUESS
FISH FISH
I MEAN: AS LONG AS WE HAVE THIS THING WE'RE IN NO REAL HURRY...
SPOFFORD

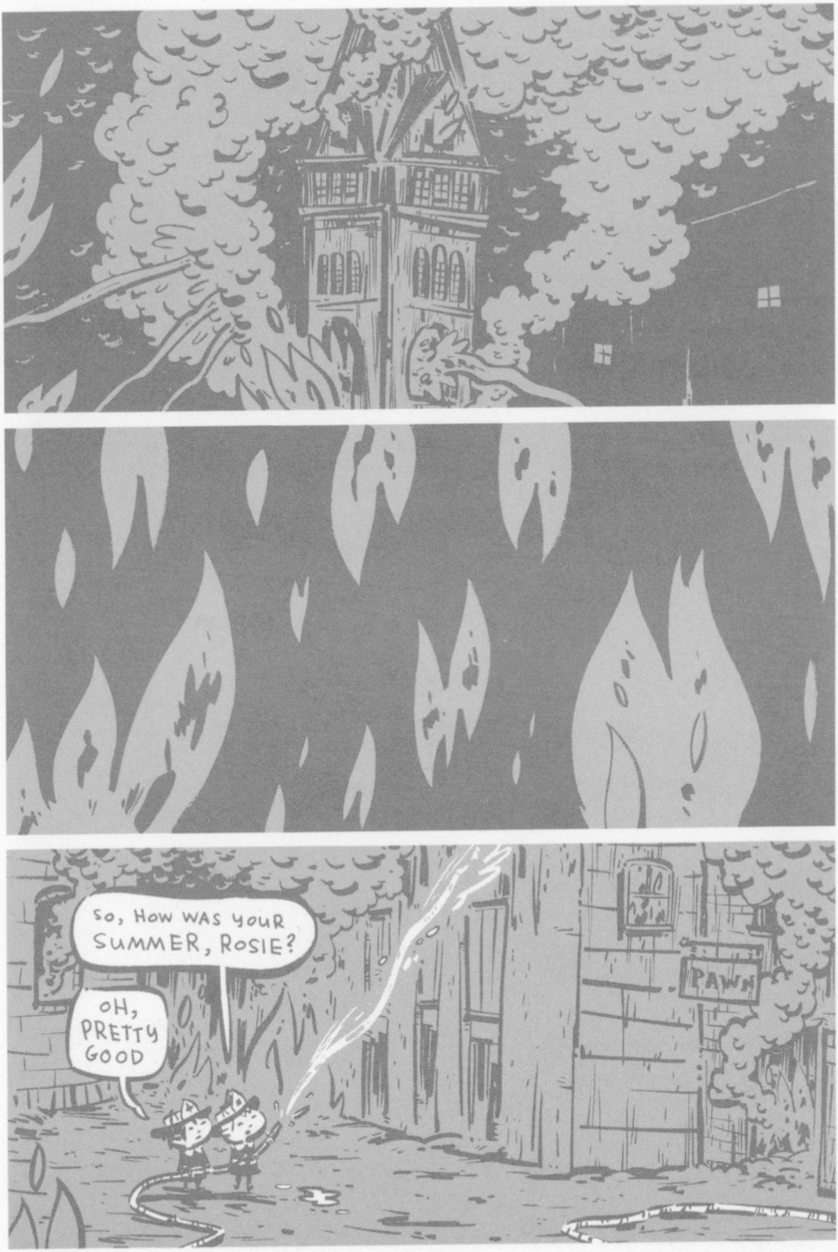
PAWN
SO, HOW WAS YOUR SUMMER, ROSIE?
OH, PRETTY GOOD

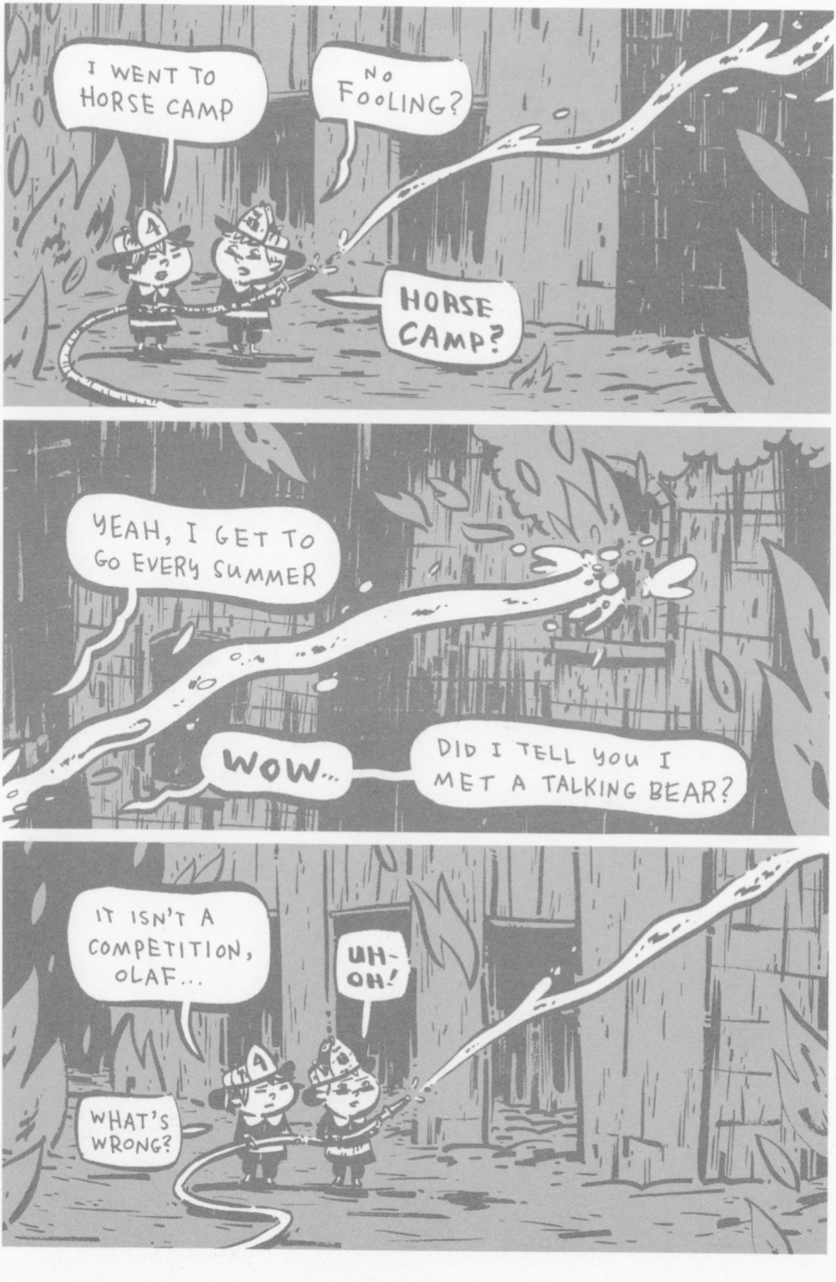
I WENT TO HORSE CAMP
NO FOOLING?
HORSE CAMP?
YEAH, I GET TO GO EVERY SUMMER
WOW...
DID I TELL YOU I MET A TALKING BEAR?
IT ISN'T A COMPETITION, OLAF...
UH-OH!
WHAT'S WRONG?

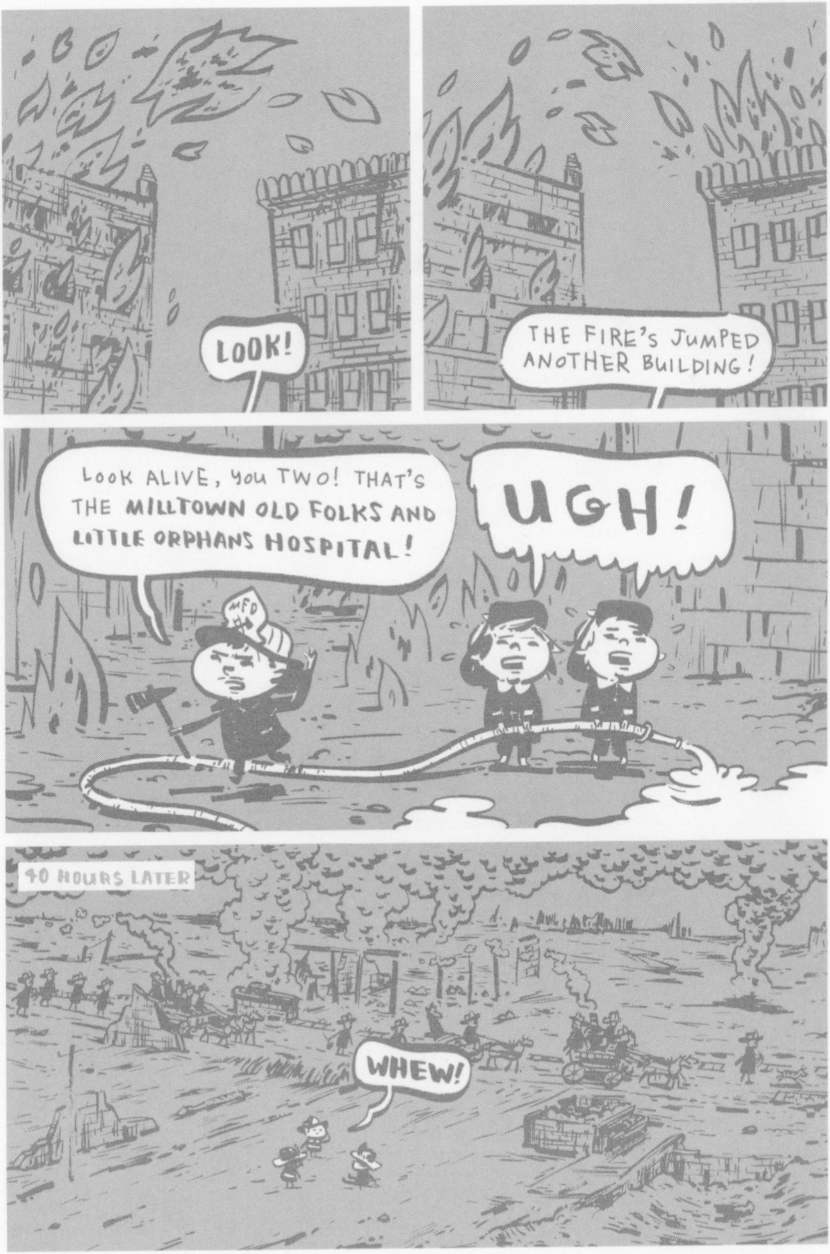
LOOK!
THE FIRE'S JUMPED ANOTHER BUILDING!
LOOK ALIVE, YOU TWO! THAT'S THE MILLTOWN OLD FOLKS AND LITTLE ORPHANS HOSPITAL!
UGH!
MFD
40 HOURS LATER
WHEW!

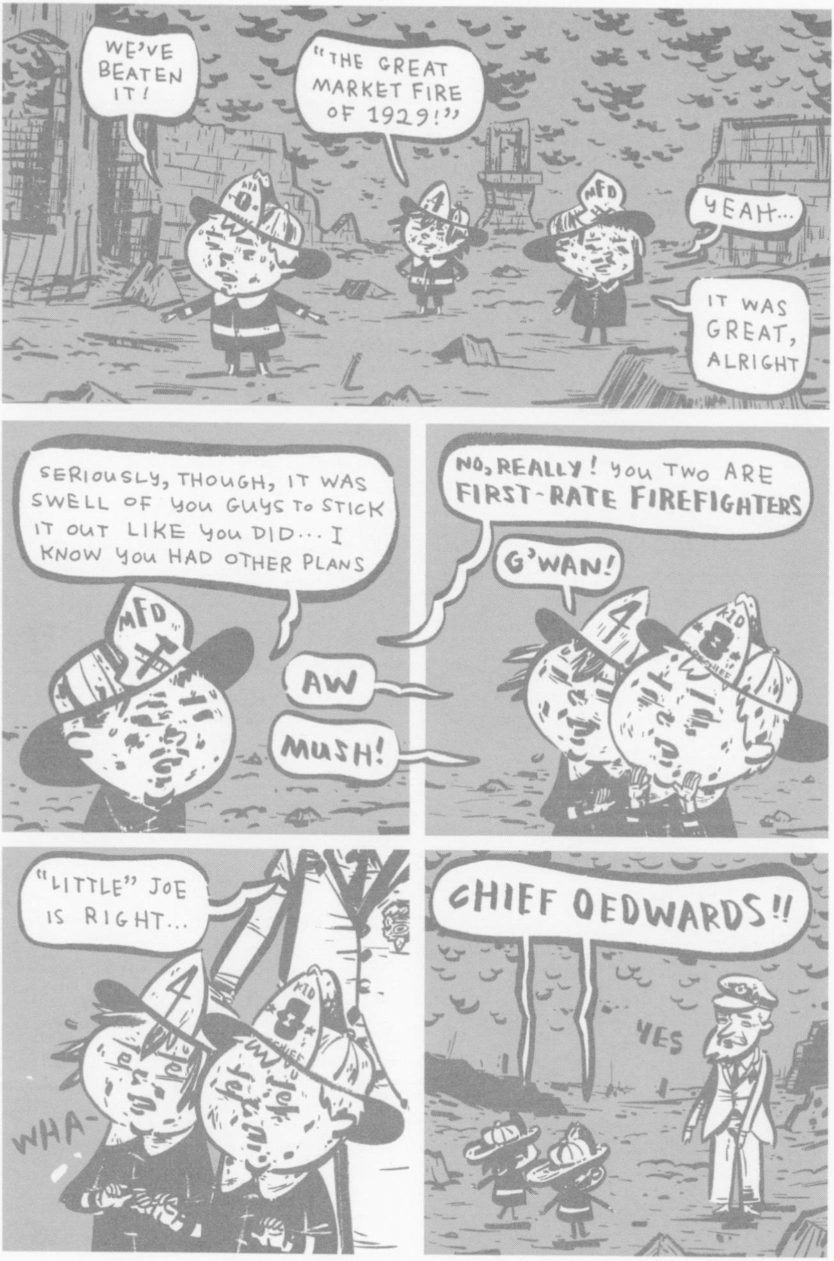
WE'VE BEATEN IT!
"THE GREAT MARKET FIRE OF 1929!"
YEAH...
IT WAS GREAT, ALRIGHT
SERIOUSLY, THOUGH, IT WAS SWELL OF YOU GUYS TO STICK IT OUT LIKE YOU DID... I KNOW YOU HAD OTHER PLANS
AW
MUSH!
NO, REALLY! YOU TWO ARE FIRST-RATE FIREFIGHTERS
G'WAN!
"LITTLE" JOE IS RIGHT...
WHA-
CHIEF OEDWARDS!!
YES

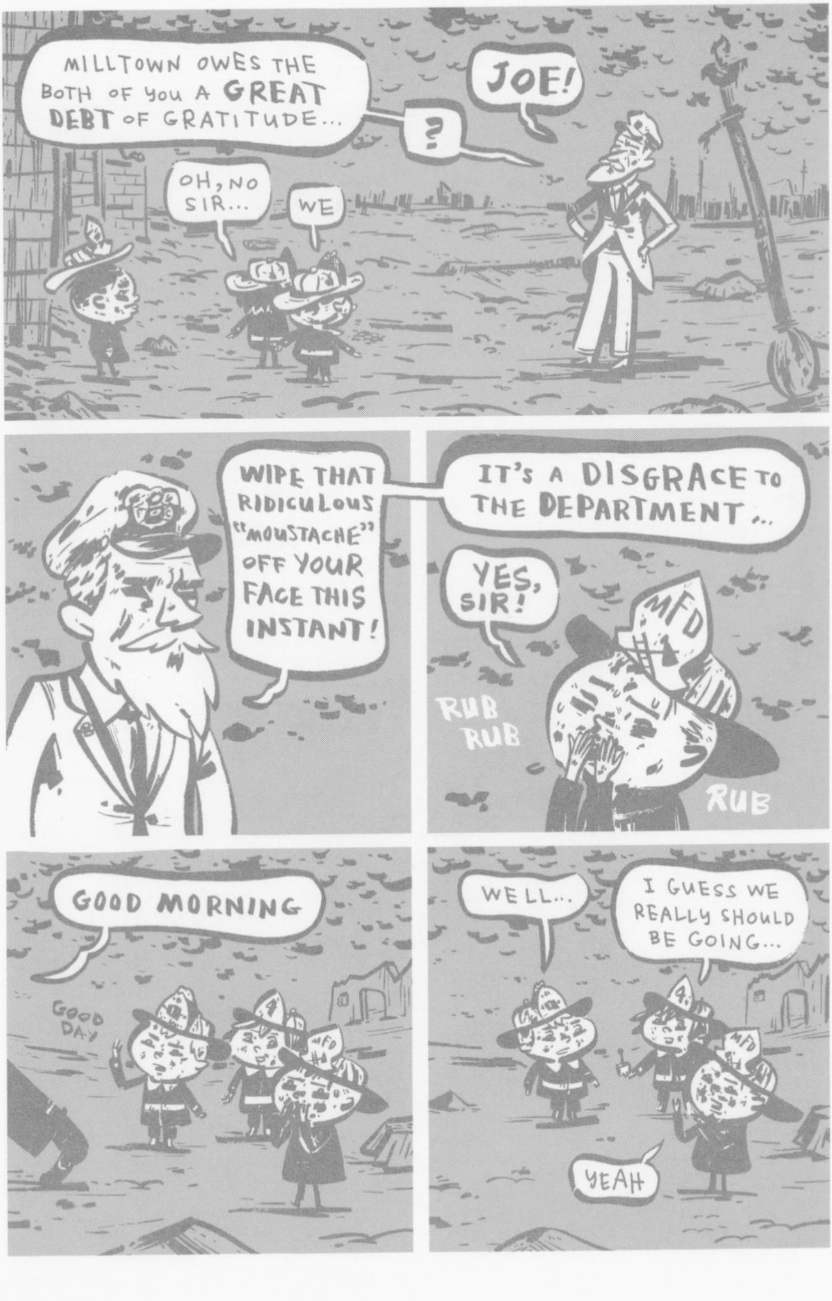
MILLTOWN OWES THE BOTH OF YOU A GREAT DEBT OF GRATITUDE...
?
JOE!
OH, NO SIR...
WE
WIPE THAT RIDICULOUS "MOUSTACHE" OFF YOUR FACE THIS INSTANT!
IT'S A DISGRACE TO THE DEPARTMENT...
YES, SIR!
RUB RUB
RUB
GOOD MORNING
GOOD DAY
WELL...
I GUESS WE REALLY SHOULD BE GOING...
YEAH

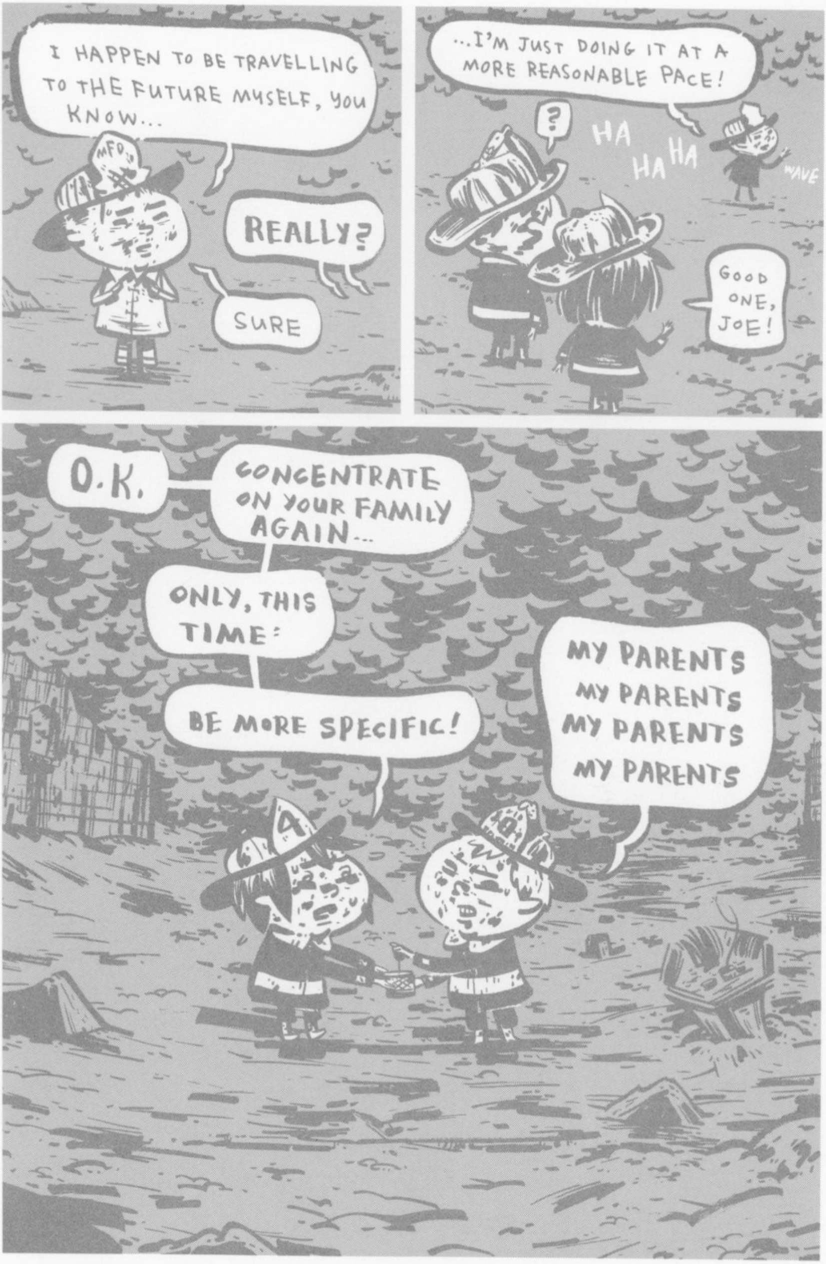
I HAPPEN TO BE TRAVELLING TO THE FUTURE MYSELF, YOU KNOW...
REALLY?
SURE
...I'M JUST DOING IT AT A MORE REASONABLE PACE!
?
HA HA HA
WAVE
GOOD ONE, JOE!
O.K.
CONCENTRATE ON YOUR FAMILY AGAIN...
ONLY, THIS TIME:
BE MORE SPECIFIC!
MY PARENTS MY PARENTS MY PARENTS MY PARENTS

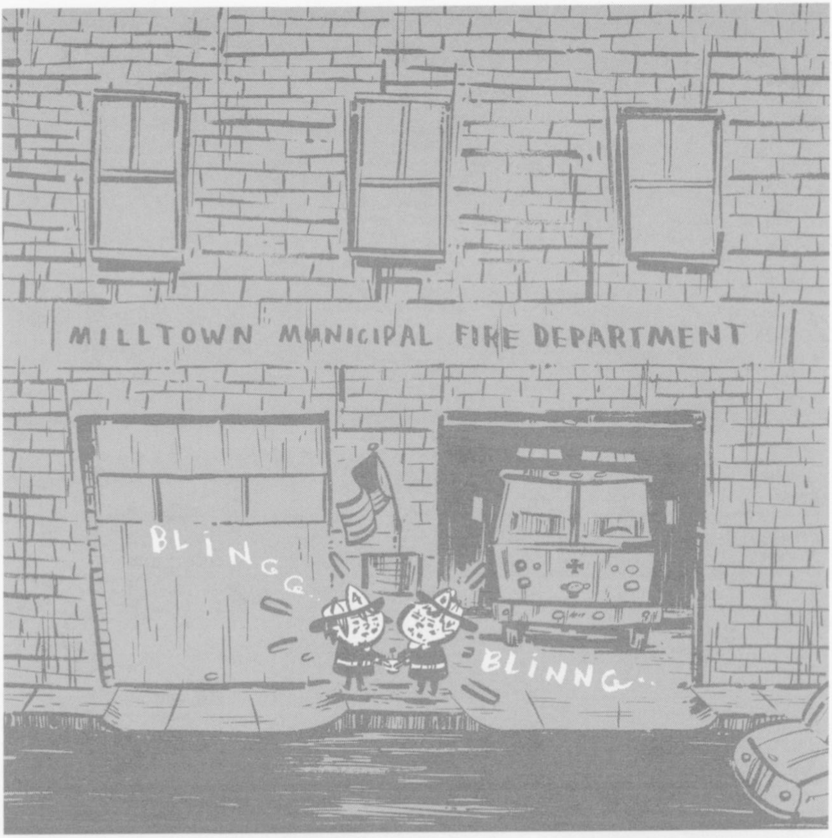
MILLTOWN MUNICIPAL FIRE DEPARTMENT
BLINGG..
BLINNG..

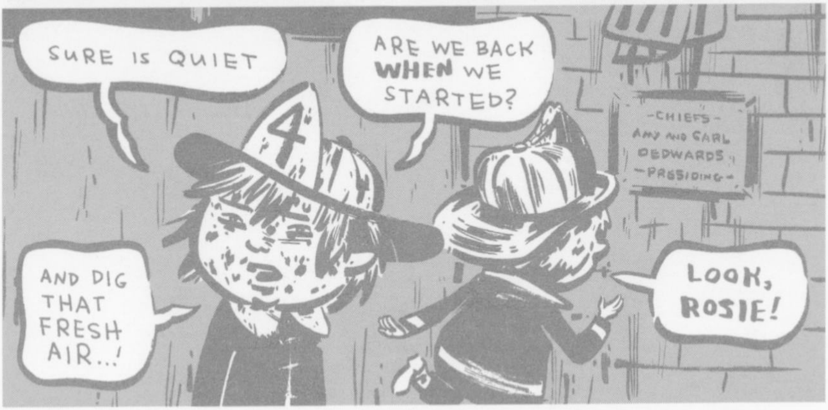
SURE IS QUIET
ARE WE BACK WHEN WE STARTED?
-CHIEFS- AMY AND CARL OEDWARDS -PRESIDING-
AND DIG THAT FRESH AIR...!
LOOK, ROSIE!

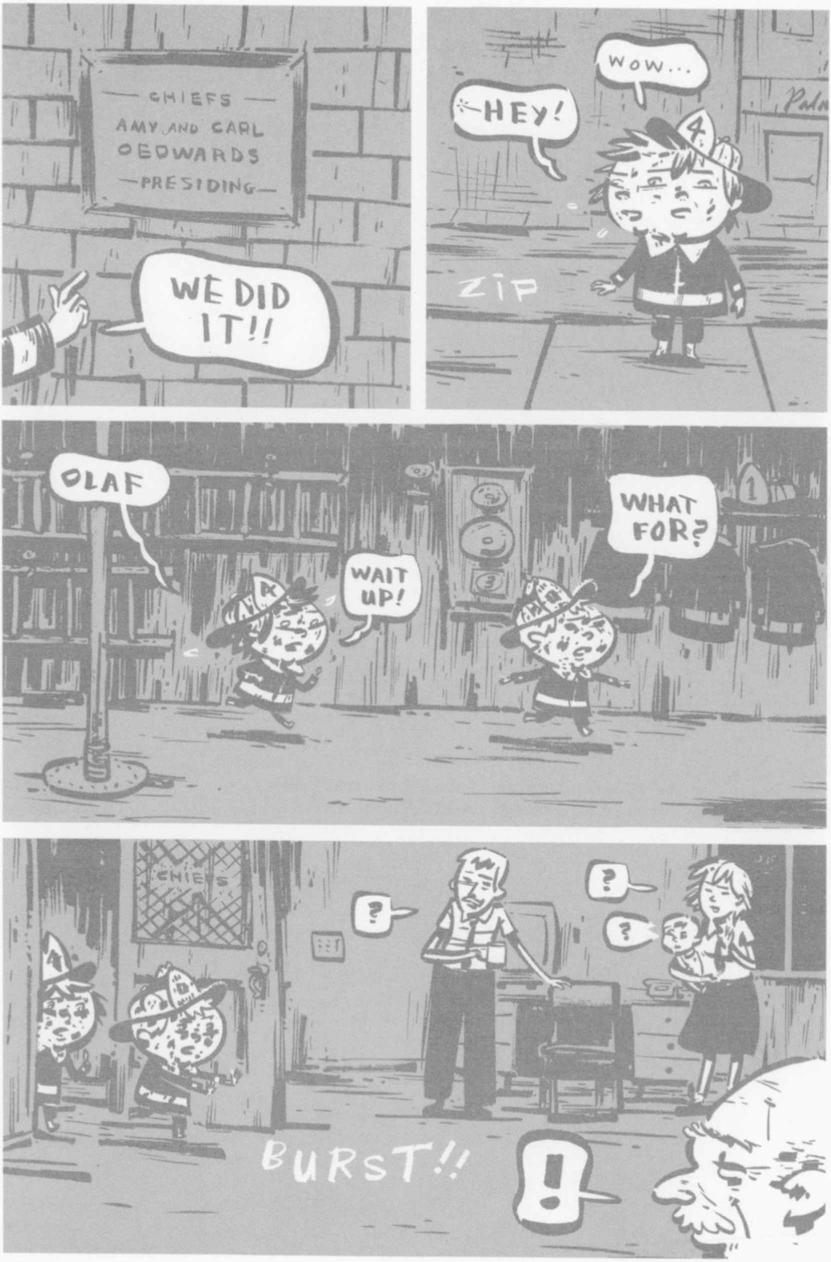
CHIEFS AMY AND CARL OEDWARDS PRESIDING
WE DID IT!!
WOW...
HEY!
ZIP
OLAF
WAIT UP!
WHAT FOR?
CHIEFS
?
?
?
BURST!!
!

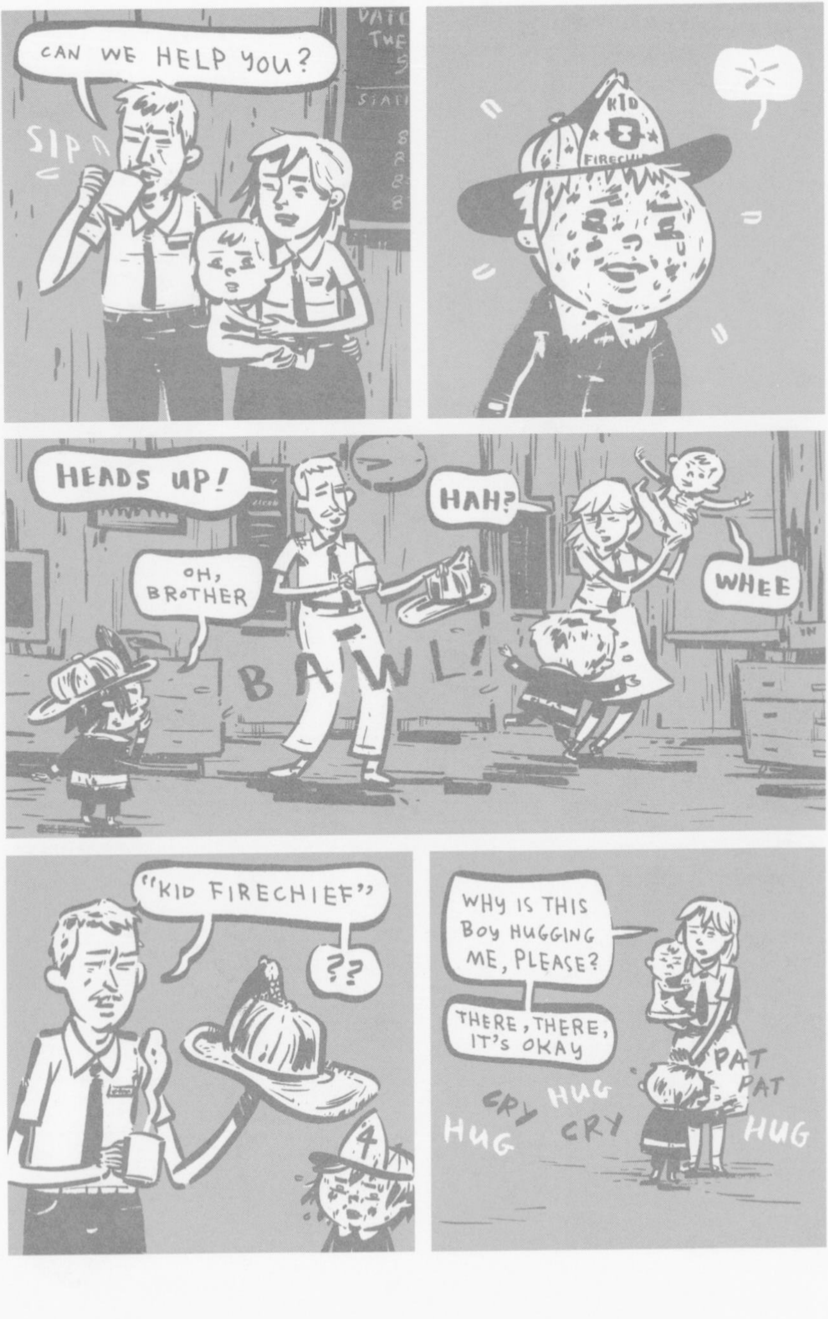
CAN WE HELP YOU?
SIP
KID FIRECHIEF
HEADS UP!
HAH?
WHEE
OH, BROTHER
BAWL!
"KID FIRECHIEF"
??
WHY IS THIS BOY HUGGING ME, PLEASE?
THERE, THERE, IT'S OKAY
PAT PAT
CRY HUG
HUG CRY
HUG

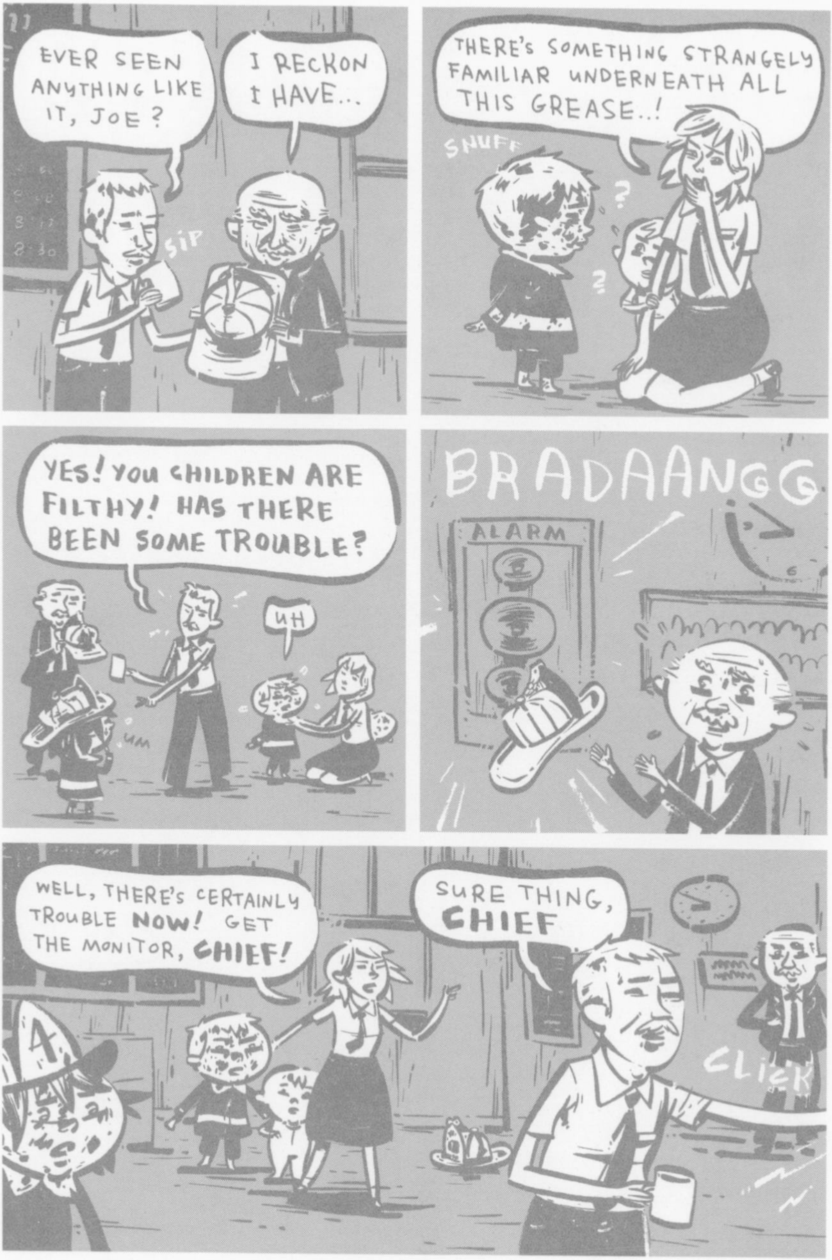
EVER SEEN ANYTHING LIKE IT, JOE?
I RECKON I HAVE...
SIP
THERE'S SOMETHING STRANGELY FAMILIAR UNDERNEATH ALL THIS GREASE..!
SNUFF
?
?
YES! YOU CHILDREN ARE FILTHY! HAS THERE BEEN SOME TROUBLE?
UH
UM
BRADAANGG
ALARM
WELL, THERE'S CERTAINLY TROUBLE NOW! GET THE MONITOR, CHIEF!
SURE THING, CHIEF
CLICK

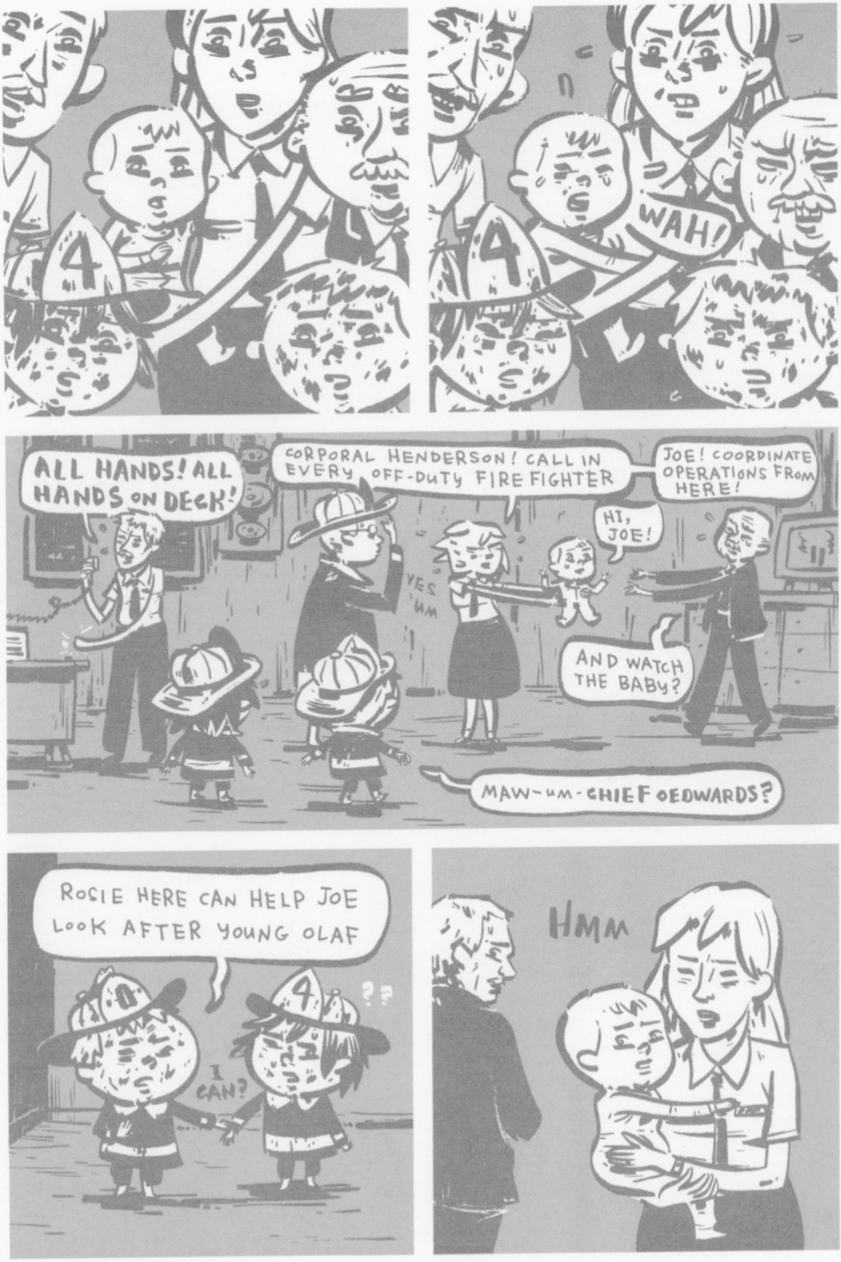
WAH!
ALL HANDS! ALL HANDS ON DECK!
CORPORAL HENDERSON! CALL IN EVERY OFF-DUTY FIRE FIGHTER
YES UM
JOE! COORDINATE OPERATIONS FROM HERE!
HI, JOE!
AND WATCH THE BABY?
MAW-UM-CHIEF EDWARDS?
ROSIE HERE CAN HELP JOE LOOK AFTER YOUNG OLAF
I CAN?
HMM

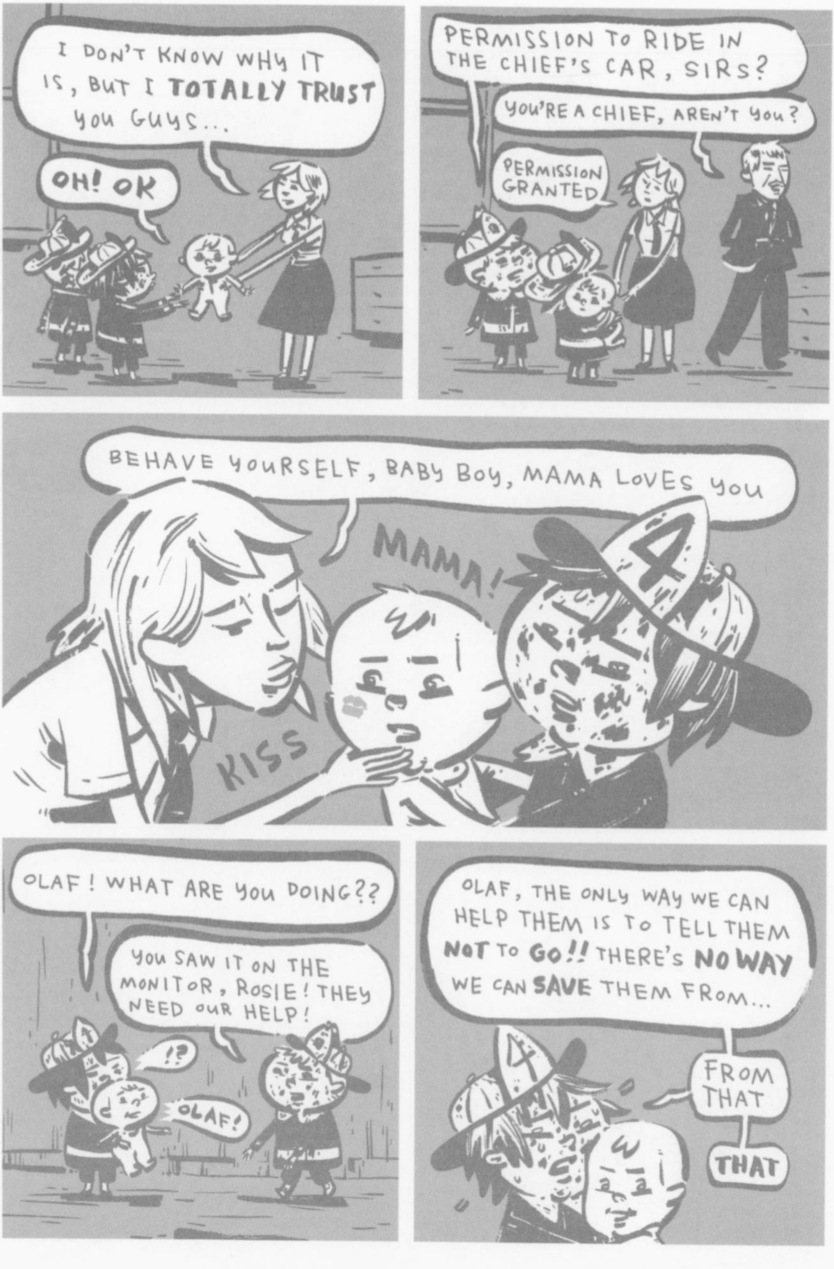
I DON'T KNOW WHY IT IS, BUT I TOTALLY TRUST YOU GUYS...
OH! OK
PERMISSION TO RIDE IN THE CHIEF'S CAR, SIRS?
YOU'RE A CHIEF, AREN'T YOU?
PERMISSION GRANTED
BEHAVE YOURSELF, BABY BOY, MAMA LOVES YOU
MAMA!
KISS
OLAF! WHAT ARE YOU DOING??
YOU SAW IT ON THE MONITOR, ROSIE! THEY NEED OUR HELP!
!?
OLAF!
OLAF, THE ONLY WAY WE CAN HELP THEM IS TO TELL THEM NOT TO GO!! THERE'S NO WAY WE CAN SAVE THEM FROM...
FROM THAT
THAT

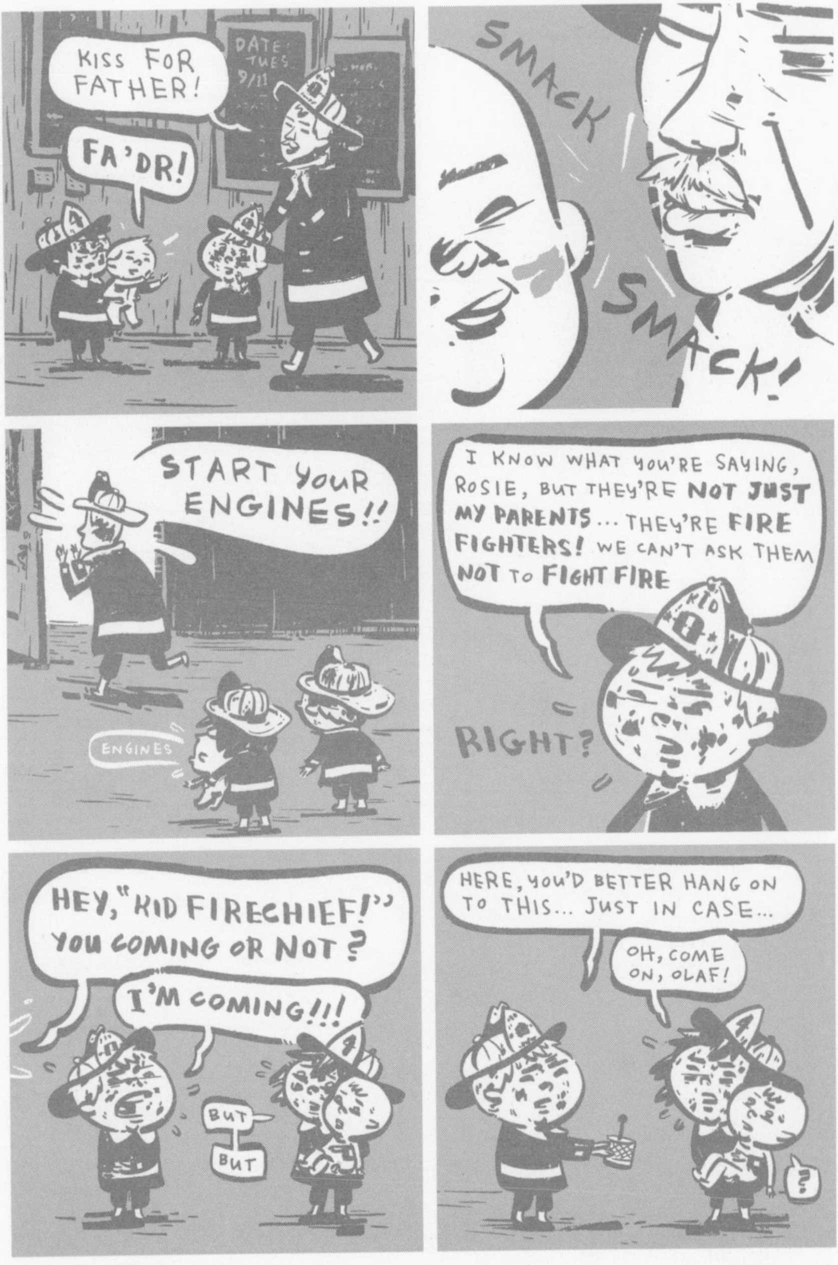
KISS FOR FATHER!
DATE: TUES. 9/11
FA'DR!
SMACK
SMACK!
START YOUR ENGINES!!
ENGINES
I KNOW WHAT YOU'RE SAYING, ROSIE, BUT THEY'RE NOT JUST MY PARENTS... THEY'RE FIRE FIGHTERS! WE CAN'T ASK THEM NOT TO FIGHT FIRE
RIGHT?
HEY, "KID FIRECHIEF!" YOU COMING OR NOT?
I'M COMING!!!
BUT
BUT
HERE, YOU'D BETTER HANG ON TO THIS... JUST IN CASE...
OH, COME ON, OLAF!
?

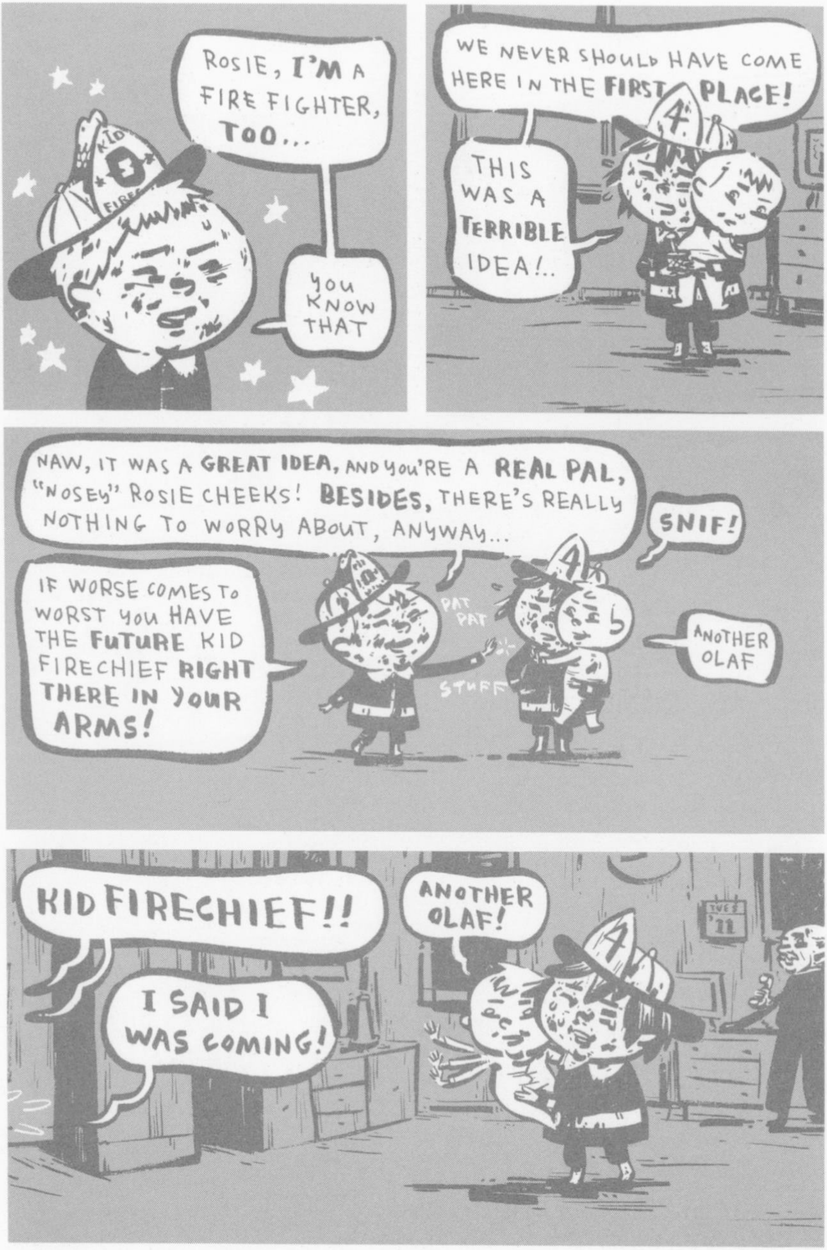
ROSIE, I'M A FIRE FIGHTER, TOO...
YOU KNOW THAT
WE NEVER SHOULD HAVE COME HERE IN THE FIRST PLACE!
THIS WAS A TERRIBLE IDEA!..
NAW, IT WAS A GREAT IDEA, AND YOU'RE A REAL PAL, "NOSEY" ROSIE CHEEKS! BESIDES, THERE'S REALLY NOTHING TO WORRY ABOUT, ANYWAY...
SNIF!
IF WORSE COMES TO WORST YOU HAVE THE FUTURE KID FIRECHIEF RIGHT THERE IN YOUR ARMS!
PAT PAT
STUFF
ANOTHER OLAF
KID FIRECHIEF!!
I SAID I WAS COMING!
ANOTHER OLAF!

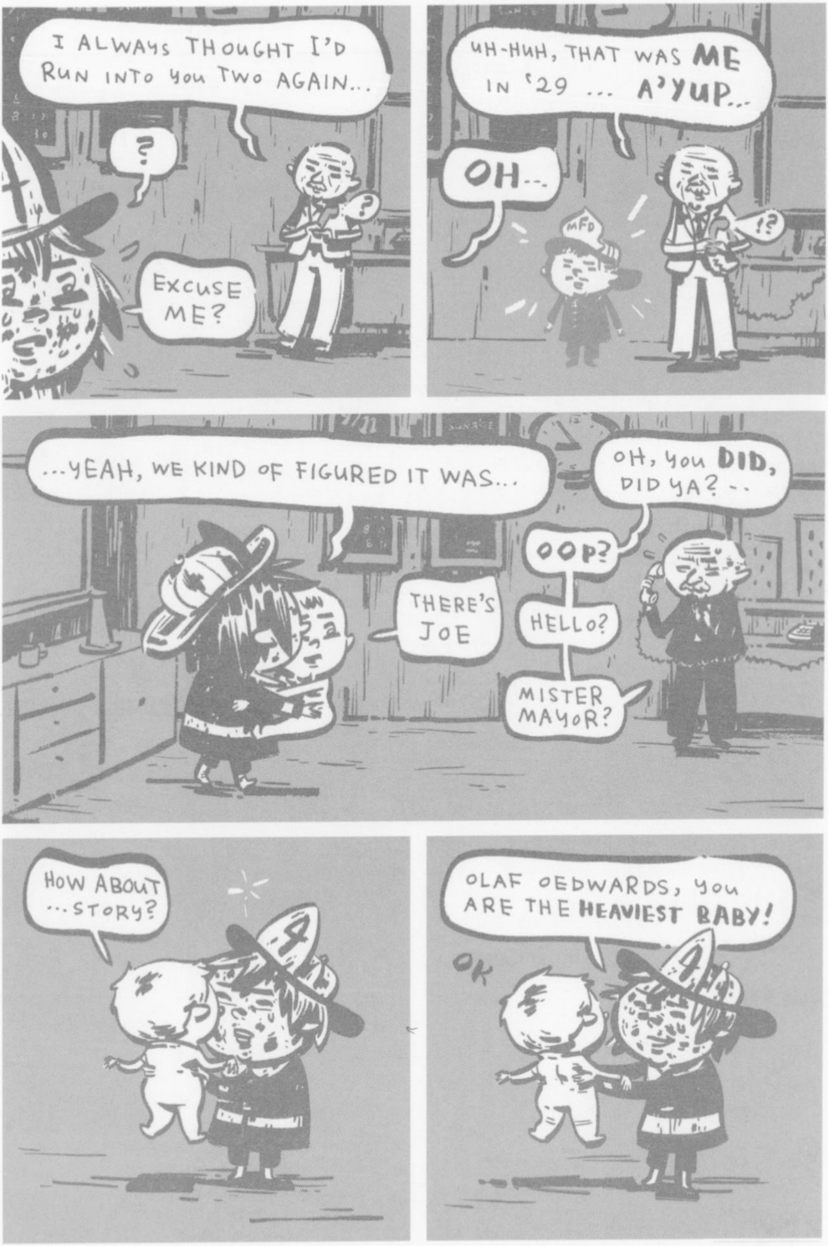
I ALWAYS THOUGHT I'D RUN INTO YOU TWO AGAIN...
?
?
EXCUSE ME?
UH-HUH, THAT WAS **ME** IN '29 ... **A'YUP**...
OH...
MFD
!?
...YEAH, WE KIND OF FIGURED IT WAS...
OH, YOU **DID**, DID YA? --
OOP?
THERE'S JOE
HELLO?
MISTER MAYOR?
HOW ABOUT ...STORY?
OLAF OEDWARDS, YOU ARE THE **HEAVIEST BABY**!
OK
¡PÅP!

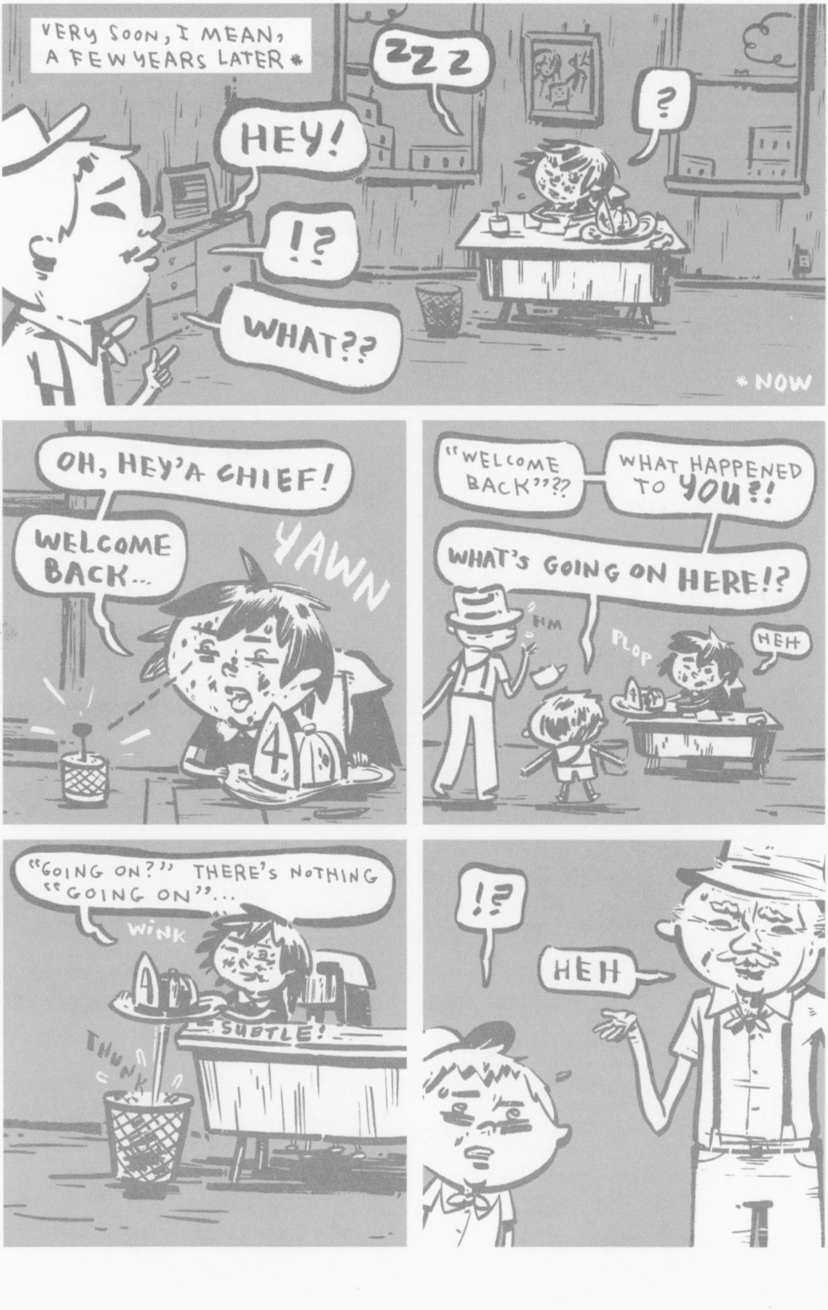

VERY SOON, I MEAN, A FEW YEARS LATER*
HEY!
ZZZ
!?
WHAT??
?
*NOW
OH, HEY'A CHIEF!
WELCOME BACK...
YAWN
"WELCOME BACK"??
WHAT HAPPENED TO YOU?!
WHAT'S GOING ON HERE!?
HM
PLOP
HEH
"GOING ON?" THERE'S NOTHING "GOING ON"...
WINK
SUBTLE!
THUNK
!?
HEH

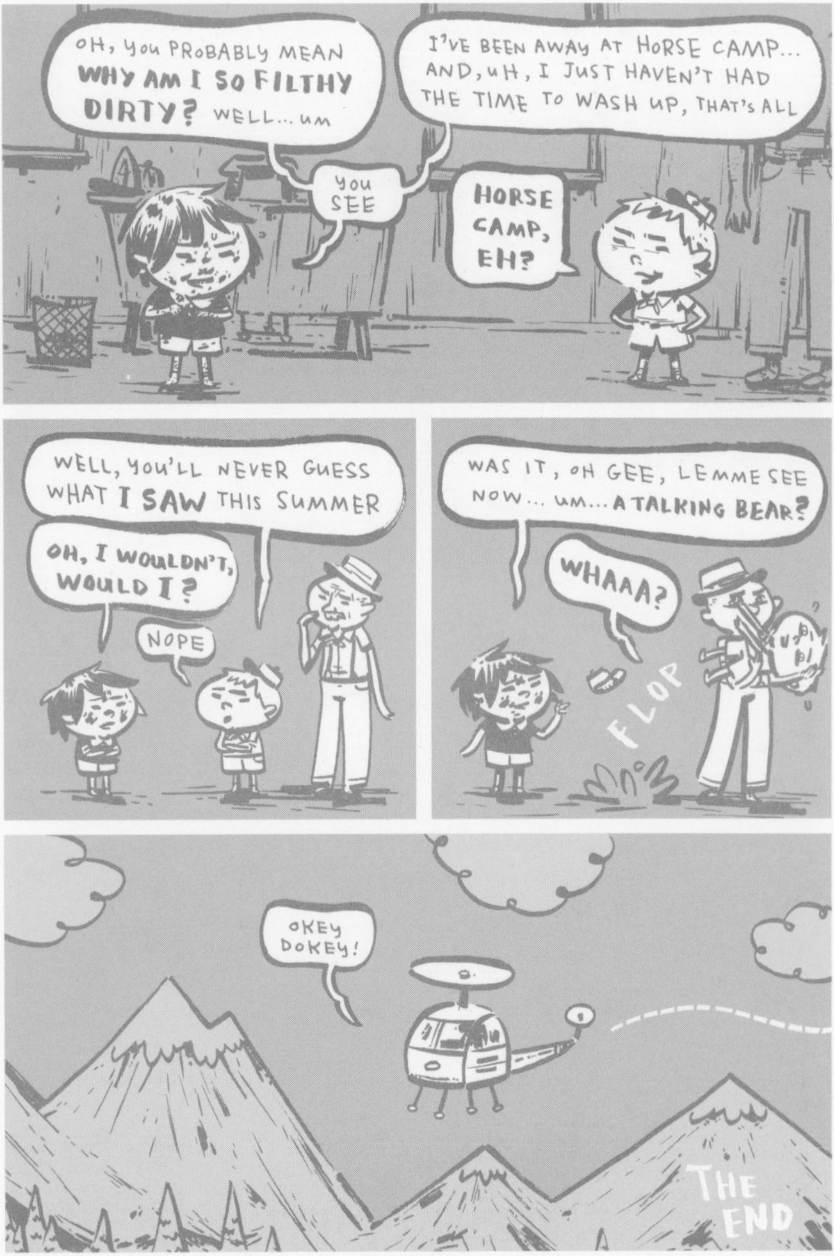
OH, YOU PROBABLY MEAN WHY AM I SO FILTHY DIRTY? WELL... UM
YOU SEE
I'VE BEEN AWAY AT HORSE CAMP... AND, UH, I JUST HAVEN'T HAD THE TIME TO WASH UP, THAT'S ALL
HORSE CAMP, EH?
WELL, YOU'LL NEVER GUESS WHAT I SAW THIS SUMMER
OH, I WOULDN'T, WOULD I?
NOPE
WAS IT, OH GEE, LEMME SEE NOW... UM... A TALKING BEAR?
WHAAA?
FLOP
OKEY DOKEY!
THE END